Tip-A-Canoe
for Two

by

Sarita Leone

Tip-A-Canoe for Two

Cover Art by *Debbie Taylor*

The Wild Rose Press, Inc.
PO Box 708
Adams Basin, NY 14410-0708
Visit us at www.thewildrosepress.com

Publishing History
First Vintage Rose Edition, 2017
Print ISBN 978-1-5092-1470-9
Digital ISBN 978-1-5092-1471-6

Published in the United States of America

The steel key stuck in the lock

as if cemented in place. It slipped in smoothly enough, but now that it shot home there was no turning the thing. And no pulling it out.

Kat attempted to twist it to the left, to no avail. She tried turning it clockwise, with the same result. Sheer frustration made her kick the bottom of the door, inches below where the plate glass met rutted wooden doorframe. The glass rattled ominously, so she took a step back.

And collided with a solid form.

"Damn!" It shot from her lips before she realized it was in her mind.

A familiar chuckle met her ears.

Double damn.

The wall she pressed against wasn't a wall at all, but the very same man she'd been squished up against yesterday afternoon. Now her backside met his front side, whereas yesterday they'd been front to front.

There was no time to contemplate which position she preferred.

"So that's how it is in the big city, then? Swearing and kicking all day long?"

The teasing made her smile. She turned to find his smile matched hers—except he had those knee-wobbling dimples she'd noticed yesterday.

Trapped between the door behind her and the handsome man in front of her. All things considered, not a bad place to be.

Dedication

As always, for Vito.
Sempre per sempre.

Chapter 1

1986

"Sometimes life sucks. Other times, it sucks you in." ~Lola Delaney

Kat should have left the skimpy bikini in her suitcase, but desperation after driving seven hours in bone-melting August heat made her hasty.

She leaned back against the flamingo-pink tiles and closed her eyes. The seen-better-days motel pool wasn't going to win any prizes for luxury, but it was refreshing. At this point, that'd do.

Life weighed heavy and pushed her shoulders beneath the surface.

She was overdue for a break from the streak of bad luck she'd had the past six months. This move was a new beginning. It was time for things to turn around in her life.

A strange sucking sound ominously close to her right ear killed her attempt at clearing her mind. She felt a tug across the center of her back. A soggy *slurp-slurp-slurp*.

Uh-oh.

Another glugging noise, a fast yank and she was topless. Instinct made her sit up straight, which brought her nipples above the water's surface. She swiveled around and stared into the opening in the pool wall.

One bra cup and the trailing end of a frayed fabric tie remained on her side. The rest had been sucked into the harmless-looking square like so much tie-dyed spaghetti.

She grabbed the end of the tie and pulled. Nothing.

Wiggling her index finger into the opening, she tried to loosen the fabric.

"Looking to lose a finger?"

The guy who appeared poolside was handsomer than any ordinary man had a right to be. A mop of thick, black curls brushed his shoulders, and his teeth were dazzling white. His eyes were such a deep shade of brown they looked nearly black. And a cleft in the chin.

Too sexy for words.

The Man Alarm sounded in her head, but she ignored it when a slow grin spread across his face.

"The view in the pool has never been this good."

She wrapped her arms across her chest and cradled her breasts in her palms. Bending her knees, she wished she'd taken the time to swim to the deep end. There was no pool filter over there.

"Glad you're enjoying yourself. Me? Not so much."

"We're in paradise, aren't we? It's cool." He swept out a hand, the gesture taking in everything within view.

She looked around.

The backside of the motel, teal-blue paint chipped and peeling in spots. Ancient lawn chairs with sagging woven seats. A trio of pink flamingoes in a scraggly flower garden.

Not the Hilton.

"It wasn't so awful until that thing ate my suit."

He leaned over the edge and stuck his right hand into the filter. "We can get your top back. It just needs some gentle persuasion."

"What about your fingers?"

He'd managed to extricate the inch or so of string that separated the bra cups, so now there was a tiny bit more showing.

A nod toward the shed just a few feet from the pool's edge. "I flipped the switch."

An industrial-size lever was mounted on the wall with a hand-lettered sign above it. *Do Not Touch Unless You Want to Wake Frankenstein.*

How had she missed *that*?

"When?"

"Just before."

"Just before it ate my suit, or just after?"

His hand was too large for the space, so he pulled it out and shook his head.

"My timing was off. Your top was gone before I could hit the disconnect." His gaze dropped. "Guess I was distracted."

Chapter 2

"Looking without touching is like eating without swallowing. It's safe—but safe? Now that's completely overrated." ~Lola Delaney

Jake pulled off his shirt, tossed it on the edge, and jumped in. Getting soaked wasn't in the plan for the day, but there was no other way. He wasn't sure he'd be able to rescue the bra top at all, but he at least had to give it a try.

The woman was a knockout. Black curls framed her face and tumbled from an untidy bundle on top of her head. He wondered if women knew how suggestive that was, to have a clip hold masses of curls begging to be released. Her eyes were the color of emeralds, and even the pink creeping up her neck and across her cheeks was a turn-on.

They were shoulder to shoulder. She took a step to the side, putting some watery distance between them.

"Now you're all wet."

Her observation was sweet, but there wasn't much to say to that, was there? He smiled. She was, after all, topless.

"Looks that way, doesn't it?"

All he could think was that she realized they were standing nearly skin to skin because she took one large step sideways. It would have been fine, except that the pool shelf dropped suddenly. No gradual slope, but a full-on, three-foot drop.

"Ooh!" Her arms circled once before she went under.

There was nothing graceful about her fall into the deep end. She took in a mouthful of chlorinated water before her toes hit the bottom. Maybe two mouthfuls—it was hard to tell with all the splashing.

Years as a lifeguard at the town pool let him hold back for a minute. She was panicky enough, but survival instinct should kick in. It always did.

Most always.

So he waited. It would happen.

Any minute now. Soon.

Or not.

Jake dove, swam down to where she flailed. He put an arm around her from behind and kicked hard. They broke the surface, and she gulped fresh air in loud, sputtering mouthfuls.

He took her to the side.

Her hair had come undone and now streamed in tight ringlets across her shoulders. She grabbed the edge with one hand and tried to push the curls off her face with the other.

"You okay?" He knew she was—or would be, once she caught her breath and realized she hadn't drowned. "Just breathe—that's it, nice and slow."

He swept a hand across her forehead, pushing wet tendrils off her brow.

A fast nod. Then she gasped, "Fine."

"Can you swim?"

The pink tiles were just inches from their faces, but he hadn't released her. Their hips nestled together and their upper bodies were tight.

For a day that had started out so lousy, this was a pleasant surprise.

One hand had the edge in a death grip. She'd put the other on his shoulder.

Another nod.

Yes, she could swim. But she'd done a damn fine imitation of nearly drowning.

Her breasts jiggled when she moved, her nipples brushing his chest hair and sending a jolt of electric lust up his spine.

"I, ah, just took one step too many…"

"It's not your fault." He nodded toward the shed. A vibrant teal square stood out against the rest of the faded space. "I keep telling him he's got to put a new sign up there."

"Him?"

"My uncle. Unless it's one that catches his funny bone the right way, like that one"—he tipped his head in the direction of the Frankenstein sign—"it could take forever to fix."

He was only human. When she made no move to extricate herself from his embrace, he lowered his gaze. There, the point just beneath the water's surface, where her breasts pressed against his chest, was perhaps the realization of every teenage fantasy he'd ever had.

Lord have mercy! How much could a man endure?

"I can't believe this is happening." She let go of the pool edge and gave him the whole weight of her body.

"Me, either. Not that I'm complaining."

"No, I don't hear you complaining."

Now he forced himself to look up. "Why should I? Hell, I kind of wish you would splash around every day, just so I get the chance to rescue you again. And again. And again."

"Listen, I'm not usually the damsel-in-distress type."

"A Gloria Steinem follower, eh?"

She scowled, and even that did something strange to him. Low in his gut—and hot where it counted.

"Listen, while I appreciate your rescuing me, I'm sure that sooner or later I would have rescued myself." She pushed hair off her brow with the back of one hand. He noticed the salmon fingernails. Each pinky finger sported a flower decal. "I always do."

He studied her eyes. "I believe you would have, but I've got to say this is more fun, don't you think?"

"I don't even know your name."

His hand moved up her back, his thumb tracing a lazy circle in the spot where her bikini top would have tied, had she been wearing it.

"Jake." He inclined his head slightly. "And you?"

"Kat Delaney. Strange way to meet, but nice to—"

A cackle of laughter startled her so thoroughly she nearly jumped out of his arms. He tightened his grip, squashing her breasts against his chest and doing his best to conceal her from prying eyes.

Damn it—just when the conversation was going so well!

If he didn't have bad luck, he'd have no luck.

"Looks like you caught yourself something real pretty in the water."

"This is Kat."

Uncle Gordon stood on the edge of the pool. The old man wore pink plaid Bermuda shorts, magenta polo shirt, white buckskin loafers, and black socks. He

7

clapped like a drunken sailor. The first laugh had been the warm-up act. Now, he threw his head back and let loose a loud peal as he raised one fisted hand in a victory salute.

"Looks like you caught the prettiest *cat*-fish I ever saw! Any more of 'em splashing around in there? Can you catch one for me?"

Chapter 3

"Never mix business with pleasure—unless part of your business involves a handsome man. Then, it ain't nobody's business but your own." ~Lola Delaney

The steel key stuck in the lock as if cemented in place. It slipped in smoothly enough, but now that it shot home there was no turning the thing. And no pulling it out.

Kat attempted to twist it to the left, to no avail. She tried turning it clockwise, with the same result. Sheer frustration made her kick the bottom of the door, inches below where the plate glass met rutted wooden doorframe. The glass rattled ominously. so she took a step back.

And collided with a solid form.

"Damn!" It shot from her lips before she realized it was in her mind.

A familiar chuckle met her ears.

Double damn.

The wall she pressed against wasn't a wall at all, but the very same man she'd been squished up against yesterday afternoon. Now her backside met his front side, whereas yesterday they'd been front to front.

There was no time to contemplate which position she preferred.

"So that's how it is in the big city, then? Swearing

and kicking all day long?"

The teasing made her smile. She turned to find his smile matched hers—except he had those knee-wobbling dimples she'd noticed yesterday.

Trapped between the door behind her and the handsome man in front of her. All things considered, not a bad place to be.

"What makes you think I'm from the city?"

The move from Manhattan to Mill Pond only put a couple hundred miles between her Upper East Side apartment and this stubborn door, but it felt like two entirely different realities. Which it was.

"Don't try to hide that city accent."

She bristled. "I'm not trying to hide anything."

The grin fell from his face. "We all hide something."

It was true, especially in her case, but she didn't intend to reveal herself to a man she barely knew. "Not me. Nothing to hide." Waving her arms wide, showing she didn't have anything in her hands or behind her back, didn't bring a return smile.

He quirked an eyebrow, his disbelief as readable as a Broadway marquee.

"Then you're a pretty unusual woman."

How had they gotten on such a serious note so quickly? Just a minute ago, she had been kicking a door like some spoiled juvenile delinquent.

"Just telling the truth."

They stared at each other for a long moment. A pulse beat in his throat, beneath the tanned skin. It was crazy, but the thought to lean in and kiss the spot crossed her mind.

Finally, he showed the dimples again, ending the

spell his masculine neck had cast.

"Always a good thing, the truth." The words sounded hollow, but the smile seemed genuine.

Her gaze still drifted from his face to his neck, then back again. Damn, but the man was good looking!

"So, what's the deal?"

"The deal?"

He nodded to the door behind her. "The door? I saw you doing your citified kung-fu move on it. Problem is, this is upstate New York and doors here don't drop like Central Park muggers."

"So you're a comedian, eh? Are you one of those street performers, telling jokes for pocket change?"

"Wrong guy. The mime went that way." A fast jerk of his head to the sidewalk behind them.

It made no sense. They barely knew each other, yet the banter came naturally.

She dropped her glance downward. His faded blue jeans were tight—and low. Scoping out his pockets—and giving his zipper a fast gaze—before looking back into his shocked eyes was dangerous, but she couldn't resist. "Empty pockets, then?"

She bit her lower lip to keep from laughing at his expression. Mr. Country expected Ms. City to be different, didn't he? It served him right, getting the tables turned.

Surprise vanished, replaced by a look that melted her insides. Obviously, he could take it as well as give it.

"Want to check?" It was more challenge than question.

Chapter 4

"The thing about small-town living is that it's done in a small town." ~Lola Delaney

Jake loved Mill Pond like a bear loves salmon fishing.

He hadn't planned to return, but remaining in Texas proved impossible. The dreams he'd had vanished—blown away on a wave of heartache colored by tragedy.

It had taken time to reach the philosophical stage. He'd licked his wounds. Taken to his cave and hibernated for a stretch. Finally he'd emerged.

If he'd had his way, he'd have hunkered down for a while longer. But Uncle Gordon's health made that impossible.

This morning he'd been minding his own business. Plans for the day included paint and caulk, but when he'd seen pretty-as-a-picture Kat wrestling with the shop door, he had to offer help.

It's what people did in the tiny town. Especially when the troubled lady had eyes the color of exotic emeralds.

She lit a spark in him. No denying it, even to himself. He had no intention of letting that spark grow...but the warmth after so many cold, lonely seasons was a welcome change.

Now his jeans tightened—a result of the mischievous sparkle in her eyes.

For an instant he thought she just might do it. Search his pockets. Here on Main Street, sheltered as they were in the doorway. The thought made a certain part of his anatomy swell still more.

She glanced down, then looked up and met his eyes. A head shake sent a curl bobbing beside her left ear.

"No."

He wasn't used to getting turned down.

Who was he kidding? The last time he'd propositioned a woman he'd been too drunk to remember whether she said yes or no. And he'd been put up to it by his buddies. A leave in the Middle East; two nights off base before being sent on a mission. He hardly remembered anything of those precious few hours.

He wished he was able to forget the operation that followed the escapade. No hostages had been rescued in Iran, and the men he'd been with had perished. One of the skeletons crowding his closet that he tried to forget.

Put your mind back on the pretty lady.

"No? Just no, that's it?"

"That's it. Just no."

Chapter 5

"I always prefer a hands-on approach...especially when it comes to men. And, their anatomy."
                                      ~Lola Delaney

Placing a hand on the doorframe behind her, Mr. Tall and Tanned leaned close. Flecks laced his irises, the gold like stardust in the night sky.

A smorgasbord of male scents swept up her nose. Spice, an exotic variety, brought images of sheiks and elaborate desert hideaways. Chlorine, a reminder of the way he felt, water-slickened against her. Musk, pure male and so seductive, sent her heart beating double time.

A single bead of perspiration slid down her spine. Her left shoulder fit snugly beneath his wrist. The skin-to-skin contact burned. It was a good sting, but it still caught her off guard.

"You sure you don't want to do a fast pocket check?"

He was dangerously close, his face mere inches from her own. It occurred that this man was *exactly* the right height for kissing.

Most of the resolutions she'd formulated on the long car drive in the beat-up Camaro, those about new horizons, less interference by men who clearly didn't get her mind or heart—and didn't deserve her time—

were close to being forgotten.

Pulling every ounce of composure from the bag of professional tactics she'd assembled, she replaced the wobble in her voice with a steely edge.

"Look, my priorities are probably different than yours. While the offer is interesting, I have to refuse. We've just met. Barely. I hope there're no hard feelings, especially since you were so helpful with my bathing suit disaster."

"No hard feelings."

Honestly, it wasn't his hard *feelings* on her mind.

Silence hung suggestively between them. When it looked like that was his only response, Kat opened her mouth. She wasn't sure what she was going to say; she only knew the sexual tension was more than she could stand.

Before she could get one word out, he asked, "What makes you think you know me so well?"

"Huh?" Blindsided, she barely breathed.

He pressed her. "As you've so aptly put it, we just met. *Barely.* So, how can you presume to know anything about my priorities?"

He had her. She hadn't expected to be called on it, either.

"I-I—"

Twenty-eight years of effortless speech, and at crunch time she sounded like an idiot.

"You what?"

"I—ah, I…" How could one man have such dark eyes? Illegal eyes, for the sins they encouraged without any effort on his part. She had to pull herself together and stop ogling him as if she'd run from a fat farm and he was an all-you-can-eat buffet. "I, ah, don't know your priorities."

He raised a questioning eyebrow. A curl had fallen onto his forehead. Her fingers itched to wipe it back, but she fisted her hand.

Kat swallowed. Cleared her throat. "But, ah, I do know mine, and they don't include—that is, they don't include…"

Penises. But she couldn't say that.

"They don't include me?"

Uh-huh. You. Or your penis.

She nodded. "Right." She tried to sound firm but not like a bitch. It was a hard mix, but she did her best. "Don't get the wrong idea. It's not just you. I'm off men—*all men*."

His brows took full cover beneath the curls dropping onto his forehead. "All men?"

He got it. Praise the Lord and say halleluiah, he finally got it!

"That's right." At least now he understood.

"So you're a lesbian?"

Oh, damn—he didn't understand!

"No!" Could she dig herself in any deeper—or any faster? "I'm just not getting involved now. With anyone."

Anyone with a penis.

"So it's not just me?"

"It's not just you. It's…" She searched for a way to explain without going into details. She didn't want to remember the bullshit she'd lived through this past year. She especially had no desire to hear it all spoken out loud. Sighing, she said, "I've got too much else to deal with. Some heavy stuff. I can't let anything—or anyone—bring me down. Understand?"

His eyes searched hers. Again, she was pulled in to the rugged good looks of the man. This time, she indulged herself and fell under his magic. No need to fight the attraction, not now. She'd made her point.

"I do."

If he was disappointed, he hid it. He straightened, taking his hand from the doorframe and breaking contact with her shoulder. Immediately she missed his touch.

"Thank you."

He nodded, a slow, deliberate movement.

"It's cool. So, anything I can do for you?"

She shook a thumb to the stubbornly locked door. Getting her new gig up and running was impossible when she couldn't even get the damn door open.

"The lawyer dropped the key off this morning. It doesn't work."

She took a step back.

"May I?" Taking the tarnished handle in one hand, he held the key with the other and gave both a forceful jiggle. Sounds came from within the ancient lock, metallic noises that made the prospect of the door actually opening seem even more remote.

The key turned and the tumblers rasped against each other before they released. The door swung in. He held out one arm and bowed. "After you."

"You made that look easy."

"It wasn't tough."

She stepped past him, over the threshold and into a crowded, dark space. Tiny motes swam in the stale air.

Her nose wrinkled. Dismay mingled with dust, both hitting her hard.

"What do you think?" He stepped in behind her,

forcing her to take yet another step into the derelict interior.

The answer came fast. Turning and hiding her nose from the swirling dust, she sneezed. The force sprayed his dark blue shirtfront with tiny dots of moisture.

Glancing from his shirt to her embarrassed gaze, Jake shook his head.

"So tell me what you really think, why don't you?"

"I'm sorry. I didn't mean to—I just—"

"It's okay. Everyone sneezes."

She turned back to the crowded room, took one step forward and tripped, falling backward so fast that all she could manage was a loud gasp.

Before she hit the floor, Kat hit the wall of temptation behind her. His arms wrapped around her waist, catching her lightning fast and holding her hard against him.

It was at that point she knew that despite his charm and casual air, Jake was as affected by the attraction between them as she was. The bulge pressing against her ass was impressive, and it had nothing to do with his pockets.

Chapter 6

"Everyone's looking at everyone else's laundry in a small town, which is a fine incentive to keep your drawers clean." ~Lola Delaney

Jake left her to "settle in" on her own. It was a good thing, because hiding her shock would have been impossible.

Inheriting the Tip-A-Canoe Art Gallery had been the answer to her immediate issues. Or so she thought. She'd been under the false impression the place was an actual art gallery. As in pictures on the walls and sculptures on marble pedestals.

Reality was so skewed she could hardly breathe— and it wasn't because of the dust.

"Shit," she whispered, making a slow circle on the heel of one clog. "This sucks."

A garage sale explosion surrounded her. Floor to ceiling, piles of junk represented, at the very minimum, the last five decades. She spied a casserole dish with gaudy fuchsia flowers on its side atop a bamboo table. A life-size mannequin wore a beaded silver Flapper dress.

She'd been robbed. Aunt Lola promised to leave all her worldly goods—and the hope for a secure life. The old woman finally went to her reward, and all she'd passed on was this mess. Clearly, Kat had been duped.

19

How the hell could she begin to pull her life together surrounded by tons of useless garbage?

Before Henry's deception and her subsequent job loss, she had been one of the city's most respected window dressers. She ordered not only her own life, but the fantasy lives of everyone passing the giant display windows on 42nd Street.

Now, her life was in ruins and her surroundings were crap. Could it get any worse?

Something from above, in the ceiling or maybe a wall vent, sent a cold burst of air into the space. Gooseflesh rose on her arms, a sudden chill in the otherwise-warm shop.

"Un-fucking-believable." There was no reason to bother keeping her words low. The expletive had a degree of satisfaction to it, so she repeated in a louder voice. "Un-fucking-believable!"

Qu-quack. Quack-quack. Qu-quack.

She whirled. Her arm hit a pile of boxes and sent them crashing to the floor. Dust rose, she sneezed and something—or someone—quacked again.

Quack! Qu-quack!

She followed the sound, weaving through the labyrinth of boxes.

A small brown duck sat as serenely as a stone Buddha just inside the open front door.

She stopped, keeping her distance. It appeared calm now, but who could tell what a wild duck might do? Its long, orange bill looked hard. Did ducks bite? Kat had no idea, but before she could decide, she realized she was trapped. Trapped in her own second-rate rubbish store by a duck.

"In-fucking-credible." She wanted to shout, slam

something hard, throw things—but she didn't know if the duck would charge, so she kept her voice low.

Quack. Q-q-qua-quack.

Great. A duck with a speech impediment.

A woman appeared in the doorway. With a wild expression on her face, she scooped the stuttering duck into her arms and held it tight against her chest.

The newcomer looked like the wrong turn between fetching and far-out, but Kat didn't care. So what if her salvation wore green-striped capris with sparkly gold stars dancing up each outer thigh and a lime-green tank top covered with butterflies beneath a thick woolen cardigan that at some point in time might have been red but was now Pepto Bismol pink? On her feet, suede peek-a-boo pumps, circa nineteen forty-five. Also green, although it was questionable whether they left the factory that shade of puce or were dyed afterward.

It didn't matter if her rescue party arrived buck naked, just as long as she took the duck with her when she went.

Kat walked to the doorway and gave a friendly smile. It didn't escape notice that she was suddenly enveloped in a frosty current.

Where the hell can the breeze be coming from?

"Thanks for rescuing me."

The woman looked the far side of sixty, with frizzy white hair and enough wrinkles to give her a hangdog expression. Her mouth set in a disdainful line, lips so tight they seemed sewn shut. She glowered so hard, Kat's lips fell at the edges.

Great. Now a crazy woman and a vicious duck trap me in this dump.

It flashed though her mind that she could probably

knock the woman over if she gave her a good shove, but knocking down old ladies—to say nothing of trampling ducks—wasn't her thing. She tried again, fixing a wide smile on her face and hoping it would melt the flamboyant, duck-toting icicle.

"Apple trees make apples."

The woman was truly mad.

"Excuse me?"

"You're just like your aunt." She clutched the duck so forcefully against her chest that it gave a strangled quack.

"I don't know what you're talking about. I don't even know who you—"

Duck Woman cut her off. "That's right, play dumb. Already heard you cussing in here—like I said, apple trees make apples. All I've got to say to you is—" She tucked the duck beneath one arm and waved an arthritic finger in the air close to Kat's face.

She took a step away, wondering how quickly help would find her if she screamed.

"Keep away from my duck. And if you even think of going near my man I'm going to make you wish you had never come to this town." The captive fowl squirmed, quacking more loudly now, so she shifted it and used two hands to restrain the animal. Before she walked out of the shop, she glared. "I'll make you rue the day you set foot in Mill Pond. And that's a promise."

She stared at the empty spot after the woman disappeared.

Then, she rushed the door, slammed it shut, and slid the deadbolt home.

She sneezed. Running a finger beneath her itchy

nose, she muttered, "I already rue the day, Duck Lady. Believe me, I rue it—big time."

Chapter 7

"Everyone's born with style. There're those who just have to dig deep to find their stylin' gene."
~Lola Delaney

It took four hours to clean the apartment above the mess—Kat still couldn't bring herself to call it a "gallery"—but when she snagged the last cobweb from the final corner, the compact space was tolerable. Fifties-era time warp tolerable.

There wasn't much to the place. A small living room with an avocado green sofa and gold throw pillows. Along with two matching side chairs, it created a cozy area around a squat coffee table. A floor-to-ceiling bookcase, stuffed to overflowing with hard covers, paperbacks, magazines, and ratty wicker baskets. There wasn't time to explore its contents—not if she wanted dinner before midnight. A table lamp with a fringed lampshade and a gangly looking floor lamp completed the room.

Two bedrooms, both undersized and sparsely furnished. Chenille bedspreads, blond furniture, and braided floor rugs made them look nearly identical, although the one facing the rear of the building had obviously belonged to her aunt. A peek into the closet confirmed that the more lived-in bedroom had been Lola's.

She chose the front bedroom. The closet held four cardboard boxes that she pushed to its back corner, a row of bent wire clothes hangers dangling from the wooden rod, and a pair of high-heel sandals. She tossed the hangers and shoved the shoes inside one of the boxes.

She'd put most of her stuff in storage so there wasn't much to unpack. When her duffel, two small suitcases, and cosmetic bag had been emptied into the closet and single chest of drawers, she crossed her arms and looked around the room.

The flowery wallpaper grated on her nerves, and the cream-colored chenille bedspread—complete with pom-pom fringe—was enough to make her cringe, but it would do. For now.

In other words, it would all work until she figured out how to get the hell out of here.

Or how to stay. That option played in the back of her mind, a mental radio station with the volume set just barely above a whisper. She heard it, but most of the time it was a distant noise, which suited her fine.

Just off the *Leave It to Beaver* living room, the kitchen looked like it came straight from a nineteen fifty-seven *Better Homes and Gardens*. Chrome, almost as wide as a Buick's grille, rimmed a flecked gold Formica countertop. White round-top refrigerator. Black-and-white linoleum checks made the floor a giant chessboard. A rectangular red enamel table, with matching chairs. A black rotary dial telephone.

Everything fit in the place. Except her.

The sturdy old-fashioned furnishings and fixtures cleaned up swiftly and, after just a bit of elbow grease, gleamed. She stood back, her hips against the chrome counter rail, and surveyed the scene.

Not her style—correction, not Henry's style, which is how their apartment had been decorated. Her style? Did she even have one?

Not really.

She pushed her hair off her forehead, skimming her fingers through the strands. Satisfied that it was sleek, she twisted the length into a tight bundle, gave a sharp twist, and pulling a silver barrette from the front pocket of her Jordache jeans, secured the whole shebang on the back of her head.

It was as good as it got. Maybe she was cut out for country living after all. She'd gone from city chic to country casual in hours. Could hip boots and a manure shovel be far behind?

Chapter 8

"Never eat with someone who turns your stomach." ~Lola Delaney

New York's finest restaurants hadn't prepared her for the Nothin' Fancy Diner.

In the city, she'd know what was expected. Here, it looked like anything went. Booths, tables, and the long counter were filled. Noisy. Crowded.

Kat felt invisible standing beside a stack of menus just inside the door. And, for the first time since she'd hit town, lonely.

Stop it. She pulled her shoulders back and reached for a menu. She'd be damned if she was going to let a diner full of small-towners drag her down.

A door slapped open directly across from where she stood. She stepped back and held the menu flat against her middle as a teenage girl carrying a tray that looked heavier than her hurried over. Enticing aromas streamed from the plates, making her mouth water like Pavlov's dog's.

When the waitress spied Kat's menu, her free hand stopped midway to the pile. She put it under the tray and jerked a smile. "Sit anywhere there's a free seat. I'll be over in a sec…"

They scanned the room in tandem. It was packed. Almost every spot filled.

A redheaded woman sat alone at a table for two near the beverage station. Kat took a step in that direction, thinking she'd ask if anyone planned to occupy the seat, but the waitress reached out and grabbed her forearm. Hard.

"Not there."

"Is she expecting someone?"

A snap at a wad of pink gum before the reply. "That's a big no. I could let you sit there, but I'd have to go straight to St. Mary's after my shift ends, drop to my knees, and beg Father Greg to absolve me. Father would have me Hail Mary-ing for a week. Find somewhere else to sit. Any place but with her."

The woman's closely cropped hair contrasted sharply to her ghost-white skin. Overweight, wearing a drab brown pullover and matching stretch pants. Twin dark brown arcs, pencil-thin and halfway up her forehead, moved up and down as she chewed. Her scowl seemed permanent. Her nose twisted, nostrils flaring, as if she smelled something rotten.

She reminded Kat of a ferret. A large, fat one—pointed face and all.

It didn't say a lot for ferrets, but once the impression hit her, there was no shaking it.

She tore her gaze away, searching for another empty space. She'd have to wait for someone to leave before claiming a seat.

"Bad timing." The girl snapped again with the wad of gum in her mouth. "We're always full on Wednesdays."

"That's okay."

The waitress shifted the heavy tray to her opposite shoulder. Then, she gave a half-smile and nodded to the far corner booth. One bench was occupied. The other, empty. The back of a man's head faced them.

"That'll do. I'll be there in a flash to take your drink order."

"I don't want to intrude." What if this was another scary townsperson, someone who made the redhead look like an angel?

Something about the tilt of the man's head set off an alarm in her mind.

"I'll wait." Just then her stomach rumbled—loud and long—and the waitress raised one perfectly-groomed eyebrow.

"Doesn't sound like you can afford to wait. Really, he won't mind." Raising her voice to be heard above the din, she yelled, "Hey, Jake—got a dinner date for you."

Instantly the crowd hushed, and Kat felt every pair of eyes turn on her. Worse, the man in the corner booth stood. He spun and flashed a welcoming smile.

What could she do?

Chapter 9

"It's not hard to get a man's interest. The tricky part is keeping it." ~Lola Delaney

It had been a long time since a woman intrigued him the way Miss Big Apple did.

"Thank you for sharing your booth with me."

Her voice was like twelve-year-old scotch. Smooth. Rich. Velvety. And just a hint of heat.

"You're welcome."

He watched her slide onto the bench across from him. A slow, fascinating move.

She opened the menu and scanned the pages.

"Hungry?"

Shutting the menu with a decisive slap, she met his gaze. "Starving."

Good. A woman with real appetites appealed to him.

"Let's see if we can't grab Destiny's attention." He caught the waitress's eye and waved her over.

Destiny popped the pink blob in her mouth, held a pen above her order pad, and asked, "So? Whaddaya want? Jake? The usual?"

He'd been about to have a bacon cheeseburger, but he was peeved by the way she so smoothly pegged him. He shouldn't be so damn predictable.

"I don't think so. Tonight I'll have…" He searched

his brain for an alternative. "Turkey on rye."

Destiny gave him an eye roll, swallowed a smirk, then asked, "Coleslaw or macaroni salad?"

"Slaw."

"Fries or onion rings?"

"Rings."

She knew all this but was making him answer for her own benefit. He knew it; she knew it. The only one out of the loop was Kat, who looked like she didn't care whether he had motor oil or dressing on his side salad.

"Italian." He answered the next question before it left the waitress's mouth.

"Another iced tea?"

"Please."

She turned to Kat, who ordered like a woman who hadn't eaten in days.

"Grilled cheese—white cheddar if you have it—on toasted—toasted, not pan-fried—wheat. A side of applesauce—with cinnamon on top—but only if it's unsweetened, otherwise I'll have two sides of vegetables. Whatever you've got, as long as it's not fried. No potatoes, either."

Destiny scribbled on her pad, crossing a word out before adding another. "So, two veggie sides and applesauce?"

"No, just one side of vegetables—preferably steamed, with a splash of vinegar—with the applesauce. If the applesauce is sweetened, two sides of veggies but no applesauce."

"Got it." The young woman tucked her pencil behind an ear, grabbed their menus, and asked, "And to drink?"

"Water—bottled."

"All we got is what's on tap."

Kat scrunched her nose.

"Ooh, fine, then. A Tab—but only a couple of ice cubes." A heart-stopping grin as the waitress left. "It's hot as hell in here. Might as well cool off somehow, don't you think?"

Oh, he did think. A lot. But none of what sped through his mind—or surged lightning-fast through his body—had to do with cooling off.

Every impulse he had, each half-formulated thought and decadent desire brought heat with it. Lots and lots of heat.

Too-hot-to-handle heat.

Chapter 10

"Every family tree has a nut in it. Don't believe anyone who says their family tree is nutless. They're lying." ~Lola Delaney

As much as she didn't want to admit it, life without a man wasn't great. Sure, the confession wouldn't win her any kudos from *Cosmopolitan,* but Kat didn't care what anyone thought. Especially since she kept the cloak of silence covering the needy confession. No one need ever know, but it was the solid truth. She craved a man in her life.

And it had only been a matter of months since the last creep had departed. How sad was that?

Jake's smile made it hard to concentrate. She wanted to listen to him, but her eyes just kept going back to the straight pearly whites surrounded by lips that looked too kissable.

Folk music filled the air, background to the clatter of forks and knives against chipped plates. Concert posters, some framed but most just thumb-tacked, covered the walls. Laid back yet bustling, a contrast that somehow felt homey.

He'd kept up a steady stream of conversation before their meals arrived. Very little speaking during the actual eating portion of the dinner, which suited her just fine. But now that was unofficially over—the

33

meager remnants of the delicious food forlorn and forgotten on their plates—and they began phase two of the getting-to-know-you dance.

Out of the corner of her eye, she caught a red-and-brown movement. Ferret Woman rose and brought the bill for her meal close to her face. With a frown, she dropped two quarters beside her empty plate and strode toward the cashier.

The crowd parted as if they were the Red Sea meeting Moses. People leaned as far back as possible. In one instance, a teenage girl nearly sat on a mother's lap, so fervent was her desire to move as far as space allowed.

Jake shook his head.

"Why do people act as if she's got a bad case of... I don't know. Something horrible and contagious. Like, maybe, the plague?"

"Worse." He thrummed his fingertips on the tabletop, staring at her in a way that didn't hide his weighing his next words. The desire to pass his silent judgment test, to show herself worthy of receiving confidences, kept her from pressing him.

Patience paid off. He took a deep breath, then let it out in a long stream.

"I don't make a habit of putting anyone down, but since you'll hear something sooner or later—and by sooner I'd bet within forty-eight hours of opening your front door to customers—I might as well let you in on the town's dirty little secret. Honestly, I'm sort of shocked you don't already know about—" He stopped short.

"Ferret Woman?"

"I've heard her called a lot of things, but that's a

new one. But damn, you've got a point. With her pinched face and beady eyes…yeah, I'd say that fits."

"I've met my share of characters in the city, but she's different. I feel terrible, judging a book by its cover and all that, but she gives me the heebie-jeebies."

"Don't waste a minute feeling bad over it. Triple T doesn't give one thought to anyone else's feelings but her own."

"*Triple T?*"

"That's right." He leaned close, lowered his voice and said, "Truly Terrible Teri. Everyone calls her Triple T for short. Just saves time and energy, and we all know who we're talking about."

What did it take to make such a dreadful reputation? Especially in such a small town, where everyone seemed Gomer Pyle friendly.

She pushed an olive pit around on her empty plate with one fingertip. Sometimes not saying a word spoke loudly.

Jake opened up. "Don't think we're all heartless. If anyone wants what's best for Mill Pond, it's me. I've given a lot of myself to this town, but even I know my limits. There's no changing that woman. She's just…well, there's only one word for it."

Kat wanted to crawl inside his mouth and pull the words from him. Leave it to a man to slow the story when it got interesting.

"Well? You've come this far—spill it. Tell me what everyone else knows."

He spread his hands before him as if that answered her question. "There's no other way to say it. That woman is pure evil."

Not what she expected.

"Evil? As in hocus-pocus evil?"

She thought she could read people pretty well. Ferret Woman gave off a nasty aura but witchy?

Bitchy with a capital B was more like it.

"I don't think so. But who can tell what goes on behind closed doors? She treats everyone like trash. No thought for anyone but herself. When push comes to shove, she's all about her needs—I've seen her turn her back on a kid with a broken leg lying at the curb. She's mercenary, thoughtless, cruel, two-faced—"

She held up a hand. "Whoa. I get it."

A sheepish grin brought his lips high at the corners. "Sorry. Where she's concerned, it doesn't take much to get any of us started. It's hard dealing with someone so heartless. Teri isn't nice, and she doesn't care about anyone. Don't let your guard down—not even for a second."

Her gut gave an unpleasant lurch. "Thanks for the warning."

"I like you too much to let the Evil One dry gulch you."

"Dry gulch?"

"You city slickers must have a similar term. You know, when someone slams into you from left field, smacking your blindside and knocking you on your butt?"

"That's a dry gulch?"

"You betcha."

"I might need to take a course in country speak, just to understand what's going on around me."

"Listen, if you need a tutor…"

Her belly did a flip-flop. "You offering?"

"You know it."

"I'll keep it in mind." She pushed the olive pit around one more time before crumpling her paper napkin and tossing it onto the center of her plate.

Lessons from this man couldn't be anything other than sheer pleasure—whatever the topic.

Jake crossed his knife over his fork on the edge of the sturdy plate in front of him. His precise arrangement as he sat back gave the impression that he'd dined in much fancier places.

"Food okay?"

She looked down. The only things she'd left were two olive pits and a sprig of thyme.

"Amazing. Now I understand the reason for the long line." The crowd had dwindled, but only slightly. A line still formed while empty tables were bussed and reset. "No one looks like they mind waiting."

She counted three couples, a family of four, and a small swell of other bodies farther back near the doorway. The sound of gentle chatter filled the room.

"We all wait our turn because the food is so good."

"I didn't notice anywhere else to eat in town. Is this it?"

"It is. There used to be a place at the end of the street, down that way." The gesture toward the wall behind her brought Jake's arm across the table. The scent of cedar came, then went, in the small space. "Food was good, but after the Olympics were over, tourists stopped coming. There was no way the locals could support a fancy-schmancy French restaurant on their own. So, Le Bon Pain closed down."

"Sad," she said without filtering the thought.

"You that crazy about French cuisine?"

She instantly regretted she'd spoken without

thinking. Her guard was too low for her own good. The lessons she'd learned from her last disastrous relationship had vanished on a wave of cedar and cinnamon.

She met his gaze. The silence stretched until it felt awkward.

Chapter 11

"There's no good time to derail a party. No good time at all..." ~Lola Delaney

Something had put the brakes on what was, for him at least, a great dinner. Jake wasn't sure what had turned her off.

He placed his elbows on the table and folded his hands in front of his chest. "So, you don't dig French food? Don't worry; your secret is safe with me."

"I like French food." She pleated the thin stick of paper from her straw. "It's just..."

"French men? You don't care for them? Really, I won't tell anyone." He mimed zipping his lips shut.

She shook her head. The hasty updo loosened, so she pulled the barrette out of her hair, allowing the strands to fall around her shoulders.

He watched every tendril drop.

She leaned forward conspiratorially.

"It's not the men."

Damn.

"So you're saying you have a thing for French guys? Got to admit, I hate to hear that."

"Why?"

"Well, it puts me out of the running." Casual flirting, that was all this was. No harm, no foul. Right?

"There is no running."

"There's always a run. And you still haven't told me why you think it's sad that Le Bon Pain closed. How could it matter to you?"

"It doesn't." Tossing the straw paper accordion down onto the tabletop between them, she shook her head. "It's just…"

"Sad?"

"Exactly. I think of the jobs lost, dreams shattered and well…" Her voice trailed off.

"It is sad, when you look at it that way. But most of the wait staff at LBP works here now." He nodded to their waitress, who held up a finger and kept writing on her order pad. "Did you take a good look at your menu? Ray was the chef down the street. Lots of non-traditional diner food on his menu."

"I didn't notice. The colors hurt my eyes."

He shook his head. Ray refused to tone down the psychedelic menus which was cool for the locals, but out-of-towners didn't find them hip at all.

"Next time, put your shades on and give the options a fair shake. Some great stuff to choose from."

"But your 'regular' order is a burger?"

She caught him, so he shrugged. "What can I say? I'm an ordinary kind of guy."

Destiny appeared beside the table in time to hear his last comment. She snorted. "Yeah. You're, like, so ordinary. And there's this bridge I was trying to sell. What do you think?"

"I think you're a smartass."

They watched as she stacked their empty plates, then placed them on the edge of the table near her hip. She did it all while giving him a series of air kisses.

"For example, take Destiny. Oh, please take her, I

beg you." When she raised a fist, he waved her off. They'd had many heart-to-heart talks, so she got that he was just pulling her leg. "I was just saying that most of the staff here came from the French place. You like it here, don't you?"

"I do. My uniform doesn't need to be starched and I don't have to wear a dorky name tag on my boob." She looked down at her snug scoop-neck t-shirt. "See? No nametag. And no nametag means no stupid questions."

Kat didn't ask and he knew better, but the waitress, however, seemed compelled to explain—bare boob or not. "Listen, I get every stupid question in the book. It works for me, not having to admit that my mother is"— she brought an index finger up alongside her head and twirled it—"crazy enough to give her only daughter such an idiotic name. But hey, at least I'm not my brother. He's got it worse—lots worse."

Jake caught Kat's gaze, trying to warn her off. Not a good question to ask.

Fortunately, Destiny chose that exact instant to look around. The crowd had grown in the time she'd spent talking. All business, she whipped her pad and pencil out and asked, "Dessert?"

"Ray makes his own ice cream. No choices, though, on flavors. Whatever he made today is the daily special. You up for a surprise?"

Kat nodded.

"Good. Make it two."

A fast note on the pad before it was stuffed it in the back pocket of the waitress's tight jeans. She leaned down to pick up their dirty plates, and asked, "Extra nuts?"

"You know it."

"Speaking of nuts, you're about to get more than your share." She straightened, smiled, and walked away, calling over her shoulder, "Two sundaes, extra nuts, right away!"

There wasn't much time to wonder about the implication of her words. Before either of them could turn around a pink mini-tornado sped to their table on a blast of cold air.

Oh, shit.

He hadn't planned on having to deal with this tonight.

"Jake! What in Sam Hill are you doing cavorting with the enemy? Good Lord, have you no sense at all?"

He ignored the figure standing beside his shoulder. At least she wasn't carrying the duck.

Destiny wasn't far up the aisle, so he called, "To go, please." Then he met Kat's gaze. Or he attempted to.

She stared—wide-eyed and open-mouthed—at the space beside him.

No. Just, no.

His aunt snorted. She poked a finger, almost touching his shoulder. All he felt was an icy prickle at the spot where she would have connected, had she been able.

"Don't tell me you're all googly-eyed over this little tart already." She jabbed him again, sending a cold pinprick up his shoulder. "Come on, boy—stop thinking with your weenie and use your mind. Can't you see she's just a piece of eye candy—one good suck and she's gone in a flash?"

Kat gasped. The bronze glow paled, and color rose

high on her cheekbones. She looked at him, her eyes showing complete mortification. To her credit, she closed her mouth and did not comment.

Most women wouldn't have allowed themselves to be insulted by a stranger. He wondered why she did, but there was no time to give that much thought.

Almost hating himself for having to ask, he ticked his head to the standing figure and asked, "Can you see her?"

Kat's brow furrowed.

There was no need for a reply, so he turned to the pink lady. With a wink, he said, "Aw, come on. Don't make Kat think you're a meanie. I was hoping you two might get along, but before she can like you, you've got to show your good side. What do you say?"

"I say no!" Waving a gnarled fist, the old woman raised her voice.

His dinner partner cringed, but she was the only one to react. The commotion in their corner didn't raise one single, solitary eyebrow.

Chapter 12

"At least the cheese gets a nibble. The mouse? Nothing but a broken neck!" ~Lola Delaney

Her mouth went dry the moment she saw the old woman. Had there been an exit nearby, she would've gone for it.

Now I know how a cornered mouse feels.

Jake did not look at all perturbed by the wiry-haired woman's rant—not even when she poked one scrawny fingertip into his bicep.

Destiny carried their sundaes held high in huge takeout bowls. The treats looked out of this world, but her appetite had taken a hike.

The man from the motel was right behind the waitress. His attire wasn't as garish as the duck woman's, but with high, black dress socks, black-and-white oxfords, blue tennis shorts, and a yellow-and-pink striped rugby shirt, he wasn't a candidate for anyone's best-dressed list, either.

He stopped beside the table. With the pink woman and Destiny, the space was crowded.

"Oh, good. Jake, you're here—and with that darling catfish of yours, too." Jake's uncle reached out and took her hand. His was warm and dry with a papery feel to his fingertips. He raised her fingers and would have kissed her knuckles had his hand not been slapped down.

The pink tornado gained momentum. "Stop that foolishness! This whole town is going to hell in a handcart when both of my men fawn over the enemy. Catfish—*hmmph!*"

"In a fine state tonight, isn't she, Uncle Gordon?"

"All day, my boy. All damn day."

New York City had its share of oddballs. No one blinked when people meandered down sidewalks talking to themselves. Or rambling on street corners about whatever cause they favored.

A live-and-let-live sort, if ever there was one, she accepted all and did not pass judgment. But this small-town kind of kooky was altogether different from anything she'd witnessed in the past. The two men seemed unfazed. The other diners paid the woman no mind at all—and they'd been the ones who gave the Ferret Lady wide berth. Pinched face and nasty was wrong, but pink whirlwind was cool?

There was more to learn about Mill Pond than she imagined. Hopefully she'd be able to blow the dust off her sandals and leave the place before she figured it all out. Or worse. Before she became one of them.

Jake looked at the enormous sundaes, then met her gaze. "Do you mind taking the ice cream to go? That way my uncle and his lovely companion can have the table. And I'll show you the perfect place to eat an ice cream sundae on a hot summer night."

Dinner companion? Jake's uncle didn't act like the brightest bulb in the light fixture but couldn't he tell his date was a bona fide lunatic?

The only thing she wanted was to escape the glare being shot her way from the old woman, so she nodded.

Better to get out while the getting was good.

"Sounds great."

Destiny winked. "I added extra nuts."

Chapter 13

"One woman's junk isn't always another gal's treasure." ~Lola Delaney

Twilight softened the edges of Main Street's shops. They hadn't spoken since leaving the diner, and she was glad Jake wasn't pushing conversation on her. What could she say that didn't sound awful if he tried to explain the eccentricity that appeared to be part of his family tree?

Kat paused outside The Stitching Post and scanned the arrangement of fabrics in the large window display. They'd done a good job, but she could have done better. It was simply a matter of placement; put things where they caught a shopper's attention and merchandise sold. Hide it, or as in this case, bore passersby with humdrum, and buyers went elsewhere.

"Do you sew?"

She looked up, gave a sheepish grin. "Not a stitch."

They walked to the end of the sidewalk. Just like that—concrete squares ended, and grass began.

Past the shops, Sentinel Park. Flanking curlicue wrought iron gates, brilliant orange cosmos, petals fluttering in the warm breeze. The sun's final rays cast the waist-high flowers in a red glow. Walking into the park was like stepping through a ring of fire.

Few people lingered inside the gates. Two teenage

boys wearing faded jeans and sneakers zipped past on bikes. They flashed smiles as they sped by.

Jake pointed. Beside a grove of trees, an empty bench.

"How about right there?"

They made their way over and sat side by side. One of the limbs from the huge maple tree behind the bench hung low, scraping the back of the seat with its leaves.

He handed her a covered container and a plastic spoon from the bag. He uncovered his sundae and placed the lid in the grass by their feet.

While she uncovered hers, she watched. And waited. He'd say something about what happened in the diner eventually. She didn't want to hurt his feelings. It wasn't his fault he knew a nasty, duck-carrying woman.

The ice cream looked amazing. Thick and creamy, so tempting her mouth watered. She raised a spoonful. A chopped walnut slid perilously close to falling. Before it could drop, she stuck out her tongue and caught it, drawing the morsel into her mouth.

Then, she licked her lower lip.

She caught him staring. "Have I got something on my chin?" She stuck her spoon into the sundae and swiped at her chin with her palm. It came away clean. "On my nose, then?"

When she went for her nose, he chuckled.

Her hand stopped an inch from her skin. "What?"

"Not a thing. I don't know why you're feeling self-conscious." She opened her mouth to protest but he went on before she could say a word. "How's that taste? Ray makes some killer ice cream, doesn't he?"

Kat resumed eating. One spoonful. Two. Luckily, nothing else threatened to embarrass her. No errant nuts or kamikaze cherries.

"He does." She had nearly demolished the sundae. "I'd love to see what he does to a cheesecake."

"Nothing. Ray doesn't do cakes." He ran the spoon along the bottom rim of the container, catching the last few nuts. The container and spoon he deposited near his feet. "He's strictly ice cream."

"You're kidding."

She finished hers, stuffed the spoon into the container, and smashed the lid on top. He held out a hand. She gave it to him, so he dropped it beside his.

Jake leaned back, watching geese glide across the pond, and put one arm on the back of the bench.

"He doesn't do cakes. Just ice cream."

"That's crazy. Every diner 'does' cakes. It's a… a…ah…"

"A rule of diners?"

"That's right. A hard, fast one every self-respecting diner owner knows."

The geese swam from one side of the wide pond to the other.

Kat pressed him. "But really, Ray only makes ice cream for dessert? That's it?"

"That's it."

Chapter 14

"There ain't no way to run..." ~*Lola Delaney*

"A diner without desserts?"

"Ray is one helluva good cook but a crummy baker. When he took over the diner, he made apple pies that gave the whole town the runs. Since then, no one asks for baked goods. Ice cream seems like a no-fail deal. Safe. And sometimes safe is good." With a fast shrug he said, "Sorry to shock you."

Her shoulders lifted, then dropped. The movement was smaller than his but carried more heaviness. What had happened to make her so weighed down?

"That's all right. I'm used to people shocking me." She sighed. "It happens all the time. All the damn time."

"I'm sorry to hear that."

"Don't be."

An expression swept over her face, pulling a mask of something—sadness? anger?—across her features. He wished he knew what hit her so hard, but since the look in her eyes as she stared at the geese didn't seem happy, he changed the subject.

"How do you like town?"

"I haven't seen much of it yet." She swiveled, facing him, and the glint in her gaze lifted his heart. The sadness was gone. "All I know about Mill Pond could fit in a pool filter."

"You're still not over that, are you?" He'd finally rescued her bikini top, but it was far worse for the wear. The bra cup that had been sucked into the filter came out shredded. He thought it would still be worth wearing but knew better than to suggest it.

"Why should I be? My first hour in town my bathing suit gets eaten, a man I don't know manhandles me in a swimming pool, and a crazy—ah, an unusual old man calls me a catfish. Catfish are, if I remember high school science correctly, bottom feeders, so it's not like I was falling over a compliment on that one."

"It was one interesting welcome, wasn't it? We could do it again, if you want. Just for laughs." His hand found her shoulder and gave a quick squeeze. She didn't pull away, so he ran a fingertip along the top of her sleeve. "There aren't many guests at the motel, so I'm pretty sure we could find some time in the pool for a private walk down memory lane."

The sun had fallen and darkness closed in around them but her green eyes seemed to sparkle. They tugged at him—everywhere and anywhere, all at once. He could lose himself in eyes like hers. Lose himself and never look for a way out.

She smiled, muddling his mind even further. The fact that she even had the ability to confound him was mind-boggling. His focus was usually dead on, his powers of concentration unwavering.

"What part of the memory lane trip, exactly, did you have in mind? The losing-my-clothing part? The cackling uncle bit? The graceless splashing moment? Which is the element that you most want to relive, Jake? Hmm?" Her teasing turned him on.

He leaned close. "This."

Between her velvety lips and the scent of roses coming from her hair, his body came to instant attention. She didn't try to pull away so he deepened the kiss, nudging her mouth open with a flick of his tongue. When she gave him entrance, he explored the warmth. She tasted like cherries, sparking a vision of her naked, cherries and ice cream drizzled over her skin.

Jake groaned, the sound muffled against Kat's lips. He shifted, his erection pressing against the zipper on his Levis. He wondered how fast they could hightail it back to his place, doing mental calculations while his hand slid lower on her shoulder. Three minutes, maybe four, he figured. Two if they ran, although running with a hard-on wasn't a piece of cake.

Kat nipped his lower lip between her teeth, biting down just enough to tantalize. She licked the spot, then plunged her tongue back into his mouth.

The last time he'd kissed anyone in the park he'd been a high school senior. His prom date, Chelsea Drake, was known for being free with her hands, and that night was no exception.

Chelsea had been willing and eager in her limited way, but they were young and inexperienced. Their fumbling was nothing by comparison to this scorching connection.

He moved his hand lower, grazing the side of her breast. His thumb brushed her nipple, pulling a small moan from her.

Self restraint, all he possessed, kept him from divesting her of her clothing. He wanted to slip his hands onto her body, feel her skin against his. Taste the sweet, private parts. He wanted to—

He wasn't the only one who wanted.

Kat's hand cupped his crotch. Her fingers molded around him, tracing the outline of his penis and stroking him through the denim. Instinctively he pressed hard against her palm, loving the delicious sensations spiraling through his body.

He couldn't run back to the house. Not now. Not with her hand massaging his already throbbing cock to a near frenzy.

They'd have to stop. For a few minutes, anyway. Until he could walk.

Shit. He didn't have a condom. No condom. No sex. It was a rule, one that he only deviated from once. Once had been enough to convince him it shouldn't happen again.

His dick didn't swim in any pond without a wetsuit. *Ever.*

She pulled back with a groan. Sexy bedroom eyes met his gaze, shocking him by the regret he saw in their depths. Her hand left his crotch just as suddenly as it found it. Without the massaging touch, he stayed rock hard, but the shivery delight shooting through his veins turned off in a burst of clarity.

She was sorry. Damn it, she was sorry.

"I…" She looked to the sky.

His fingertip stilled on her nipple. The stiff peak begged to be fondled, kissed, stroked, but he had another rule about women: Never physically push in the face of rejection. No was no, and there wasn't any debating the point. Not even if the point was warm, hard, touchable—and still pressing against his thumb.

He took his hand off her breast and sat up straight,

something that proved difficult given the state of his jeans.

"It's all right." He stood and offered her his hand. "I think we should head back, don't you?"

Chapter 15

"Confusion is a natural state of mind for some and, really, it's not all that bad. At least the confused ones have a state to call home. Others? Completely homeless—and completely clueless." ~Lola Delaney

She sipped from an ivory cup, grateful the dented percolator knew how to do its job. The coffee was good, a hint of sugar leaving a pleasant aftertaste on her tongue.

Her tongue. The one she'd practically pushed down Jake's throat.

What had she been thinking?

Not a damn thing, that's what. Her hormones had merged with moon glow and turned her into some crazed nymphomaniac.

She lifted the heavy receiver and dialed.

Two rings. Then, a lifeline.

"How're things in the mountains treating you?"

Her mood instantly lightened, a trick only someone near her heart could bring off with any degree of success. Joann Fernandez nailed it without fail—every single time.

She kept her tone casual. "Okay, I guess."

Only three words, but Joann wasn't fooled. Their history went all the way back to diapers, which meant no degree of camouflage could conceal the truth.

"What gives, sister? And don't waste our time with fluff, either. I don't want to hear you saw a big, brown bear last night or heard an owl this morning."

Jake wasn't a big bear, but he was large in a certain area. That knowledge accounted for some of her sleepiness. She'd lain awake for hours, revisiting the details of their encounter. They were the type of memories that left her hotter rather than cooled, and the apartment lacked the modern conveniences, including a fan, so her rest had been anything but peaceful.

"Nothing, exactly. And everything, somewhat." Thoughts ran through her mind like mischievous children under a water sprinkler, zigging and zagging, and all vying for space beneath the cool spray. She had the beginnings of a headache.

"Just spill it, Kat. Don't pull a Jena Rose on me."

Jena Rose, Joann's three-year-old daughter, was notorious for meandering explanations. Pointless stories were endearing coming from a toddler but not so terrific from a grown woman.

"Where is my goddaughter?"

"With my mother at the Macy's summer sale, probably getting too much stuff and eating more sugar in a day than I allow in a week. But hey, what can I do about it? At least she's with Mom, and I've got the kitchen to myself."

Joann, Jena Rose, and Juanita, Joann's mother, lived in an apartment in the Howard Beach section of Brooklyn. Kat tried for years to talk them into moving into Manhattan, but their apartment was rent-controlled. Too good a bargain to walk away from, especially when the price to rent anything near Kat's place cost more than either Joann or Juanita could afford.

"What's on today's to-do list?" Having the kitchen meant Joann had a mission.

"The Goldberg bar mitzvah. You remember Debra Goldberg, right? From the slim-down class we took last winter?"

"Of course I remember. The redhead with wide hips who thought wearing a tight leotard cancelled out eating Twinkies. She kept getting caught in one of the weight machines, right?"

"That's the one. The last time she managed to jam her breast between the vibrating hip bands she almost lost a nipple."

Heat flashed low in Kat's belly at the word. Her right nipple pebbled, the feel of Jake's touch still imprinted on her memory.

"I remember." She tried to keep her voice neutral. "They had to call for help to get her out, didn't they?"

"As a matter of fact, they did. So scary, those machines. I pulled my enrollment that very same afternoon." She paused, then said, "You did, too. Remember that? What a fiasco!"

She remembered. What Joann conveniently forgot was that neither of them liked their instructor, a young man who desperately wanted his own set of breasts and made no bones about it. That wouldn't have mattered had he been able to keep his ogling—and hands—to himself, but he never let the chance to grab any part of a woman's anatomy pass him by.

"So, Debra's got a son who's having a bar mitzvah?"

"This Saturday, in their temple's conference room or something like that. I'm not sure of all the details, but it's…you know…"

"Oh, no. Don't say it. Please don't tell me you're doing another—"

"You got it. It's supposed to be 'modest' but you know what that means."

"Cheap. Not again. You promised you weren't going to take any more of these money-losing propositions." Joann was known to cave in to a fast-talking party organizer. "Tell me you're not losing money on this one. Please, just say it ain't so."

"It ain't so." The smugness in her voice came across the miles loud and clear.

"Thank God! At least you're not losing money this time."

"Well…"

Uh-oh. She knew that well all too well.

"What?"

A small silence, then, "I'm not making any money, either."

Kat would have slapped her thigh in frustration had she not been holding a hot cup of coffee in her hand. How the hell would Joann ever make enough money to get her and Jena Rose out on their own? It was impossible, given their circumstances and Joann's inability to charge a fair price for her work.

She counted to three. It was all she could ever complete in the count-to-ten-before-speaking bit.

"Why don't you move up here? Bring that sweet child of yours out of the city and into…" She looked around. "The country. There's a park here."

"You know I can't. Besides, we've got Central Park here, or have you already forgotten your roots?"

"I haven't forgotten anything. But there's no need for mounted police in this place. Think about it. That's all I ask."

"I will. But I can't promise anything. You know that, don't you?"

As much as she wanted her best friend and godchild near, she understood that it wasn't a lark to just pick up and move. If anyone understood that, she did.

"I know."

"Listen, I hate to cut you short, but I do have the Goldberg affair to deal with. Things don't just whip themselves up, you know. Was there something in particular you called to talk about? Or did you just miss hearing me complain about my life?"

"That's it. I just missed you."

It was only a half-truth, but she couldn't begin to lay the goods on her friend. Especially not when she had a gratis bar mitzvah to bake for.

Joann laughed, not fooled at all. "Oh, no you don't! I know that tone of voice—you're keeping something to yourself. Juicy, too, I bet."

"I'm not hiding anything." It wasn't a lie. Not really.

"Just tell me one thing. Are you doing it yet?"

"Doing it? What 'it' exactly are you referring to?"

A short laugh. "Not 'it' it. I know you better than that. I'm sure you're not doing the bop with anyone yet. It's not like you to jump from one guy to another without some lag time in between. No, I want to know if you're doing it yet—and don't play dumb. We both know how you self-medicate."

She drained the coffee cup and stood. The space from table to sink wasn't far, but it was farther than the telephone cord.

Again, trapped. The story of my life.

"No. I'm not doing it. In fact, life here in the boonies is pretty damn dull."

Joann was like a poodle who sniffed a hambone. She wouldn't give up until she got at least a taste.

"Come on, give. We both know you're not telling the truth. There's something going on up there in the mountains, isn't there? Something fun?"

"Maybe. I think so." She reached for the sink, held the cup out and let go.

Stupid move.

"What was that? Something broke?"

Kat sighed. A splay-bristled broom hid in the pantry closet, along with a metal bucket and a stack of paper grocery bags. Time to pitch the cup pieces into a bag and sweep up near the sink. The crash sent shards skittering along the linoleum.

Just before she put the handset back in its cradle, she promised, "I'll tell you later."

Chapter 16

"Therapy is different for everyone. Some find it in a bakery. Others, a bottle of rum. Still others, in the arms of a handsome man." ~Lola Delaney

The peace and solitude she hoped to find? Lost to the trio of boys flying past on hopped-up Schwinns, an elderly woman calling geese she apparently thought were stone deaf to feed near her ankles, and a loose cluster of stroller-pushing mothers loudly comparing the effect of breast milk on the contents of a baby's diaper. Lingering on the bench within earshot of the confusion nursing a cup of take-out coffee from the diner wasn't going to soothe her mind.

Her gaze shifted to the park entrance.

Oh, hell no. Not before the caffeine kicks in.

Her heart thudded into the pit of her stomach. Her fingers tightened on the disposable cup so hard coffee splashed over the top.

She stood, ignoring the sting of hot liquid on her wrist and walked toward the center of the park. There had to be a back exit.

She didn't look over her shoulder but prayed she wasn't being followed. Moving as fast as her Candies allowed, she held her cup away from her body. Coffee splattered the concrete walkway, leaving a trail even a blind man could follow by its hazelnut scent.

Walking in four-inch heels inside a building was talent. Practically running over uneven park walkways in the same heels was sheer madness.

A stone beneath her left heel almost sent her sprawling. She regained her balance, but just barely.

There definitely was something moving on the path behind her. And if that something was, in fact, someone, she couldn't very well admit she'd escaped to ponder the madness that had overtaken her and made her fondle the bits and pieces of a man she barely knew.

Especially if her suspicion was correct and that very same man—and his glorious bits and pieces—followed right behind her.

How on earth had she gone from Manhattan to running in a heartbeat? Her life was a shambles—and she had no idea how to put it in order.

Joann was right. Time to self-medicate.

Chapter 17

"Ain't no way to decipher a woman unless she wants to be deciphered. And that, my fine friends, is a fact." ~Lola Delaney

Intuition and excellent problem-solving skills, two talents that had served him well in the past, were of no use at all when it came to figuring out women. Jake already knew that.

Every man worth his weight in beer nuts knew it. Those who still wrangled with trying to unravel the female mind were hopeless. They sought the Holy Grail of relationships. Nice in theory, but unattainable.

But most women could be at least understood. Not completely, but enough to share some sort of logical relationship—even if it was only a platonic one. It was an unwritten rule of the male-female dynamic, that there should be common ground somewhere.

Mill Pond's sexy-as-hell newcomer was a man stumper. He'd lain awake most of the night, working the Kat issue over in his mind. But despite pulling out all the problem-solving tricks in his arsenal, he had no idea what made the woman tick.

Hope of making progress with her still burned but not as brightly as it had yesterday, although his desire for the woman grew with every passing hour.

Funny how aching testicles put a damper on his

outlook.

Kat-astrophe.

He pulled into the only empty slot in front of Maxwell's Grocery. Wishing he'd remembered dinner earlier, when the store aisles would have been empty enough to use as bowling lanes, he got out of the car and headed for the automatic doors. He'd considered going to the diner but the thought of dealing with Destiny's inquisition—and there was sure to be one, considering Kat was the only woman he'd dined with in longer than he cared to admit—convinced him to cook his own meal. No questions. No knowing looks. No defending his position against dating.

Maybe that's where he'd gone wrong last night. He'd forgotten one of his rules.

He had a no-dating policy, implemented when he realized every single woman in town was either looking for a sex toy or angling for a trip to the altar. Not that he had anything against sex—hell, he loved sex—but even casual encounters eventually turned serious. And serious? That tugged a man to his last mile and a position in front of a priest who droned on about sickness, health, better, worse...no matter how sugary it sounded, it all boiled down to one thing: responsibility.

Jake didn't want anyone depending on him. Not again.

Air-conditioning hit him like an Arctic blast. Grabbing a cart, he pushed it toward the dairy section.

He exchanged greetings with several people but didn't stop to chat. Hunger made him less social than usual.

Until he passed the baking aisle.

It was a good thing no one was behind him. He

stopped. Backed up and wheeled toward Kat. She held a red plastic shopping basket draped over one arm. In her hands, two bags of chocolate pieces.

A pair of cross trainers replaced this morning's killer heels. And the black skirt, white blouse ensemble was gone. White jeans and a midriff-baring sleeveless navy-blue tank top inspired pure desire.

He reined in the lust galloping through his veins.

"How're you doing?"

She dropped the bags of chocolate into her basket as if she were a thief and he the store detective.

Guilty pleasure?

"Jake." She met his gaze. The corners of her lips turned up but her smile didn't hit her eyes. "I'm fine, thanks. You?"

Huey Lewis cheerfully sang about going back in time while he wished he could turn the clock back, too. Not all the way back to the future, like in the movie, but back to their first meeting. In the pool.

He wasn't dumb. She couldn't hide her dismay at seeing him behind a veneer of politeness.

Letting her off the hook with a couple of random sentences was an option he wasn't inclined to take. The more she avoided him, the more determined he was to put himself in her face. It was stubborn, purely selfish, and defied rational explanation but he didn't care.

"Not bad." Then, because he hated the way she looked so uncomfortable, he nodded to her basket. "Doing some baking?"

"Not exactly."

She didn't offer anything else so he waited. She shifted her weight from one foot to the other. The basket held a five-pound bag of sugar, a couple pounds of butter, corn syrup, chocolate, and several large bags of nuts.

Jake took it off her forearm. He set it into his shopping cart, pushing a six-pack of Coors to one side.

"You don't have to do that."

She reached toward the basket, but he began wheeling, leaving her no choice but to trail behind him. She did, so he slowed his step so they could walk side by side.

"I know I don't." If she wanted to act like last night had never happened, it was fine by him. Honestly, he still wasn't sure exactly what went wrong in the park, or why she'd run like all the minions in hell were hot on her heels this morning when she saw him, but that didn't matter now.

He was just glad to see her.

They passed the cashiers, and she would have stopped but he kept moving.

"I was on my way out." Kat pointed at the checkout sign. "Really, I'm done shopping."

Jake regarded her basket, compartmentalizing all the items and finding no logical explanation for their pairing.

"Did you hear me? I said, I'm done. Shopping. Done. Finished."

"I heard you. I'm done too, right after I get a thing or two."

Hijacking her groceries hadn't been a conscious decision, but it was amusing watching her try to distance herself from him while he pushed her food around.

He made a beeline for the fresh peas, snagged a handful and stuffed them into a plastic bag. Then, he moved to the broccoli and chose a bunch. They hit a bag, then the pile of groceries in the seat part of the carriage.

"You're a vegetarian." It was the first thing that came to mind, so he said it.

"I know." She scrunched her nose. It was an incredibly sexy, crotch-tightening gesture.

"Where are the vegetables?" He pointed to the evaporated milk and nuts. The chocolate bags had slid beneath a container of espresso powder.

Kat grabbed the bunch of broccoli closest to her, shoved it into a produce bag and tossed it onto her things. "There."

"Fruits? Isn't fruit one of those big vegetarian must-haves?"

Messing with her felt good. Almost like payback for the way she'd played with him.

A display of bagged oranges lost one bag as she grabbed it and dumped it onto the broccoli. With a quirk of an eyebrow, she reached for a second five-pound bag of oranges. She almost squashed his loaf of Italian bread when she dropped it onto his grocery pile.

"You look like the kind of guy who likes oranges. Now that we're both eyeball deep in fruits and veggies, can we please check out? This place is like a meat locker—I'm freezing."

Jake glanced down and saw she was, indeed, cold. It crossed his mind to say he had a few more groceries to get, but he chased the devil off his shoulder.

"Let's go."

Chapter 18

"Men—there's only one way catch them, and that…well, now, that's all about the birds and the bees…" ~Lola Delaney

"Where's your car?"

"I don't have one."

"But you had one when you checked into the motel." Her sign-in slip had listed a license plate number.

"Right. I don't have it here."

When he looked down at her as if she'd lost her mind, Kat sighed. Things were simpler in the city. No one cared about anyone else, really, so there were no explanations to be doled out.

For what felt like the thousandth time, she reminded herself that this wasn't Manhattan.

"In the city there's really no need for a car. Subways, taxis, the train…all work better than having to pay a mint for parking and constantly wondering when—not if—your vehicle's going to lose its cassette deck. So, I'm used to not having a car. I left it at the…ah, at the gallery."

It was still hard to call the shop a gallery.

"I'll drive you." Jake put all the grocery bags in the back seat of a shiny Mustang. He'd left the top down so the switch from carriage to car took only a few seconds.

"Anywhere else you need to go before you go home? Any other stops to make?"

She didn't make a move to get into the car. He went around and opened her door.

"No, thanks. But really, I planned to walk back to the apartment. It's only a few blocks." She pointed to the sneakers. "See? Prepared to walk."

He had hijacked her groceries, but he couldn't abduct a woman from the parking lot. "Why walk when you can ride? What? Don't like convertibles?"

"No, it's not that. The car is gorgeous." She ran a palm across the black leather passenger-side headrest.

"Then get in. We'll go for a ride, you and me. What do you say?"

What harm could there be in taking a ride from the guy? The day was gorgeous, the car a dream, and Jake's good looks and charm made the offer too good to turn down. Kat shrugged, and moved closer to the passenger seat. She bent her knees to sit.

"Yoo hoo! Oh, Jake, is that you?"

The sound stopped her cold. The look on Jake's face told her all she needed to know.

"Oh, Jake, honey, don't pretend you don't hear me." The woman who ran up to the car apparently didn't have an ounce of embarrassment in her genetic makeup. She boldly pinched his ass before he turned around.

"Chelsea, stop it!"

The newcomer grinned. "Don't pretend you don't like it. I remember some things, and that's one of them."

Jake looked from the blonde to Kat, then back again. His eyes flashed.

If looks could kill.

Kat stepped away from the car. Removing her groceries from the back seat, she said, "You look busy, so I'll go home the way I planned. On foot. And alone."

"Wait—"

There was no sense waiting for an explanation. Besides, as she turned for the sidewalk, she heard the other woman giggling.

It was obvious the pair had history. Maybe even current events.

While her heart inexplicably sank, it was a relief. As long as Jake was unavailable, following her no-penis rule was definitely going to prove less challenging.

Chapter 19

"Oh, sure, you can catch more bees with honey than vinegar. But who wants bees when you can have men instead?" ~Lola Delaney

Kat tucked the receiver against her chin, mixing syrup with one hand and searching the kitchen cupboards for a candy thermometer with the other.

She tugged one chrome door handle after another, rifling the contents of each cabinet as if they were display cases at Bloomingdale's. She pushed all sorts of Pyrex bowls, ramekins, and casserole dishes to the back. A cupboard filled with turquoise, red, ivory, and yellow Fiestaware made her smile. The unexpected tropicality of the assortment was super, but the mélange of colors did not hide a thermometer.

Not that there wasn't an assortment of kitchen equipment. There was. Aluminum pots and cast-iron pans took up so much room that she had to shove them back into their space before slamming the cupboard door closed.

Great. A must-have turned no-show made a challenge near impossible.

"How can a kitchen not have a candy thermometer? It's a joke, having all these colored plates and matching glasses. What good are they if there's no thermometer? I should've brought my own."

71

Golden liquid bubbled in a pot on the stove, releasing a scent of sweetness each time she swirled her stainless steel spoon through its creamy goodness. Her mouth watered.

She loved creating new tastes from basic ingredients, then watching those she cared for enjoy the products of her efforts.

"You don't need a thermometer anymore. You can just eyeball it and figure out what to add—or take away—by the consistency. Come on, have faith in yourself. You're way beyond thermometers."

"Really? Like you're 'way beyond' measuring cups?"

"Touché. But you'll know when it's reached the soft crack stage."

"I don't know. I seem to have lost part of my mind up here in the Adirondacks."

"What's going on?" Joann hit the opening like white on rice, but Kat wasn't ready to change topics. Not when her goddaughter's college fund was on the line.

"Not so fast." She had an eye on the bubbling liquid. "We're not done with your cake business, sweetie. How do you expect to move forward if you're holding yourself back?"

Hypocritical, talking about moving forward in the middle of the old-fashioned kitchen, her biggest-ever backward move.

"I know, I know…I get it, really I do. But I just can't seem to formulate a workable business plan. I'm trying, but just not getting very far."

The discouragement in Joann's voice tore at her heart. She wanted the world for her best friend, without a hint of sadness.

She spread toasted hazelnuts, almonds and walnuts on a greased baking sheet, pressing the nuts into the corners to cover the entire pan. She looked at the pot and gave it a fast stir. The caramel hadn't thickened all the way. It was close, but not to the stage she needed.

"How did the bar mitzvah cake turn out?" She shifted the subject a little and left out all references to money. It wouldn't help to bring up lousy career choices. When Joann decided to make a move, she would be supportive. Until then, she would keep her opinion to herself. "I bet it's gorgeous. Vanilla or chocolate?"

"Chocolate, with butter cream frosting. And it is something else, even if I do say so myself."

Those amazing cake skills came naturally. Juanita had clothed and fed her children after her husband's early death by baking and selling custom wedding cakes. She made them in her Brooklyn kitchen, the way her daughter did now.

Their baking chops were undisputed. Not so much their business acumen. Anyone with a couple hundred could learn business basics in night school. But talent like the Fernandez women possessed wasn't for sale.

"Wish I were there to lick the spoon." Loneliness for the familiar rushed over her. She hated her neediness, especially when she couldn't help asking, "Have you heard...um, well, have you?"

"You mean have I heard any news about that dickhead you were living with?"

"That's the one. I hate that I'm asking, but have you heard anything?"

"Not much. I did run into Jenny Albanger, who

said the scuttlebutt at the office is kind of hush-hush. Apparently no one, not even the guys he worked with, wants to say a word about what Henry did. Kind of worried they might pick up something nasty, just by being associated. That's what she said, anyway. Sorry if it hurts you, Kat."

Nasty by association? When she'd first learned what her "perfect" boyfriend had been doing in his spare time, she barely made it to their bathroom before she got sick. Then, she'd taken the longest shower in her life, hoping to wash away the creepiness coating her like slime after an oil spill.

Yeah, she understood nasty by association.

"Don't be sorry. Nothing he can do or say, or anything said about him, can hurt me. I'm over letting him hurt me." She twirled her spoon in the caramel. "If I'm honest, I really feel detached. I didn't know him. He wasn't who he pretended to be. When we were together, I wasn't the woman I wanted to be, either. It's better this way. I hate what he did, but I'm glad we're done."

"You're getting a whole new view on things. I like it. Keep it up, sister. So—done with Henry, but I know there's another man on the hook. I can feel it."

The spoon left a trail in the hot sugar. She dragged it so there were streaks, then squiggles and finally a heart on the surface of the mixture.

"Is that right? You feel my love life, long distance?"

"Uh-huh. Who is he, this mountain man? And just so you don't think I'm naïve down here in Brooklyn, I hear in your voice you're ready to deny it. Don't tell me you're already running away from love. Head toward the man—especially if he's real. Not like the last asshole. Is this one real?"

Kat considered. Was he? He seemed genuine but so had Henry early in their relationship. It was only later that she discovered his lying and cheating. So, real? Who could ever tell about someone?

"I don't know."

"Fair enough. You've only been in the sticks for what, two days? You probably need longer than that to decide about someone."

"Three days. Tomorrow is four. And it's not the sticks. It's the mountains—rural living at its best."

"Listen to you—the city is washing right out of you, isn't it?"

"Maybe." She stirred the syrup. It was almost thick enough, nearly at the scorch-or-perfect stage. "I don't know anything. The gallery's a mess, my boyfriend turned out to be a jackass, and now I'm here trying to pull it all together. It's just so…"

"Overwhelming," Joann finished.

"Don't you know it. And all I want…"

Really, what did she want? It was hard to tell at this point. For so long, and in so many discouraging ways, she had let other people dictate the direction of her life. It had been a cop out, not standing up for herself and just going where the stream took her.

And where had it taken her? Not on an exotic, heart-stopping adventure or an amazing, life-altering journey. No, floating along on the current of Henry's life had given her nothing like that. While the journey had altered her, in the end it left her alone, in the middle of nowhere surrounded by the remnants of a life lived by a woman she wouldn't have known had she stumbled over her.

"You know, I'm not sure I know what exactly I want," Kat admitted.

Chapter 20

"There's nothing like a woman scorned."
~*Lola Delaney*

Not so long ago, hers had been a ho-hum existence. Growing up in an ordinary, middle-class family in East Northport, one of the sleepy coastal towns on Long Island's North Shore, she'd never yearned for anything great. Her dreams didn't include someday becoming a spy, ballerina, novelist, or rocket scientist. All she'd ever wanted was to be happy. That's it. Nothing more.

Now it looked like even the deceptively simple life request was denied. She felt like a form at the Department of Motor Vehicles—denied for insufficient whatever, a bright, red circular stamp across her brow.

Joann was so reasonable and reassuring. "Remember, it isn't your fault life your life got so convoluted. You're a passenger on the roller coaster, not the operator."

"I think that's part of my issue." The truth stuck in her throat, but she coughed it out like a cat with a hairball. "I've been a passenger for too long—for forever. I've got to learn how to either get off the roller coaster or take the controls. One or the other—it's my only chance at surviving the damn ride."

"You go, girl! I love it when you take charge." High school cheerleading paid off, still. "You get yourself straightened out. We'll all celebrate!"

"Not so fast." Kat gave the caramel a vicious stir. "Don't go popping open any champagne just yet. I'm far from success. One minute, I'm sure I'll sell this so-called gallery, pocket the money, and start over where nobody knows me."

"Like Mill Pond?"

"Don't confuse me with the facts, because other times—like every other damn second—I think I've got to figure out how to make this dump into a profitable business. It'd be nice to have something to call my own. Just mine, with me in charge."

"I like the way that sounds."

"Me, too. But this place is such a disaster. And to add to it—but in a nice way—I met someone. Not just any someone, but a sweet guy. He's funny. He teases me, and I like it. You know, Henry never teased me. Or me him. We never did that. I know I shouldn't compare men, but really, is there anything wrong with having fun?"

"You don't have to convince me you're entitled to have some fun. Believe me, I've been praying you'd meet Mr. Perfect. But tell me one thing, if you don't mind."

"What?"

"Is he hot?"

She stirred hard and fast, deflating sugar bubbles as they rose to the caramel's surface. "Almost too hot to handle."

"I hoped you'd say that." Joann's laugh was gentle.

Kat was louder, giggling away tension until happy tears slid down her cheeks. She reached up to wipe them away, but her finger stilled on her skin. Had it been her imagination, or had she heard a voice? Not hers or Joann's but someone else's? And not too far away, either?

Noises downstairs made the laughter die in her throat.

"Oh, boy," she lowered her voice. "Quiet—I hear something."

"What?"

She searched for a weapon. She pulled hard on a drawer handle, rummaging through the assortment of kitchen utensils so fast she nicked a fingertip on a vegetable peeler. Unless she could kill someone with a potato masher, she was out of luck on the weapon front.

"Kat—are you okay?"

She grabbed the largest item in the drawer, leaned close to the phone sitting on the countertop, and whispered, "If I don't come back, call for help. Someone's downstairs in the shop."

"But—"

"Not now." She turned toward the staircase that separated the living space from the rest of the building. Then, she turned back, leaned close again and added, "If anything happens to me, you'll make sure Jena Rose doesn't forget me, right? Promise."

"I promise. But—"

Without waiting for the rest, she hit the stairs on tiptoe.

No time for buts. Now or never—and if she didn't act on the adrenaline rush surging through her body, she'd end up on the never side of bravery.

For an insane instant, it crossed her mind that now was all she had.

Chapter 21

"Smokey the Bear wasn't all wrong about fire. He wasn't all right, either. If you don't want to get burned, don't play with it. But if you think you can take some heat, stand real close...and let the flames lick you all over." ~Lola Delaney

Jake tripped. Knowing Lola's mess, which her niece hadn't disturbed as far as he could tell, anything could be responsible for his stinging shin.

He moved more cautiously, but it didn't stop him from ramming his hip into a different obstacle. This time, he knocked something over. No breaking glass, but there was a large, dull thud.

Why hadn't he bothered to turn the lights on? If he had, he might stand a chance of getting to the stairwell without damaging anything—including his own body parts.

Keeping to what he hoped was the middle of the aisle, he placed one foot before the other and made his way to the light pooling on the floorboards just a few feet ahead of him.

He was about to turn the corner when something leaped at him from the steps. He dropped the sack and held his hands up in front of his chest. He caught the flying dervish just as he felt a crack across the forehead. Fortunately, the blow was superficial.

Grabbing Kat—as soon as she was on him he recognized her rose-scented perfume—he pulled her against him. She struggled, trying to wiggle from his grasp like a mouse stuck to a sticky trap. The thrashing about wasn't at all unpleasant, especially since she only wore a tank top and barely-there shorts, so he held her close and let her resist for several heartbeats.

It was shameful, holding her against him while she wiggled, but he didn't feel one bit sorry. He hadn't lunged at her, had he? And any means of defending himself was fair, especially when she had a weapon.

When she hit him again on the head, he pulled back but didn't let her go.

"Quit hitting me, okay?"

She froze mid-wiggle.

And relaxed her lush body against him. He dipped his nose into her hair and inhaled. So sweet. Damn it if she didn't smell good enough to eat...

"Jake?"

"Expecting someone different?"

His eyes acclimated to the darkness. He caught her shocked expression. She wasn't expecting anyone at all.

"You shouldn't sneak in here like that! I thought you were a burglar. You're lucky I didn't hurt you." It obviously hadn't hit her that he still held her close, because she didn't demand release.

"With what?"

She held up her hand and he burst out laughing.

"You tried to brain me with a turkey baster? Is that how they do it in the big city?"

Kat's creamy complexion turned darker in the dim light. It could have been a touch of embarrassment, indignation, annoyance...whatever it was that caused her cheeks to bloom made her sexier than ever. Heat—a different sort of warmth—suffused his body, and he ran a thumb beneath her jaw and nudged her chin up.

Her eyes sent silent questions he couldn't answer.

Electric questions.

He didn't know what this was between them, only that it was.

"I didn't know it was you." A shake sent her curls tumbling against a cheek. "It was the first thing I grabbed."

"And now that you know it's me?"

"Hmm?"

His heart skipped a beat. "Would you still try to stop me with that silly thing? Or would you grab something else?"

It was a risk. She still held the baster in her right hand, but her left was down on his hip. Either one could do damage—one more seriously than the other.

She rose to the bait like a hungry minnow.

"Are you offering something?" The question was bold, her voice so low and sweet he wanted to lick her. All over. And, hell, she really *did* smell temptation good.

"Would you say yes?" Loosening his hold just a touch, he leaned close and looked into her eyes. They'd lost the shock from when he grabbed her. Good. He hated to think he was flirting with a woman who still reeled from his sudden appearance.

She looked fine, so he stroked a slow line along her left cheek, down the slope of her delicate neck and lower. He stopped at the top of her shoulder. She trembled in his arms, and he responded the way any man would. Especially a man who'd gone so long without physical intimacy with a gorgeous woman. His cock thickened enough that his jeans tightened.

Damn jeans. He'd rather they were both naked, or at least as nearly naked as they had been in the motel swimming pool. An image of Kat's firm breasts flashed through his mind, bringing more blood to his throbbing penis.

"What do you say, Kat? Would you say yes if I offered more than just this?"

"What is this, anyway?"

Good question. It wasn't what he'd expected when he'd come through the back door.

"What do you want it to be?"

"You broke into the gall—the store." She choked on the word gallery. He couldn't blame her.

"The door was open."

Her head turned toward the front of the store.

"Not that door. The back door. Closed, but unlocked, the way Lola always had it. Didn't you know?"

She shook her head. "I would have locked it. So why did you come through my back door?"

"Why did you leave your oranges in my car?"

"I...ah, right. I forgot one grocery bag, didn't I?"

"That's right. When you ran from me," he reminded her.

"I didn't run."

God, but she was adorable when she pulled her lips into a straight line. On someone else, it would have been horrible and unflattering, but she pulled it off—and then some. Beautiful, sexy, and stubborn—three items Jake never minded on a woman.

"I don't know what city slickers call it, but when

someone dashes across a parking lot like their ass is on fire, around here we say they're running."

"My ass wasn't on fire." She lifted her chin, bringing her lips closer to his. Dangerously close, unless she wanted him to claim them. "And even if it was, I doubt you'd have noticed. You were busy, remember?"

"I'd never be too busy to know if your ass was on fire." His arm was still around her waist. It was a risk, but he let his hand drop so his palm spread across her lower back, just above the gorgeous body part that was the topic of conversation.

"Hmm…" She lowered her voice, the sexy purr making him harder. "Maybe you should let the bombshell know hers isn't the only behind on your fire watch list."

"She's not on the list." He went the final few inches, cupping one cheek in his hand and pulling her hips against his. "There is no list. She's just an old friend, that's all."

"And us? We're new friends, then?"

"I hope so. Don't you?"

Kat didn't answer right away. She scrutinized his face, and he let her. He didn't move as her gaze roamed from his forehead, to his eyes, to the rest of his features. Then, she met his gaze again. Serious replaced shock.

The purr was gone, too. "Just friends. That's all I can deal with right now. I'm…"

"Off men, I know."

She might be "off men" in her mind, but everywhere else, she seemed turned on. He couldn't be wrong about the signals. The way her fingers twisted in the curls just above his collar wasn't a hands-off message.

She looked like it had been a long time since she had been loved.

Too much thinking.

Jake kissed her, his mouth open and gentle on her lips. The chance to pull away was hers, and he gave her time. She kissed him back, and this kiss was even more forceful than the one in the park had been. This time, they knew each other's mouths. Without any need for tentative explorations, their lips parted, their tongues found their way and heat flared between them.

Kat tasted sweet. Like spun sugar. His heart hammered against his chest, his penis throbbed hard and insistent in his Levis and all he could think of was getting her naked and beneath him. Need made his kisses insistent, and when she responded in kind he gave in to his desire.

His hand slid beneath one strap on her tank top and pulled it down. Then, the bra strap, not much more than a flimsy length of ribbon, tore as he pushed it aside. He didn't care. He'd buy her a new bra—a dozen new bras.

Breaking their kiss was tough but he had to taste her. Could she be so sweet everywhere? A groan tore from his throat when he leaned down, cupping her exposed breast with one hand and dipping her backward in his other arm. The nipple was so stiff he suckled hard, loving the sigh that escaped her open lips. He rolled the delicate flesh across his tongue and took her breast into his mouth. The discovery that her sweetness extended far beyond her lips nearly made him explode.

"Oh…" Her moan filled his head.

He pushed her back against whatever cluttered counter stood behind them. When something crashed to the floor it didn't break their concentration.

"Too many clothes." He grabbed the bottom edge of her shirt and pulled it over her head. What was left of her lacy bra took only a second to unclasp. One swift turn of the wrist and he had both items dangling from his fingertips. He dropped them to the floor.

So beautiful. He wished for more light, so he could see her clearly, but the silhouette of the slope of her breasts and her tiny waist made him growl.

"I want you."

She grinned up at him as she did some fancy wrist turning of her own. The button on his fly posed no challenge. Then, still keeping her gaze locked on his, Kat pulled his zipper low, inch by inch. She stopped midway.

"Baby...don't torture me..."

She kissed him, pushing her tongue between his lips and swirling it around in his mouth. The kiss turned him inside out. When she slipped a finger into his jeans, it was his turn to moan. "Oh...oh, yes..."

A fingertip grazed the tender tip of his penis. Her touch sent sparks up his spine. He'd grown rock hard, and with his fly half undone, he was nearly out of his jeans. Freedom—frustratingly close...

A second finger joined the first inside his pants. He swiveled his hips, helping her slide her fingertips down the top few inches of his erection.

Desire became a demanding need. They had to move on or he was going to go insane. Every instinct urged him to find a way to bury himself deep into her warm center, hold her close, and make her cry his name as she fell over the edge.

"Sweet Jesus, Kat..."

"I know…Oh, God, I know…"

Her shorts were tiny, so short he wiggled a fingertip up the inside seam. A scrap of fabric covered her, but he pushed it aside.

"Oh…" The whimper sent chills up his spine. She wriggled, pressing her hot skin against his finger.

God, but she was magnificent.

Reluctantly he removed his hand and went for his wallet. In his back pocket, the condom he had stashed behind his drivers' license just this morning. Ribbed, for her pleasure. He couldn't get it out fast enough.

He tore the wrapper with his teeth. Spit the foil over his shoulder.

Slow it down, man. Just slow it the hell down.

No sex for so long put a guy at a disadvantage. If it was over before the earth moved for her, he'd be pretty damn embarrassed.

But her fingers were working magic on his skin. Nerve endings came alive. Heat coursed through his body but he forced himself to slow. Her neck, sweet against his lips. Breathing in the scent of her, he focused on keeping his heart from galloping out of his chest.

Angels. The high-pitched sound of angels singing in the background—something new but hell, if heaven above thought this was a divine match who was he to dispute it?

He swept his lips up her neck. Along her jaw. His lips found hers as his fingers pulled the condom out of the wrapper.

Angels—with a one-note melody that was distracting…

Kat pulled back so quickly their lips made a weird

sucking noise when they separated.

"Shit!" Her fingers tightened around the tip of his cock and squeezed hard when she swore. The sensation wasn't unpleasant but before the full effect of her touch registered, she removed her hand. "Damn it! Do you smell that?"

Now that she mentioned it, he did smell something—

Chapter 22

"A lover should look at you as if you are magic."
~Lola Delaney

A smoke detector shrieked. Near-paradise turned to purgatory, and sirens blaring outside the shop sent a frigid blast that chilled their passion.

Voices, loud and tense, gave him barely enough warning to turn to face the door before it came crashing into the dark space. Flashlight beams played over them, so Jake put his body in front of Kat's. She swatted his shoulder, trying to push him aside and go somewhere—he hadn't a clue where she thought she was going without her shirt but it wasn't the time to ask—so he stood firm.

The overhead fixture went on, bringing them face to face with Mill Pond's three-man police force. A long moment passed before the trio lowered their department-issue service pistols.

The chief of police fought to keep his lips from twitching. "What the hell is going on here?" His gaze swept over the half-naked woman, down to the partially unzipped fly, then back up to meet his eyes. "What's with the smoke? And the stink—what is that?"

Jake had been best man at Tom and Kathy's wedding, and he'd been a pallbearer when cancer stole Kathy a scant year later. They'd been buddies for so long they were almost brothers.

Kat pushed Jake aside, cupped her breasts in her hands and ran to the stairway leading back to the apartment. "My candy is burning!"

For several long moments, the four men stared at each other.

Tom was the first to break into a grin. To his credit, he held in the laughter as he ushered the other cops out the front door.

Over his shoulder, he asked, "Need any help turning the smoke alarm off?"

The noise ceased. Loud metallic banging, muffled-but-understandable curses, and the sound of rushing water followed.

Holstering his weapon and fighting so hard to contain his amusement his shoulders shook, Tom said, "Well, it sounds like you don't any help from us. Your friend seems to be, ah, taking care of her own burnt candy. 'Night, Jake."

They left as fast as they'd arrived. No sirens when the cars started but laughter carried on the night air. Damn it.

He zipped his fly and picked up Kat's discarded clothing.

Any chance of satisfying their mutual hunger was gone. He'd be lucky if she even looked at his crotch again after this fiasco. Regret deflated him, in more ways than one, as he took the stairs upward, praying she wouldn't hit him with more than a turkey baster when he reached the top.

Chapter 23

"Embarrassment? Might be uncomfortable, but won't kill you. Regret? Now, that's another story altogether." ~Lola Delaney

The sun was barely up before Kat faced her so-called inheritance. She'd been sleepless all night anyhow, tossing and turning for hours after she'd sent Jake—and his, she now knew, impressive penis—on his way.

She shoved a dusty stack of comic books into a cardboard box. The shelf below the counter where they had been body wrestling was nearly empty. Looking at the place where they'd been nearly naked sent a surge of heat to her cheeks.

She'd almost melted on that counter, almost died from lusting for his body. It would have been a damn fine way to go.

Back to business. Slipping and sliding in the almost-sex memories wouldn't get the crap cleared out of the place.

Lola's Folly. That's what Kat's mother had called her older sister's business.

The siblings hadn't been close. Lola's husband hit on his sister-in-law shortly after Kat's parents married. Her father and uncle had come to blows while the sisters exchanged harsh words. Kat's grandmother had done her best to intervene, but there was no calming the waters. The damage had been done.

Eventually Lola's husband took off with a cashier from the hardware store in town. He'd drained their joint bank account, stolen her treasured red Buick Skylark, and set off for parts unknown. He was never heard from again.

Broke and humiliated, Lola reached out to her sister, but there was no repairing the rift between them. Left on her own and with very little to show for her efforts, she put all her energy into the one thing that remained. The gallery wasn't much, but it was better than nothing.

Kat would have liked to have known her aunt. Wishing didn't change things, so she didn't dwell on what she hadn't had. Still, when she let herself, she wished...

But yearning wasn't going to pull the shop into shape, so she shook her head to clear it.

A square of yellow foil caught her eye. She bent down and picked it up.

Condom wrapper. Her gaze swept the dusty floor. No condom. That, at least, was something.

She jammed the wrapper in her pocket.

When she swiped a palm across the shelf she'd just emptied, it came away nearly black. It would take more than a little effort to clean the joint. It was going to take buckets of bleach and endless rolls of paper towels.

Time. And elbow grease.

But it wasn't as if a better opportunity waited for her. This was it. Crunch time. Either she'd make a success of the mess or she'd sink further into the abyss called her life.

Resolve to straighten out her circumstances—inch by inch and dirty, dusty artifact by artifact if she had to—spurred her on. She grabbed a handful of theater programs and glanced at the date on the top one—nineteen sixty-eight—before tossing them into the box. In the far corner of the shelf, one lone hardcover stood against the wooden sidewall.

The cracked, blue leather-covered cookbook got her full attention. Old cookbooks were a passion. It was like reading the evolution of man—from the stomach's perspective.

It looked as if it had been bound by hand and its pages, crumpled in the corners and spotted with who-knew-what, were typewritten sheets cut to fit between the cover. It was strange, but she ignored the book's handmade elements and focused on its contents.

Every recipe so far, and she'd skimmed through more than half of the titles, was meatless. They weren't vegan, since many used milk, butter, or some kind of cheese, but there wasn't any meat, poultry, or fish in any of the recipes.

She stuck a finger between two pages, contemplating the merits of two similar dishes. Pasta Primavera. Vegetable Lasagna. They both sounded scrumptious, but she would probably never bring them to her dinner table. Who had time for cooking with a dump to revive and a life to reconstruct?

The front door to the shop stood wide open. She hated risking another encounter with the vicious duck—or the even more formidable Duck Lady—but between last night's smoke and the dust coating everything around her, keeping the door open and fresh air circulating was her only shot at breathing.

She heard footsteps an instant before she heard the call so she shoved the scrap of foil from her pocket into the book and turned.

"Hello? Anyone here? Miss Delaney?"

"Right here."

The police chief stood a few feet inside the doorway. She smiled and waved him inside.

Just last night they'd stood in practically the same spots, he wearing a crisp blue uniform like the one he had on now while she was topless, her hand tangled in Jake's pants. It occurred to her that since hitting Mill Pond, she had spent a lot of time topless.

Heat suffused her cheeks. What to say to someone who'd witnessed such an embarrassing moment?

He held his right hand out as if last night had never happened. "I don't believe we've been introduced. I'm Tom Preston, the Chief of Police around here. And you're Katherine Delaney, our newest resident. Nice to meet you, Miss Delaney."

A web of fine lines radiated from the corners of his cornflower-blue eyes. Short, sandy hair liberally laced with gray made him look older but she guessed his age to be right around Jake's. The smile was kind and friendly, but didn't reach his eyes.

She was staring. Quickly, she shifted the book to her left arm and shook his hand. "Kat, please."

"Kat. I like that. And everyone calls me Tom. We don't stand on formality much around these parts."

"Nice to meet you."

Kat leaned one butt cheek against the counter behind her. He looked every bit the part of small-town police chief, with a long, rangy build and inquisitive gaze. His eyes swept the room, and she got the impression he catalogued every item in the store in one fast perusal.

Then, the cop's gaze met hers. He smiled again, and as before the expression didn't reach his eyes.

"How do you like our little town?"

She lifted one shoulder, then let it drop. "I haven't seen much of it yet. Just the motel and the diner. And the park." She gestured to the mess around them. "And this. So, really, I'm not in much of a position to like or not."

"Fair enough. I'm just thinking this must be an awful large change for you from big city living. Do you think you'll grow accustomed to our slower pace? Or will you yearn for the bright lights again?"

It was a strange question. Hadn't she just told him she didn't even know what the damn town had to offer? How could she tell what she'd miss? Or not?

Too little sleep, for the second night in a row, left her grouchy. "You know, that's another thing I can't answer. As I said, I'm not in a position to decide what I might miss but there are...ah, there are things I left behind which I have no desire to revisit. I'd really like to make a go of it here. That is, if I can figure this mess out."

Their heads swiveled. Piles of random objects surrounded them.

Tom indicated the one empty shelf behind her. "You're making headway."

"A small start." She looked over at the bare spot in a sea of disarray. "It's going to take a lot more clearing to decide a direction for this place."

He studied her face. Then, he nodded. "You'll do it. You seem like just the kind of woman to pull order from chaos. Besides, that's what you do, isn't it?"

So her old life hadn't been left as far behind as she thought. She wondered just how much he really knew. And if he was aware of the whole story behind her flight from the city, would he hold it against her?

Only time would tell.

Until she was sure, she'd have to be careful. Very careful.

"Obviously, you know my employment history. It included being a professional organizer, so you're right. I do tame clutter, although this job certainly tops any other I've undertaken."

"You seem very capable, Kat. From what I've seen so far." He paused, the corners of his lips pulling upward ever-so slightly. "Ahem, I meant to say that it looks like you're skilled at handling anything that comes your way."

The double entendre surprised her. He appeared so sedate, even with the service revolver slapping his hip, that a sexual innuendo—even a small one—caught her unawares.

A compliment or veiled invitation? Tom certainly wasn't pushing himself at her but the reference to her handling skills couldn't be plainer.

Maybe she just had sex on the brain. Celibacy never agreed with her, not for the long term. Even before she'd begun—well, whatever it was she and Jake were doing—but, before that, she'd felt an all-too-familiar itch that screamed to be scratched.

Chapter 24

"More people die regretting what they didn't do than what they did. Treat regret the way you'd treat any other unwelcome visitor. Tame the bastard, and then move along. You won't regret it." ~Lola Delaney

"Kat? Are you okay?"

She'd been daydreaming again. Of sex. Or her lack of.

Hurriedly, she shook her head and smiled. "Fine, thanks. Just tired, I guess. Lots to do, and just me to do it all."

Tom walked toward the door. A breeze lifted his tie, so he covered it with a hand against his torso. No wedding ring, but that didn't mean much. Maybe he didn't wear one.

"I won't keep you, then. Just wanted to let you know I'm here if you need anything. Any questions about Mill Pond or the services the community offers, just holler. Although you've already hooked the best guy for that job. Jake's the go-to man about town. He'll shape the place up in no time."

She let the hooked comment pass.

"What do you mean about Jake and the town?"

Tom grinned. "You mean he hasn't reeled you in yet? You haven't been sold, hook, line and sinker on his pull-tourists-from-Placid schemes?"

Lake Placid, the next town over, had been the site of the nineteen eighty Olympics. When the games were going on, hundreds of thousands of visitors filled the area. They spilled over into neighboring towns. But that was a while ago, and Kat didn't realize any tourists still took notice of Lake Placid.

"Nope. I didn't know he had a scheme."

"Oh, Jake's always had an agenda. Always. About everything." It wasn't said with malice. Tom just put the statements out there as if they were fact. "Don't get me wrong. Jake's agendas are never self-serving. He's the kind of guy who does for others before he thinks of himself. But you two seem pretty close, so maybe you already know what makes him tick."

She had no idea what made Jake tick but had a damn good start on being able to wind him up.

"I was going to say that about you. You sound like his brother."

He smiled, and this time there was pleasure in his eyes. "Close. Known each other since first grade. We used to play cops and robbers down by Bear Spring Lake. Have you been there yet?"

"Haven't had the pleasure. But let me guess…you were the cop and Jake was the robber?"

"Not quite. I was the robber, and he didn't hesitate to put me down any way he could. Including tying me to a pine tree and leaving me there for about four hours one time. Ask him about it. He'll tell you how it was." Tom shook his head, his smile making him very easy on the eyes. "When Jake takes you to the lake, make him show you the pine tree. It's still there."

"What makes you think he'll take me to the lake? I'm not much of a lake person, to tell the truth. More a swimming pool kind of gal, if you get my drift."

He brought two fingers to his brow and shot her an informal salute. "I get your drift just fine. But I've known him almost my whole life. He'll take you up there. And he'll make you like swimming there, too. Just remember what I said about the tree. Nice chatting with you."

And before she could open her mouth, he walked out the door, leaving her with more questions than answers.

Kat looked around. The drive to tackle the mess no longer existed. She tossed the blue cookbook onto the counter and headed for the apartment to grab her purse. There was only one thing that would hold her interest.

In a time like this, with no official man in her life and everything around her in shambles, it was a good thing she had a hobby. One that didn't include needing a penis to pursue.

First, the purse. Then, the grocery store. Finally, if she was more attentive than she had been last night, chewy goodness.

Chapter 25

"Respect the past. Look toward the future. If you're lucky, Macy's could be having a shoe sale soon. So keep looking..." ~Lola Delaney

One of the last vestiges of his old life was the thirty-two foot vintage wooden boat. Paying for it signified years of hard work, dedication and long, mind-numbing hours behind a drafting table. With its chrome finishes and polished teak deck, it was grander than his current lifestyle afforded, but he kept it tarped and hanging in his barn.

It owed him nothing and asked nothing of him. And if it was a reminder of the man he once was, so be it. He could live with that—as long as he didn't dwell overmuch on the way things had ended up.

He checked the lines threaded through the heavy, stainless steel pulleys securing the boat to the wide ash rafters. So many ropes held the vessel aloft that if one, or even two, snapped it would stay secure.

Still, he checked.

Satisfied it wasn't going anywhere, he climbed down the aluminum ladder beside the starboard side. He folded the ladder and leaned it against a wall. Stood back and considered the boat. She begged to be taken out, silently beseeching him to set her in the water and hoist her pristine sails.

Sailing was almost like sex—waves of pleasure, intense gratification. Both stole his breath whether he rode waves beneath his boat or above a woman. Nothing compared to the rush and excitement, to the total surrender of falling into bliss.

Dependability was the difference between a boat and a woman. The boat, whether hanging from the ceiling or sitting high in the water, didn't depend on him for anything more than an even sailing hand. Women? Not as forgiving.

Jake sighed, the breath coming from low in his gut. When had his life changed so drastically?

Stupid question. He knew the answer, down to the precise moment of impact. The nightmare never left his mind entirely, hardly ever gave him a respite from the guilt that ate a hole in his soul.

Three lives were lost because of his miscalculation. They had depended on him, and he'd let them down. It would never happen again. Ever.

Something brushed up against his ankle. He jumped in surprise and dropped his gaze.

A tiny gray kitten stared up, big blue eyes wide and whiskers twitching.

"Where'd you come from?"

He looked around. The barn door stood open, but his place was acres away from the next house.

The kitten twined around his ankle.

He picked it up and held it against his chest. It was a tiny thing but possessed a deep rumble.

"Whatcha got there?" Tom, still in uniform, walked through the wide door. He stopped beside Jake, reached out a fingertip to stroke the kitten between its ears. "A pet? About time, if you ask me. Though I'd have figured you'd get a dog, not a cat. Especially not one that tiny. Hell, that's hardly a handful, is it?"

Tom's habit of stopping in for a fast beer before heading home was an old one, started just after their college graduations. Their houses were barely a mile apart, and it was a convenient arrangement. Just before Tom and Kathy married, Jake accepted an engineering position in Texas, which put a stop to it for a while. But after he returned to town, with Kathy gone and both men living alone, there was no reason not to reinstate the beer-and-bullshit hour.

He held the animal in one hand. The other he raked through his hair.

"It just arrived here, the way you do."

"Huh. What're you going to call it?"

"Nothing."

"Shitty name for a cat." Tom made himself at home, taking two Coors from a fridge in the corner. He popped the top off one, handed it to Jake, then opened the second bottle. He took a long pull, motioned at the cat with the beer. "Cute, in a piss-ant kind of way. Now that's a name for it. Why don't you call it Piss-ant?"

He swallowed a mouthful of beer before answering. "What the hell are you thinking? I can't name a cat that. Besides, I'm not keeping it, so I'm not naming it."

Tom settled onto a church pew that lined the closest wall. The pew had been in front of a church in Lake Placid that was in the process of being renovated. It had a "free" sign taped to it, so Jake had wrangled it into the bed of his pick-up and brought it back to the barn. It took up some space and gave him a place to sit and think—and admire the boat.

"What're you going to do with it?"

Jake held it away from his chest, closing the distance between himself and his best friend in two long strides. He tried to hand the cat off, but Tom held his hands high and refused to take the animal.

The cat landed gently on the wood bench seat beside them as he sat. The animal walked to Tom, sniffed his shirt, and purred when it got a gentle rub between its ears. Then, it turned tail and came back, curling up beside his hip and closing its eyes.

Tom motioned with his bottle. "Looks like you got yourself a pet whether you want one or not. Cats are self-sufficient. I don't think it'll break your no-dependents rule."

"Nope. You know I don't break the rule, not even for cats."

"It's not a cat. That there is one itty-bitty kitten. Can't see how it'd be too much trouble, especially for a guy with a boat tied to his ceiling."

"Now you're being an ass." He looked down at the mound of fur beside him. It went against the protective wall he'd built around himself to even contemplate letting something into his life that might rely on him. If the cat—correction, *kitten*—knew how he'd already failed miserably, it wouldn't be snoring, its nose pressed against his jeans. He tipped his bottle to the rafters. "What's the boat got to do with anything?"

Tom drained his beer. He set the empty on the bench, then leaned back and put his hands behind his head. "Seems to me a smart guy like you would see the connection, but I don't mind enlightening you." He smirked. "You run like hell whenever anything looks like it might even be thinking about depending on you."

"But—"

The cop in Tom came out. A hand went up between them. It stopped dialogue as effectively as it did traffic.

"I don't want to hear any shit about what went wrong the last time people depended on you." He locked Jake with a steely gaze. "That was a long time ago. You've got to forgive yourself and move on."

Neither spoke for several heartbeats.

"What about the boat?"

"Now, I was getting to that." Tom turned his attention to the underside of the large vessel. "That boat, whether or not you realize it, is one big dependent item."

"It's just a—"

"Bullshit. That boat is more than 'just a boat'. It's part of who you are, a reminder of who you were. And maybe, it's a little promise about who you might be again—if you forgive your damn self and let that happen." A wave to the ceiling before he went on in a quieter tone. "You're taking good care of the boat, Jake. You can take care of other things, too. It'll be all right this time."

He didn't know he had been holding his breath until he released it one long, slow stream. Trying to argue was pointless. They both knew the truth. If anyone had insight into how he felt about the disaster, it was the guy beside him. He'd helped pick up the pieces after the tragedy. He'd witnessed the fallout.

"You can't guarantee it'll be all right." The words were low and slow, but something in his tone woke the cat. It looked up at him, stretched out one paw and placed it on his thigh.

"There are no guarantees about anything."

Kathy. Tom still suffered her loss, and reminding him didn't help matters.

Damn it.

"Listen, I didn't mean…" He didn't mean what?

"It's okay. I miss her no matter what anyone says—or what they don't say. It's just part of the process. I'll miss Kathy every day for the rest of my life. I've learned to handle it—and you've got to learn to cope with what happened to you, too. It's time. And guarantees? Shit, there aren't any—for any of us. We both know that. Hell, the cat probably even knows it."

The cat. Now, that he could deal with. The rest would have to wait for another time.

Jake finished his beer and put his empty on the floor beneath the pew. He grabbed the ball of fur and stood.

Tom gave him the interrogating-cop face. "Where are you off to?"

He headed for the door. "Find a home for a wayward pussycat."

Chapter 26

"Don't kid yourself. Good girls give hand jobs, too." ~*Lola Delaney*

Humidity in her New York City kitchen had been a constant enemy during the summer months. But in the Adirondacks, the air seemed sweeter, less sticky, and infinitely more conducive to candy making.

Toenail polishing, too.

Weekly visits to the beauty salon were *de rigueur* back in Manhattan. Granted, Kat hadn't checked out every nook and cranny in Mill Pond yet, but so far she hadn't spotted a nail salon. Not that she could really afford frivolous beauty routines now. The cushion in her bank account wouldn't last forever. It would give her some time to figure out a direction to take in this new life but the fewer withdrawals, the better.

So for the foreseeable future, she'd be buffing, shaping, and polishing at home. Not that she minded. The kitchen-table pedicure reminded her of college, when anyone without a Saturday night date would pile into the sorority house kitchen, gossip, and paint their nails. Cheap wine filled Styrofoam cups. Combined with nail polish fumes, laughter chased away any angst over being dateless.

She stroked polish on the pinky toenail on her left foot and checked the others, looking for any spot that needed a touch-up. None did, so she capped the bottle. She turned it upside down and read the miniscule label on its bottom.

Scarlet Screaming Sex.

Good Lord. Sex in a bottle…almost as handy as a genie in a bottle, as far as granting wishes went.

She eyeballed her toes. Genie or no, the name suited. If her toes weren't scorching hot and sexy, she didn't know what was.

Not that it helped, she reminded herself. No screaming sex. No scorching hot anything. No penises. Not after the last penis, the one attached to a rat in disguise. Not again.

No thank you.

Why was it that every time she thought she found a guy who might be "the one" he turned out to be a jerk? Could she have such poor judgment she couldn't even choose a decent guy from the millions of eligible bachelors on the planet? Apparently that was the case, because so far she'd chosen fool after fool, enduring predictable breakups one after the other and never gaining any ground on the elusive happily-ever-after she—like every other woman she'd ever met—yearned for.

Funds were limited but she'd stopped at The Liquor Emporium after grocery shopping. The Emporium was almost as small as the front bedroom, but she had found spiced rum—and brought home two bottles. The apartment had no bar to speak of other than a dusty half-bottle of scotch tucked into a far corner of a bottom kitchen cupboard. She added one of the bottles to the stash, left the other on the kitchen counter. Now she had the rudimentary beginnings of a home bar.

A door led from the kitchen onto a wooden staircase that hugged the building's exterior. So far she hadn't ventured onto the tiny landing. She assumed it was for emergency exits, which, hopefully, she wouldn't have many of. Or none at all—that would suit her better.

Mindful of her drying toenails, she walked on her heels across the kitchen floor to the fridge. She pulled a bottle of Tab from a six-pack. A few more heel steps, and she stood beside the exit door, in front of the cupboard where she'd found drinking glasses. She opened the door, chose a squat tumbler, and set both the soda and glass onto the countertop.

She slapped the door shut. Turned—and looked straight into the eyes staring at her from the other side of the glass in the old door.

"Holy shit!" Jumping on her heels stung. Her toes slapped the tile so hard two of the cotton balls she'd stuck between them dislodged.

Kicking the cotton balls under the refrigerator, she unlocked the door and opened it into the kitchen.

"Are you trying to scare the hell out of me?"

He lifted the right corner of his upper lip, a gesture that reminded her how firm and smooth his kisses had been. How she stood on such shaky legs was beyond her, but she did. Barely.

"Not my intention at all. Now, if you asked if I was trying to scare the pants off you, I'd have to give you another answer entirely."

The guy is smooth as silk.

"Are you trying to mess with me?"

"Would it work? Because if it would, I just might try." He smiled. The nail polish fumes were clouding her head. Suddenly she couldn't concentrate on anything other than the eyes and lips on the man in front of her.

And so-help-her-God, she wanted to kiss him.

If he knew the way his presence disarmed her, he didn't show it. He held out a furry gray bundle and placed it gently in her arms. "A housewarming gift."

The kitten nestled against her ribbed tank top was so small it hardly felt real. She couldn't resist lifting it to her cheek and putting the warm bundle against her skin. The kitten sounded like a jet engine beside her ear.

She brought it back to her chest. Its heart beat against her palm. The idea that this tiny animal could really belong to her was almost too much. The child within her, the one who had asked Santa for a kitten, puppy, or even a goldfish, wanted to believe the good fortune, but she couldn't quite. Not just yet.

There had to be a catch. Wasn't there always?

"A housewarming gift?"

"Wouldn't hurt to have some company around the place. Besides, I want to make sure you feel properly welcomed to Mill Pond. You do feel welcome, don't you?" He grinned, raising one eyebrow so high it disappeared beneath the black wave falling onto his forehead.

"I do. Feel welcome, that is."

She stepped back into the kitchen, on her heels.

Jake came inside, closed the door behind him, and gestured to the soda. "Want me to open that?"

She nodded, then heel walked back to the kitchen table. When she sat, the kitten arranged itself in a circle on her lap.

Chapter 27

"Just a dab'll do…or a splash, if that's what you fancy." ~Lola Delaney

"Were you planning to add some rum?" He held the bottle up.

"Just a little splash. Grab a glass and join me. It's the least I can do for a guy who brings such an adorable gift. It—what is it? A girl or a boy?"

Kat looked down at the kitten. Its eyes were closed, and it purred, but there was no sexing it from a purr.

"Ah…I took a peek on the way over, and I'm pretty sure it's a girl." He poured two glasses and set one before her, beside the nail polish. He sat in the chrome and vinyl chair opposite hers. "She's pretty, isn't she?"

"She is, and seems like a total mush. So quiet and loving…are you sure she's mine? I mean, don't you want her?"

He shook his head. "Not me, thanks. I, ah, don't do cats."

"You're a dog man?"

Jake's head shook again, an abrupt movement that didn't invite dispute. "No, not a dog man either. I just don't do animals. I like them just fine, but I don't want the responsibility."

Hard core avoidance. No ifs, ands, or buts by the

look in his eyes. She didn't bother to try to sway him.

"I guess you really don't want her, then. I'd love to keep her, so thank you. Oh! I've got to get stuff for her. Food and toys. Cat litter and, I don't know…stuff."

The kitten pricked one dainty ear when he chuckled. "I stopped at the pet store and picked up the essentials. They're in my truck. I couldn't carry everything and didn't want to drop your little friend, so I left it all on the front seat. I'll grab it as soon as we finish our drinks." He raised his glass. "It doesn't look like she needs anything right now. She's perfectly content in your lap."

Kat grinned, genuinely pleased with the unexpected gift. She looked down at the kitten, then up at Jake. "She does, doesn't she?"

"Who wouldn't?"

She let the remark pass, too intrigued by the prospect of having a pet to engage in flirting. There would be time for that later. Now, a more pressing question.

"What should we name her?"

"That cat is yours, so you get to name her whatever you want."

"I don't even know her."

"You'll get to know her. Just pick a name. Any name. Isn't there some secret name you've kept for a time like this? Something you've been saving?"

"Well…I always wanted to name a fish Goldie, but she's not a fish."

"Not hardly. And I have a problem with fish names on principal. I catch fish, not name them."

"You fish? Like with a hook, from a rock by the water?"

Jake swallowed hard. The rum and coke went down in a huge rush. "A rock? Don't tell me you actually believe...oh, right, I nearly forgot. Miss City Slicker, you've never been fishing, have you?"

"Not unless you count choosing a goldfish for my goddaughter fishing."

"Not the same thing." He took another mouthful of his drink. Motioning to hers, he waited while she lifted it to her lips and took a swallow. "Did your goddaughter name her fish Goldie?"

"Jelly Bean. Can you tell what I brought her in the other package?"

His smile made her tummy do flip-flops. "It's a good thing you didn't bring Rolaids or WD-40."

"Tell me about it." She lifted her glass and took another sip. He had a light hand with the rum. The apartment lacked central air so the sweet drink was refreshing. "Besides, Goldie isn't a J name, so she wouldn't even consider it."

"How old is she? The godchild, not the goldfish."

"Jena Rose is three going on twenty-three. I hate to brag, but she's so much more on the ball than I was at that age. The last time I spoke with her on the phone she told me that I should have my people call her people so we can get a lunch set up. And maybe some time at the park—if it fits into her schedule."

Joann had never been one of those push-the-kid-into-every-activity, hyper mothers, so the your-people-my-people routine had to be something Jena Rose heard either on television or in the park.

"She sounds adorable."

"I know I'm biased, but I love her. Even if she does try to weasel out of wearing anything that's not some shade of purple."

"Favorite color?"

"You got it. She's a cutie, but the purple thing can be a challenge."

Jake reached over and scratched the kitten between her ears. His wrist brushed Kat's thigh, sending a current of awareness through her.

He was so close his five o'clock shadow was visible. She remembered how his face felt pressed against hers.

"You love her a lot." It was a statement, so she nodded. Yes, she loved Jena Rose almost more than she could put into words. "What would the kiddo call the kitten? Would it have to be a J word, or could it be something random?"

"No, not a J, because the cat's mine, not hers. That is, unless you want her back?"

Jake sat up quickly and put his hands in the air. "Nope. The cat's all yours, Kat. Hey—that's not bad...you could call her Kat's Cat. KC for short."

"I can't do that to her. She should have her own name, something that fits her personality and tells the world she's her own boss." She stroked the kitten's velvety smooth nose, which brought more intense purring. She looked up and met his gaze. "Attila."

"That tiny little cat?"

"Mmm hmm."

"Why Attila?"

"Because she's got the heart of a warrior. Strong and brave. Adaptable. All good characteristics. She deserves a solid name. Attila. It fits her, don't you think?"

Jake motioned to her glass as he lifted his. They

toasted the kitten, who didn't even open an eye as they officially named her.

"Attila it is, then."

He took a drink, and she did the same. They sealed the kitten's fate with rum.

Chapter 28

"There's a perfect balance between wanting to be loved and needing to love. Hard to find. Harder to hold on to. But when it works...sheer magic." ~Lola Delaney

Heading home should be on his mind, but it was far from it. Spending time with Kat, getting to know her even a little bit, had much greater appeal than his empty house where he would eat a frozen dinner in front of the television.

Lola told him more than once that he'd love her niece if he met her. While love wasn't something he felt comfortable contemplating, the old woman had been right. The attraction was there. Kat intrigued him—a lot—so leaving before she tossed him out wasn't something he planned to do.

And she didn't seem inclined to send him anywhere.

But unless he got some food into her, she might toss something else eventually.

They had moved from apartment to the intimate garden behind the gallery. Lola's carefully pruned apple tree, perennial beds, and flagstone patio received more attention than her shop ever had. The wrought iron table, chairs, and glider were inviting. The space provided a secluded setting for their impromptu date, but they'd consumed three rum and cokes without any real food. Candy didn't count.

"Hungry?" The enthusiastic nod she gave as a reply let him know his wasn't the only empty stomach. "How do you feel about pizza?"

"I love it. But no weird stuff on it. Just cheese, please."

"Can do." Lola had installed a phone jack in the potting shed so he stood, grabbed the Princess phone, and dialed. "Hey, Gino. It's Jake. Listen, I'd like a large cheese, two bottles of root beer, and some garlic knots. For delivery, over at Lola's. Around the back, in the garden, okay?"

He dropped the receiver into the cradle.

"You seem pretty familiar with my aunt's place. Like you've been here before."

"I have, but don't go spreading it around."

"Why not?"

Before his arrival with Attila—who now slept peacefully curled beneath the table—she made chocolate-covered truffles. The remnants of the candy tray—all four or five round pieces—sat on the glider between them. She picked it up and waved it in his direction. When he shook his head, she placed it on the table beside her. It suited him fine, that nothing but space—and a small one at that—separated his thigh from her knee. With one leg curled beneath her and the toes of her other foot pushing against the flagstone, she looked comfortable.

"Let's just say that in a small town like Mill Pond, not everyone gets along as well as they should. For one reason or another, real—or imagined—issues keep people from being friendly. Not Hatfield-McCoy feuding, but enough that it pays to keep some business personal."

"How personal were you and my aunt?" Kat stuck the tip of one index finger in her mouth. The candy tray, so sweet and sticky, left its mark. He watched her lick sugar from her finger.

Looking away wasn't an option. His gaze was glued to her finger, his mind wishing her lips were elsewhere and the destination of his wish growing harder by the second.

"Jake?"

Right. She had asked a question.

"Your aunt was my mother's best friend. They, ah, worked together before either of them got married. Lola's husband worked with my Uncle Gordon. He owns the motel across the street."

She wiped the tip of her finger dry on the edge of her shorts.

"The Tip-A-Canoe Motel? The one with the hungry swimming pool?"

"That's the one."

"So your uncle is the man I met the day you rescued my bikini top? Do you work for him at the motel? And why is the motel and this place both named Tip-A-Canoe? Do you know?" Kat edged closer on the glider. He caught a whiff of chocolate when she leaned in. His stomach rumbled.

"Too many questions! Damn, but you fire them like a sharpshooter." He held the high card in this information game. "I'll tell you what I know, but you're going to have to answer some questions, too. A getting-to-know-you tit for tat. What do you say?"

She squinted, turning the seductive stare into a soul-searching weapon. His gut tightened, but he didn't blink.

"Deal. But I ask the first question."

The table turn was faster than the speed of light but he gave it to her. "Ask away."

"Do you work for your uncle? And have you always?"

Greedy with the questions. "That's two questions, but I'll let you slide this time. I don't officially work for Uncle Gordon. I just help around the place. In case you didn't notice, he's not a young man, and the motel needs repairs. I've got time on my hands, and I don't mind doing what I can." He swallowed, then said, "And no, I haven't always been here to help with the place."

She opened her mouth but he held a hand up. "My turn. Remember, tit for tat. This is an easy one. Just a yes or no answer…are you involved with anyone?"

She hesitated before she shook her head. "Not anymore. I was but I found out he wasn't who he said he was. I learned something about him that…well, it showed me that I didn't know him at all."

"Sounds rough."

"It was. I…" She searched his face, but he couldn't tell what she needed from him so he just held her gaze. She sighed. "Henry worked for a large insurance company. I found out he had a scheme to charge clients more than their premiums—in some cases, thousands of dollars more—and was pocketing the money. It doesn't sound like an enormous thing when you don't see the big picture—he had hundreds of clients, and the money added up."

"Not an altar boy, then." He whistled. Tom had alluded to her having some involvement with the law in Manhattan, but he had no idea it was this deep. "Were you…"

She didn't look away. "Involved in his deception? No. I'm the one who called the authorities when I realized what was going on. I couldn't live with someone who lied like that. I left. Gave everything to Henry. It seemed better than trying to disentangle myself from his financial mess. Fortunately, Aunt Lola's bequest gave me somewhere to begin again. Not that I'm sure what's going to go on with this gallery…but at least I've got something to keep me busy. And, thank God, I learned Henry is a weasel— before we got any further into our relationship."

"I'm blown away. You read about this kind of stuff all the time but never meet anyone who's involved. It must have sucked realizing the guy you cared for wasn't who he seemed to be."

It sucked talking about it. He couldn't imagine living it.

"It did. But that was months ago, and I'm fine, so I'm not dwelling on the past. Now it's my turn to ask a question, right?"

She bounced back. He'd give her that.

"Right."

"What about you? What did you do before you started helping your uncle out at the motel? And do you know why his motel has practically the same name as my aunt's business?"

"You just can't get it down to one question, can you?"

"I guess not." She shrugged. "So sue me. Well? What about the name? And what did you do before? Enquiring minds want to know."

A rum-induced giggle was amusing, but he wished

the damn pizza would just show up already. If he filled her mouth with food, she might not ask so many questions.

He looked over his shoulder, but Gino didn't magically appear around the side of the building. And the wide-eyed beauty beside him stared a hole in his head, waiting for what he'd agreed to give.

Shit.

Chapter 29

"The truth, or some version of it, always trumps a lie. Always." ~Lola Delaney

"This is the last time I'll give you a two-for-one deal. The Tip-A-Canoe bit came about because a very long time ago, your aunt and my mother were best friends. I told you that already. But my mother, my uncle's sister, and your aunt, along with my uncle, bought this pair of businesses right out of college. Ambitious for their day but they were a good team, apparently. That is, until your father and my aunt came along. Then, all bets were off."

She scrunched up her forehead. The tiny lines zigzagging across her creamy complexion begged to be kissed, but before he could lean in, she asked, "What do you mean, all bets were off?"

Shelve the kissing. Back to the history lesson.

"It's obvious, Kat. Your mother was pretty enough that she posed a threat to my aunt, who refused to marry my uncle unless the trio broke off their partnership. So, your aunt took the gallery. My uncle, and his new wife, kept the motel. And that, as they say, was the end of something good."

"What about my mother?"

He wished she hadn't asked that.

But she had.

Technically, it fell under the tit-for-tat question exchange, but why put it off? Better to meet the bullet head on than try to dodge it…and get hit in the ass with it later.

"Your mother met your father. From what I can tell, your father and aunt had some sort of…ah…"

She waved a hand between them. Then, she placed her palm on his chest and looked earnestly into his eyes. The alcohol widened her pupils, and she looked adorably sexy.

"I know. My mother always said nothing happened, but it was hard to be in the same space with the two of them. She and my aunt didn't see much of each other after the infamous pass-that-wasn't, and I think she regretted that. When she died, my aunt didn't come to the funeral. I didn't know it then, but she was already sick, too."

He laid an arm across the back of the glider and placed his hand on her shoulder.

"I'm sorry. Your aunt had such a big heart and was a generous, caring woman. It stinks that the heart everyone adored her for would betray her. You must miss both of them. And your father, too."

A sigh. She nestled closer to his side as a tiny tremble shook her body. Spreading her fingers wide, she looked down at them in silence.

"Hey, I'm sorry if I made it worse." Leave it to him to throw salt on her wounds. If his foot wasn't so far down his throat he'd use it to kick himself in the ass.

"You didn't. It's just that every now and then I remember I really am alone in the world. It pretty much stinks, but there's nothing I can do to change it."

"Not alone. You've got Jena Rose. And her mom.

And don't forget Attila." At her name, the kitten lifted a heavy eyelid. She blinked, then closed her eye and placed a paw across her nose. "And me," he added softly. He put a fingertip beneath her chin and tilted her face up. The sadness in her eyes tore at his heart. "Don't forget me."

"Mmm…" This sigh made a rumble as it pulled the edges of her lips into a reserved smile. "Do I? Have you?"

Dangerous territory. But his head moved on its own, nodding his surrender, and his mouth worked without consulting his brain.

"You do. If you want me, that is."

He kissed her, savoring the taste of rum on her lips. To his utter delight, Kat kissed him back. Hard. With a tiny nip, she pulled his lower lip between her teeth.

Instantly, he responded the way he'd done in high school, when he couldn't ever satisfy his teenage body's cravings. All the finesse and self-restraint he'd learned over the years sailed away on a cloud of hot steam whenever any part of his anatomy met an inch of hers.

Impulse and desire kicked common sense to the curb.

His free hand found her breast, cupping it in his palm and massaging the sensual curve of the woman. Memories of how sweet she tasted beneath her shirt taunted him. He moved his hand high, to push aside the slender strap holding her tank top in place.

"Well hello, folks! Got one hot Italian dinner here, although I'm not sure you're hungry for what I've got. Hey, Jake—"

Swallowing a growl of frustration, he removed his

hand and turned toward the voice.

Gino Cavatelli's pizzas were near legendary in Mill Pond. He even made deliveries into Lake Placid for special customers. Not with the kind of delivery style he used around town, but he consented to bring his Sicilian mama's special, top-secret recipe pizzas the extra four miles at least three, maybe four, times a week. Gino's Pizzeria was one local business that withstood the downswing in the economy.

"Your timing is amazing." He shifted, but it was impossible to get comfortable with a hard-on digging into the seam of his jeans.

"Hey, if you don't want the pie, I can leave the way I came." Short, stocky, and with so much natural charm he was born to be in the public eye, Gino smiled, revealing dazzling white teeth. They peeked beneath the fringe of black-as-midnight moustache. "You look otherwise involved. Maybe you're not hungry?"

Kat's laughter stopped him cold. She held her side with one hand, bringing the tank top flush with her skin and drawing attention to her stiff nipples.

"You've—" She pointed one unsteady, rum-affected finger as she giggled harder. "You've got a…a…"

"Haven't you ever seen a guy with a pizza before?"

He spread his beefy arms, a bag holding garlic knots in one hand and two bottles of root beer held between two fingers of his other. He stood there with a huge grin plastered on his face, waiting for her to answer.

She wiped a fingertip beneath one eye, drawing the tear onto her finger. "Never with the pizza on his head, no."

Gino shrugged. He stepped to the table and deposited their drinks and the garlic knots on its surface. He waggled his fingers at Attila, who took that moment to look up and yawn.

"Nice cat." He placed the pizza box on the table. His gaze turned to Jake and mine-swept his body. One eyebrow lifted. There was no need for words. Jake knew he'd be buried in shit as soon as he was alone with his old friend. "Listen, I'll put this all on your bill. You don't look like you're in the mood to pay right now."

Chapter 30

"Say yes. Whenever possible, simply say yes."
                                        ~Lola Delaney

The pizza was history. Attila snored gently on top of the empty box.

A fat, almost orange moon hung low in the sky. Crickets chirped and fireflies danced, but Kat barely noticed any of it.

The glider swayed smoothly beneath them. She couldn't recall when she had been this content. Not in a long time. Maybe never.

Jake's arm around her shoulder held her against his side, and she fit as snugly as if created to puzzle into him. His breathing was slow and steady, and she unconsciously fell into the same rhythm.

Contentment. That's what it was, this uncomplicated feeling filling her mind and body. Manhattan, Henry, the insurance fiasco and every bit of her old life felt a million miles removed. The burdens of a disastrous relationship and its deceptions fell away, shed as the cocoon no longer needed to weigh a butterfly to the earth.

"Jake?"

"Mmm?"

The hoarse rasp, his wordless answer, sent shivers up her spine. And heat to the lower parts of her anatomy.

"You didn't answer all my questions." The answers didn't matter. She merely wanted to keep him by her side, even if it meant prattling over random subjects.

"It's my turn." He slid a tender hand along her exposed upper arm. "You asked the last question, so it's my turn."

If you say so.

Before the pizza-balancing Gino, it was all a little blurry.

"So, ask." She leaned her head against his shoulder. A firefly flickered not far from the tip of her nose. Fascinating, to think those female insects attracted their mates by blinking their tails on and off.

"Do you plan to stay in Mill Pond? Run the gallery?"

Aside from going back to the city—which she did not intend to *ever* do again—her options were limited. And endless, considering nothing tied her anywhere.

"I don't see why I wouldn't stay. I'm not sure I'll keep the gallery operating the way Aunt Lola did. I mean, it's more a junk shop than anything else." She paused, wondering what venture the town lacked but nothing came to mind so she continued. "I just don't see myself running a secondhand store."

"Why don't you just organize the place, see what's actually in there. I wouldn't be surprised if Lola's got some treasures hidden in among the junk. Don't count her out. Your aunt was a smart woman. Whatever went on in the gallery was for a reason. I don't know the reasons, but I do know Lola didn't do haphazard."

"No? Tell that to the stack of crap we knocked over with my butt. I picked it up, and it all looked pretty hit and miss to me."

"Look deeper." His finger drew tiny circles on her skin. It sent shivers further up her spine, hardened her nipples, and made her breath catch from the sheer joy of it. "And don't remind me of your butt—not if you want me to keep my hands off. You're a lot of things. Resistible isn't one of them."

She whispered beside his ear. "Who says I want you to resist?"

The fingers on her arm stilled. Heat thrummed beneath the surface of his fingertips, so steady and undeniable it transferred from his skin to hers.

"Be careful what you wish for, Kat."

"I wish for a lot." Common sense said to press hard on the brakes. Desire urged her to ratchet things up a notch. Desire threw common sense beneath the bus with a sharp kick. "A. Lot. Of. Things."

The sharp intake of air beside her told its own story. He wanted as much as she did. His common sense tangled in a heap with hers.

Excitement moistened the folds at her apex when his mouth found her neck. Jake nibbled a ladder up to her ear, then sucked her earlobe between his lips.

Try as she might to forget it, the niggling question—the one that wouldn't quiet no matter how hard she tried to silence it—popped out even as she squirmed against the hard bench.

"My turn. You avoid the point skillfully but answer my question. It's the last one I'll ask tonight." She ran a hand up his thigh, the well-worn denim velvety against her skin. When she reached his crotch, she cradled the bulge straining his jeans. He shivered at her touch. "Tell me what you did before you became your uncle's handyman."

"Handy? I love where yours is." He ground himself into her. She massaged his erection through his jeans, her fingers trailing the steely contours of his flesh.

"Don't try to distract me." One button opened with a twist. His zipper rasped down until it went no further. Then, she slipped her hand inside and caressed him through his knit boxers.

"I wouldn't think of distracting you, honey. Not now." His hands slid beneath the waistline of her shorts and he pushed them low, stopping when he held one of her cheeks in his wide palm. "You're not going to give up on this, are you?"

She tugged him free, circling her fingers and sliding them along his rigid length. "No. I'm not, so give it up."

A tiny voice in her head reminded her she had sworn off men. And their penises.

"Shh."

"Hmm?"

Kat lowered her head, brought her lips to him, and kissed the pink tip. The groan the small peck elicited was so feral, it sounded pulled from his feet.

"Tell me." She blew warm air across his skin through pursed lips. His hands had made fast work of her shorts. They were around her ankles, so she kicked them away.

"I was…"

Kat took him in her mouth. She swirled her tongue across his salty, hot skin.

"Mmm?" She sucked harder, pleased when he groaned again.

"An engineer. Good God in heaven, Kat—I was an

engineer."

As he gasped out the answer, Jake pulled her up onto his lap. His erection lay thickly against the wisp of fabric still covering her as they kissed. His mouth was everywhere. Her lips. Her eyelids. The tip of her nose, a fast, sweet touch. Then, her neck again, all while she pressed her aching need against his hot, hard length.

Their hands were not idle.

Hers, straining to touch every inch of him, to caress the rock-solid abs revealed when she unbuttoned his shirt. To stroke his chest and biceps, to feel the strength of the man against her.

In his arms, for this moment at least, she was safe.

Jake pushed aside the scrap of fabric. His fingers separated her folds, stroked the slippery nub hidden within. A whimper escaped her when his touch sent instant pleasure zinging through her body, awakening nerve receptors long forgotten.

"Oh, Jake…"

His erection brushed her, and it was exquisite but…

"More."

She guided him toward her, but he pulled away.

"Wait." The word came on a ragged breath. He withdrew a condom from his pocket, tore at the wrapper, and then rolled it down over his penis. He flicked a thumb across her sweet spot, sending spirals of dizzying pleasure almost too intense to bear through her. A fast hip shift, and he stroked her with his length, not penetrating but so close.

He paused. Met her gaze. "Are you sure?"

She couldn't remember the last time she was this sure about anything.

"Yes. Oh, yes…"

His gaze didn't leave hers as he buried himself inside her. The first instant, when she took the full length of him, seemed endless. He filled her completely, settling her squarely on his erection and holding still for several heartbeats. The wait was glorious. The end to it, even more so. Jake massaged her with his thumb as he began to move, every thrust bringing her closer and closer to the edge of reason.

Conflicted emotions roiled within her. She wanted the dance to last, to go on forever. She wanted to ride him hard and fast, send him over the edge just to feel and watch his release. She wanted…oh, she wanted so much but wanting and waiting were two separate things.

His fingers worked her into a frenzy. Molten heat filled her veins and the insistent throbbing at the point where Jake's body joined hers couldn't be denied.

"Oh…oh, Jake…"

"Come with me," he whispered against her ear. Jake arched his back. Buried himself hard inside her. "Come. Kat. Now…"

She did, lost to sensations she had tried to deny. As she shuddered, she felt Jake's hot release.

For one long, glorious moment, nothing else mattered. Not one damn thing.

Chapter 31

"The fastest way to get around a problem is to go right through it." ~Lola Delaney

Jake had played her. And right after she'd decided he was sensitive, in addition to being intelligent, funny, and kind.

Oh, yeah. And sexy.

Attila lounged in the front window, stretched full out in a beam of sunlight. If she wasn't so adorable, Kat might have considered tossing her out with the books.

It didn't make any sense. How could a man show up with a beautiful, homeless kitten one minute and play the old *wham, bam, thank you ma'am* the next?

She'd read him wrong. Just like she'd done with every other man in her life. All the bullshit, and she hadn't learned one damn thing. She should be shot, put out of her misery and forgotten. It was criminal that a woman with an above-average IQ and more than enough good sense to deal with anything else life threw her way couldn't tell a decent man from a creep.

"It's the damn penises. They get me every time," she muttered. Attila lifted her head. Blinked. Then she put her chin back on her paws and resumed purring.

Jake's idea of post-coital snuggling had been to zip up, give her a peck on the cheek, and dash off.

Hard to believe she'd let him go like that, but it

happened so fast she didn't have time to react.

One positive side effect of the hit-and-run hook-up was the way the shop looked. She'd been decluttering, tossing and sorting since just past midnight. Most shelves were bare. The Dumpster at the side of the building overflowed. And finally, she could see what space there was to work with.

Sleep-deprived, caffeine-less, and irritated, a whirling dervish in the cleaning department but a complete mess regarding relationships.

Kat smacked the shelf she'd just cleared with her hand. The sting just added to her pissy mood.

A chill shot up her spine. Despite the warmth on her reddened palm, she was suddenly cold.

"Damn it, damn it, damn it!"

"I see you're still using vulgar language. Wouldn't have expected much else from someone with your background."

She didn't have to turn to know whose voice it was. The front door stood open again, with the hope of coaxing in any stray breeze. The danger was, an open door coaxed any stray at all.

Qua-quack.

The stuttering duck. And, to top it off, Jake's crazy aunt.

Just what she needed.

She plastered a phony smile on her face and turned to the door.

"Good morning to you, too." It was nearly impossible to keep the sarcasm to a minimum.

The duck, at least, wasn't glaring at her. It *quacked* once more, then snapped its bill shut and tucked its head into its owner's armpit.

"Hmmph."

The vision of purpleness reminded Kat of the time in college when she'd had too many—*way* too many—blueberry daiquiris. There had been much praying to the porcelain goddess that night. So much that she still refused anything with blueberries.

She wished she could just say, "No, thanks" the way she did with the fruit and be done with this woman.

"Is there something I can do for you?"

"Hmmph! As if you could do anything at all for me. No, I don't think so, missy. I for sure don't need anyone teaching me how to use profanity—something you're pretty damn good at, I see."

The white curls popping out from beneath the brim of the New York Yankees cap on the old woman's head were grandmotherly. Their owner's surly disposition didn't match them.

Snakes would be more fitting.

"Actually, I think you're right. You seem to have mastered the art of swearing all on your own. And you, too, seem pretty damn good at it."

They stared at each other across the remaining clutter.

If there was a reason for the visit, Kat wasn't going to learn it this way.

She took a deep breath and prayed for patience. "We seem to have gotten off on the wrong foot. Why don't we start over?" She smiled, but the gesture wasn't returned. But there wasn't any "hmmph"-ing, either, so she continued. "I'm Kat Delaney. I inherited this shop—actually I thought it was a gallery, but it isn't exactly what I pictured but—oh, but you don't want to hear that. Anyhow, it seems as if you know more about me than I do about you. Or your duck," she added.

Purple high-top sneakers shifted on the wide-plank wooden floor. Then, a toe tapped.

A good sign, no?

She waited. Her spiel had been delivered. Now the ball was in the purple tornado's court.

"Clarence."

"Pardon?"

"My duck. His name is Clarence." He got a swift squeeze, which made him open his eyes in surprise.

Qua-quack. Quack.

"He's a…" Complimenting a duck was a far cry from arranging a cupboard or finessing a client. "He's a handsome duck."

There. She'd just, hopefully, ingratiated herself with a duck.

What next?

"He's a wood duck, you know."

She nodded and hoped the woman couldn't see the I-couldn't-care-less stare she felt in her eyes. Evidently, it eluded the fowl's owner, because the duck got a pat on the head.

Warming to the topic, the woman took two steps inside the open doorway.

"Wood ducks are very friendly. Clarence doesn't know any better than to act like a person. I raised him up from just a little guy. Between us, he thinks he's as smart as any human."

So do you. She kept the smile on her face.

"You must have noticed his lovely voice." The woman's curls bounced when she spoke. It was like watching a dancing blueberry sundae with whipped cream, and a Yankees cap instead of a cherry, invade her space.

His voice?

Kat found her own. "Right, his voice. Yes, I heard him quacking. He's got a stutter, doesn't he?"

Bad move.

A defensive arm curled around Clarence's middle and she nearly spat the words, "He. Does. Not. Stutter."

"Oh, I didn't mean—"

"I don't give a damn what you meant. You insulted my Clarence, you hussy, you!"

"Enough with the 'hussy' business. If this is your idea of welcoming me to town, it stinks."

"Why…why…why—"

"That's the same question I've been asking myself." Kat cut her off just because she couldn't stand seeing the duck's discomfort. Every "why" brought him tighter into the purple armpit. "Why the hell did I move here? Why is everyone so crazy in this place? And why-oh-why do you keep shitting on my parade? What did I do to twist your panties?"

She sucked in a deep breath and held it.

Neither spoke. Clarence, too, kept his bill shut.

Then, a surprise.

Chapter 32

"There's no cure for crazy." ~Lola Delaney

"You're Lola's niece. She didn't tell you about me? About Gordon? Jake? Clarence?"

Her throat tightened. If she could've managed it, she would've quacked.

She shook her head.

"It's hard to believe Lola didn't say anything."

"Believe it. We didn't have a relationship. I only saw her once or twice, when I was a baby. What should she have told me about…all of you?"

The duck's owner turned away for a moment, then looked back, her eyes not nearly as penetrating as they had been. She studied Kat, taking her time without trying to hide the assessment.

Her voice softened. Not much, but enough that her tone wasn't as abrasive.

"Apple trees make apples…"

Kat sighed. "You said that the last time you stopped in. Whatever you're thinking, it can't be right. I'm as far from my aunt, personality-wise, as the moon is from Bergdorf's. We didn't know each other. Whatever animosity there was between you and her, it should be put to rest. Really, think about it. I don't know a thing about apples other than I like mine green."

"Green ones are the best for pies, you know."

"I don't know anything about making pies, either."

"That's a damn shame." She adjusted her duck, then nodded toward the far corner of the shop. Piles and boxes still filled the space, stacked haphazardly against a wall. Kat hadn't made it that far yet, so she had no idea what the boxes held. Her visitor did. "Lots of baking paraphernalia in there. Pie tins, mixing bowls, cookie cutters, and biscuit molds. Lots of stuff. Cookbooks, too. A woman should know her way around the kitchen. Wouldn't hurt to take a gander at those baking things. Might learn a thing or two. Maybe three." She paused. Then, almost as an afterthought, "You look bright. I'm sure you could teach yourself the basics from the boxes."

The compliment took her off guard. Lack of sleep made her response time slower.

"Thank you, I think." Baking had never interested her but she didn't intend to share that bit of personal news. "Maybe I'll take a look sometime. See if I can't learn how to bake…something."

"Start with cookies. They're easy. I'd say a way to a man's heart is with bread, but that's a hard start."

At that, Kat stiffened.

"I don't have to worry about finding the way to a man's heart. I've no intention of getting involved with a man."

The question was rapid. "You're one of those lesbians, then? You're not the first, so don't worry about that. No, between here and Placid—out on Route 52—there's a lesbian couple. Live in that big green house with all those hippie weathervanes on it. You'll see it when you pass. Hey, maybe you want to stop in and introduce yourself, seeing as how you're a lesbian, too."

"I am not a lesbian." What the hell was wrong with this town? Every manless woman had to be homosexual?

"Are you sure?" Pushing her cap back on her head, Jake's aunt stepped close and peered into Kat's eyes. Frostiness swept over the space. A sudden chill in the air almost made her cross her arms. She hoped her nipples weren't visible now that the temperature dipped.

"I'm sure. I don't have anything against lesbians— I don't have anything against anyone, damn it!—but I'm not gay."

Jake's aunt hugged her duck close, held up her free hand, and took a fast step backward.

"Okay, okay...I'm just trying to be friendly here. After all, you're right. You're not Lola's shadow and deserve to either sink or float on your own merits. I just meant that bread baking has kept my Gordon satisfied all these years. Thought it might work for you, too, missy."

"Kat."

"Whatever."

Gordon?

The old man with the wacky outfits?

The one Jake called "uncle"?

"You're really Jake's aunt?"

"Damn right I am." She narrowed her eyes, squeezed her pet so hard she elicited a strangled quack—all in less than a heartbeats' time. "What interest do you have in my nephew? You didn't set your big-city sights on him, did you?"

"Not a chance." Kat set her body onto his, and her mouth on his lips—as well as another, more interesting, part of his anatomy—but her sights? After last night, that was out of the question. "Don't give it another thought. I have no interest whatsoever in your nephew. For all I care, he can look up the lesbians out on Route 52."

Chapter 33

"Swearing rarely solves a problem. It's pretty damn good at letting off steam, though." ~Lola Delaney

"Son of a bitch!" Jake examined his fingertip. A crescent-shaped blood blister was already forming. He wiped the throbbing finger down the leg of his shorts.

It was his own stupid fault he'd squeezed his skin with the needle-nose pliers instead of the wire he'd wrapped around the screw he'd been holding in place with the now-damaged fingertip. Lucky he hadn't done worse. Working with electricity wasn't the most forgiving do-it-yourself endeavor.

This morning his mind was as undisciplined as his body had been last night. It went where it had no business going. While the results of his careless behavior hadn't landed him in the proverbial vat of boiling oil, either instance had the capacity to do so.

Focus.

He needed to concentrate on the task at hand. Deal with the rest another time, he told himself as he put the pliers back into the cramped junction box.

One twist. A second, smaller twist. He pulled the tools out of the filter box, satisfied the connection was secure.

"What you up to today?" The red crepe soles of Uncle Gordon's white bucks allowed him to move as silently as the wind. He appeared, wearing his signature bowler hat. His green, tropical-print shirt warred with the blue-plaid walking shorts but the multi-color striped socks on his white legs matched everything.

"Fixing this." Jake closed his eyes for an instant but the picture of his uncle in full dress chaos already imprinted on his mind.

"Didn't know it was broke."

He tipped his head toward a turquoise-and-white webbed folding chair. "Take a load off. It's going to be another hot one. Sit in the shade over there and keep me company."

He watched the old man drag the chair into position beneath a faded tin canopy hanging off the side of the pool house. The shady spot was just a smallish square, but it was enough to give shelter.

When he left for Texas, his aunt and uncle had been retired from their "real jobs" and worked full-time keeping the motel running. Aunt Pat learned how to keep accounts working for Dr. Tate, and she'd put her secretarial acumen to use sending out pamphlets about the motel and Mill Pond, setting up local charitable events and even writing the social column for *The Gazette*. Her feature had been called *The Local Happenings,* but it was widely acknowledged that it was all gossip. Sugarcoated, of course, but gossip nonetheless.

Uncle Gordon had been able to keep up with motel chores, and together their business thrived. It didn't take a bad turn until the economy dove. The fall of paying lodgers coincided with his aunt and uncle growing suddenly old and a bit unsteady between their ears.

Then, the accident that claimed Aunt Pat and her silly duck.

To top it off, the crash he'd helped engineer occurred in the very same week.

Coming home seemed logical. Necessary, even. But the reality of it was that Jake just wasn't cut out for a lifetime of coasting. Staying in Mill Pond, close to the only family he had, was non-negotiable. But there had to be more for him than fixing leaks, tightening screws, and adjusting filters. More, even than painting the motel—which was next on his to-do list.

"Like I said...I didn't know the filter needed any fixing." His uncle put his elbows on the arms of the rickety old chair and steepled his fingers. He fixed his rheumy gaze on the toolbox.

"It eats women's bathing suits. Don't tell me you didn't notice." He fit the cover back onto the gray plastic junction box. He finger-tightened a screw into the hole in each corner.

"Didn't think that was a problem. Especially seeing as how you caught such a pretty little catfish."

He tightened the screws on the diagonal, securing the box without snapping the plastic cover, with the flat-head screwdriver. Satisfied it was secure, he put the screwdriver into his back pocket, then sat back on his heels.

"You're just lucky Kat didn't sue you. I'm no lawyer, but there's probably a law against relieving a guest of her clothing against her will. Just what you don't need is a lawsuit. Shit, none of us does."

They stared into the pool, silently recalling the last tango with the law.

His uncle tipped his hat brim up a fraction of an

inch. His eyebrows were completely white, so scraggly and long that he looked like a hoot owl.

"Can't disagree with you there. So, you fixed the damn filter?" He waited for a nod, then asked, "Tell me the truth. Do you like being back in Mill Pond? Or are you still on the lam?"

The old man might give the impression his faculties were on permanent leave but there was more in his head than almost anyone gave him credit for. He'd once again out-maneuvered his nephew, turning an ordinary conversation into one Jake would rather—*much rather*—avoid.

Forever.

And ten decades after forever.

"Shit, but you're good." He wiped a hand on his thigh. It wasn't even midday, and the sun beat hot enough to fry eggs on the concrete pool deck. A rivulet of sweat snaked down his spine, an impermanent distraction.

"Glad you realize it, my boy." A brittle laugh, followed by a wheeze that sounded like it came from the old man's knees.

He instantly got to his feet but his uncle waved him back down so he complied, but only just. He didn't like the wheeze, and lately a cough, that came with some frequency.

He waited until his uncle caught his breath. "Are you okay?"

"Right as rain. Don't worry so much." He pushed his hat back just a tad further on his head. Whiter frizz poked out beneath the brim, making his thoughtful gaze look less serious than it might have had the fringe not been so absurd. "You didn't answer my question. I'm old, and sometimes I don't know whether my fly is up or not until I feel a breeze, but I'm not stupid. Are you still running? Or are you ready to settle down?"

"Why is it suddenly so important? You writing a book or something?"

The joke, told all the time when Jake was a boy spending summers at the motel, didn't bring a smile. Uncle Gordon's eyebrows came together in a flat line across his forehead. A white caterpillar walking across his face.

When he thought he was about to be melted by the stare, his uncle said, "I'm not getting any younger. A man should know how his family feels about some things. And right now, I want to know if you're still doing the anti-reality jog."

"Anti-reality jog? I can't believe you said that."

"Believe it. When I see my nephew hiding out in his dead aunt's skirts, I know he's jogging away from reality. Hell, she was my wife, and I don't even bury my head in her skirt anymore." He paused, raised a bushy brow, then asked, "You do get my meaning, don't you?"

He had to fight not to shudder. The idea of his aunt and uncle doing...even if they were both alive...well, it was just too damn much for him to take. He held a hand up, the way Tom did, and hoped the traffic cop ploy would work for him, too.

Uncle Gordon flashed a knowing grin and sat back in the chair.

"I get it. And point taken, but I haven't buried my head anywhere." Not that he didn't have a great lap in mind. "And, I'll give you, I was probably trying to hide from things when I first got here. I wanted to hide from myself, I think."

"That happens, my boy. Nothing to be ashamed of. But you can't hide forever."

Was he hiding? Not now. Not in a long time.

Stuck, maybe, but not hiding.

"I know, Uncle Gordon. I just haven't figured out where to go from here." He squinted into the shade. "Wait a minute—are you saying you don't like having me around?"

A small cackle, followed by a tight cough. Then, the wheeze. Not as bad this time, but still there.

"Now who's shitting who? You know we love having you back in town. Your aunt just about went nuts when you moved to Texas. I'm lucky she didn't insist we follow you. That damn duck is what kept her from leaving. I'd bet my last flamingo on it."

Jake gazed at the decrepit group of pink birds standing in the weedy flowerbed. Ugly. Real, headache-inducing ugly. Tacky, too. But the old man loved those idiotic birds, so they stayed.

"Don't do anything hasty. Wouldn't want to lose one of the pack."

"Flock, Jake. Flamingoes fly in a flock."

He wasn't sure he flocking cared. The worn plastic birds looked like an oversized pack of pink rats to him.

"Right."

"Anyhow, what do you think? Will you stay, or will you go back to Texas?"

Chapter 34

"Home? Anywhere you lay your head—as long as you don't lay your head on an anthill. That ain't home—no matter how high or fluffy it seems."
                                                    ~Lola Delaney

No one had come right out and asked him before. Not even Tom, who regularly made it his business to interrogate anyone he met.

"I like it here," he admitted.

"I hoped you'd say that. You know, the whole you-can't-go-home-again drivel is just crap. You can go home again—but you've got to find a reason for being home. And for making it home again. Understand?"

"I get it. I'm just not sure I know what to do with myself, now that I'm here."

"What about all that bring-tourists-to-town brouhaha? You've got people talking. I hear them, down at the diner. Your ideas are catching on, Jake. You've got folks riled up, ready to paint the sidewalks red if it'll draw Placid's overflow. Don't tell me you're gonna give up on that, not now when everyone's getting hopped up on your ideas."

He debated while he put his tools back into his dented metal box. The pliers nestled in beside a larger set, rubber grips pointing up so he could grab them without getting stuck. He shoved the screwdriver into its own divider pocket alongside a Philips'-head screwdriver. Three spare blue wire nuts went into a little compartment.

"I'm not giving up." He knelt beside the box, ready to end the conversation but aware that if he didn't give his uncle some answers, he'd have a tail until he did. "It's just that I've got to find more to do than just go to town meetings, bring up ideas for adding revenue, and gearing people up. I've got to find something real to do with my time. Am I making any sense?"

Uncle Gordon had been the most influential male figure in his life. His mother, his uncle's sister, met a moose head-on with her baby blue Nova when Jake was seven. Fortunately, he wasn't in the car. The crash didn't turn out well for either participant.

He and his mom lived in an apartment in Lake Placid, so losing her meant he'd moved into the big house behind the motel with his aunt and uncle. It hadn't been a bad life, growing up surrounded by new friends from interesting places. Even if the kids who stayed in the motel didn't stay for long, he had fun. And moving to Mill Pond meant he met Tom, the brother he'd never have found otherwise.

Confiding in the man who raised him wasn't hard to do. Especially on one of Uncle Gordon's less-eccentric days.

"You're not only making sense, you're damn near close to making dollars, too. Get it?" He began to laugh, but it turned into a strangled wheeze. Again, when Jake started to rise, the old man waved a bony hand. "Stay there, I'm fine. Don't worry so damn much. Dollars and cents—a good one, right?"

"I guess so." He inhaled, forcing his lips to curve

upward. The cough. The wheeze. Fear prodded him. "Are you sure you're okay?"

"Damn tootin' I am. And you're gonna be, too. I got a business proposition for you. Hear me out before you say anything."

"Fine. But then we're going to talk about seeing Doc Tate."

Having him checked over couldn't hurt.

"Don't bring that old fart into the conversation."

His uncle had fifteen years on the doctor, but he didn't point that out.

"So, I was thinking that maybe you'd like to take over running the Tip-A-Canoe." Uncle Gordon waggled his eyebrows, Groucho Marx style, and smiled so broadly his gold crown showed. "Not as a gift, mind you, because I know you'd never say yes to that, but a genuine business proposition. We'd be partners. You'd run the place, and send me checks when you made enough to spare."

"Where are you going?"

"Hey, I'm no spring chicken. These long winters get to my bones. Your aunt and I were thinking of going south. Florida, maybe. Or even Georgia. You know how I like my peaches."

Sometimes he wondered if his uncle remembered his wife had passed on. The spirit that popped in—unannounced and uninvited—at random times was just that, a spirit. Even though several townspeople claimed to see his aunt, the fact remained: She was dead, and her body buried in the tiny town cemetery.

"Uncle, you remember about Aunt Pat, don't you?"

A wave of an arthritic hand. "How in tarnation could I forget about the woman? She damn near trips me up, she's so close on my heels."

"It's just…"

Shit. How to phrase the reminder without breaking an old heart?

His uncle saved him. "Don't worry, Jake. I remember she's gone—from this mortal life, that is. She's here…but she's not here. I get it."

He nodded. "Okay, that's good."

"But I'm taking her ghost along with me when I go, so say your goodbyes before we head out." The conversation would have been comical had his uncle not been so serious. "Now, what about my proposition?"

The idea wasn't bad. It would take a bit of planning and some thought, but he had always harbored a desire to run the motel. He loved the place. The people. And, if he were a bona-fide business owner, his credibility would rise exponentially.

Caring for a motel wasn't like caring for a person. The human responsibility was limited. So limited, really, that it might not even be there. Too much.

"I like it." When his uncle grinned, he did the same. "We'll have to discuss money, naturally. You'll need some cash for a new home, and funds to get you set up wherever you decide to go. But yes, I like the idea."

"You'd have to take Clarence. Your aunt wouldn't leave unless she knew he was in good hands. And I don't want to smuggle that bigmouth duck into any retirement village. They have rules about stuff like that."

Retirement village. Now it made more sense. Jake liked the idea even better.

The duck went against his no-pets policy, but his uncle looked at him with such high expectations that he didn't have the heart to refuse. A duck. How much trouble could one little, old duck get into? And how hard could it be to mind Clarence?

He couldn't pull the rug out from under his uncle's dreams because of a duck.

Especially a duck who was, technically, a ghost.

"I'll take Clarence." He hoped he wouldn't regret the duck part of the proposition.

"So we've got a deal?" Uncle Gordon leaned forward in his seat, his right hand outstretched.

"We've got a deal."

Before he could shake his hand, Uncle Gordon's wobbly chair tilted, then tipped over, spilling the old man onto the concrete. Jake closed the gap between them in a heartbeat, but it was too late to catch his uncle. He'd landed atop his bowler hat, which hadn't padded his fall one bit.

The old man was down. And out.

Chapter 35

"There's not much a stiff shot of whiskey can't fix. Or a shoe sale at Bloomie's...yeah, that can do the trick, too." ~Lola Delaney

"I'm telling you, this is stupid. There's nothing wrong with me a blob of petroleum jelly and a Band-Aid can't fix."

Jake parked his truck in the Medical Center's lot, pocketed the key, and turned to his grouchy passenger.

"Stay there. I'm coming around to help you."

"I don't need any—"

He scrambled out and slammed the driver's side door, cutting off the last word. Before his uncle got his seatbelt unbuckled, Jake ran around the hood to the opposite side. He opened the passenger door and put his hand beneath the old man's elbow. Uncle Gordon protested and tried to shake him off, but he wouldn't be shaken.

"I told you, I don't need any help."

When the orthopedic shoes hit the pavement, he helped him stand. The old man seemed steady on his feet, but he wasn't taking any chances. A good-sized lump, hidden by the wild white curls beneath the hat was enough excitement for one day.

"You probably don't, but humor me." They made their way to the front door. He pulled it wide open, watching his uncle walk through. He did seem to be moving without any difficulty. Maybe—hopefully—the bump on his head wasn't serious.

He looked up when he heard his aunt's voice. She stood in all her purple glory in the center of the waiting room. Her hands were on her hips and, for once, she didn't have Clarence with her.

"What in Sam Hill are you doing here?" She met her husband halfway between the door and blue tweed waiting room chairs. Her eyes met his, and she put a hand on his arm. Without being told anything, her wife radar kicked in. She shifted her gaze to Jake. "What happened to him?"

"I'm right here, woman. Don't talk around me like I'm Casper the ghost." Uncle Gordon stopped, swaying just a bit. "But I think I'd better sit down."

Jake grabbed a chair and pulled it into the center of the room just in time to catch his uncle. When his aunt fell to her knees, pulling her husband's head against her chest and holding him steady, he dashed past the empty reception area and into the hallway beyond.

The doctor only employed one nurse. Nancy served as both receptionist and right hand to the family practitioner. When she wasn't at her desk, it meant the doctor needed her with a patient. There were only three exam rooms. Two doors were open. One, closed.

He knocked on the closed door.

Almost instantly it opened. Jake expected to find Nancy, in her old-school starched white uniform. Instead, he came face to face with a wide-eyed brunette who looked too young for the blue nursing scrubs she wore.

"Yes?" Her voice held a twang that put him off his

mark. For a moment, he stared down into her fresh face. No trace of makeup touched her skin. The only adornment were the petite gold hoop earrings dangling from delicate earlobes. "May I help you?"

The twang again. So unusual in upstate New York to hear a southern sound.

Behind the nurse, a doctor appeared. Again, not the doctor he expected.

The man wearing a white coat towered over the dainty nurse but stood eye to eye with Jake. They looked at each other for a brief second.

"I'm sorry to disturb you. I was looking for Dr. Tate." He heard talking from the waiting room. Quiet, unremarkable bits of conversation, so there was no urgency.

"I'm Dr. Jackson, doc's grandson. Grant Jackson. You're Jake Preston, aren't you? I think we met once or twice when I visited my grandfather when I was—when we were—kids."

He put his hand out. The doctor's grandson had been around a lot during their pre-teen years. Then, nothing. Being a boy, and not real conscious about things like that, he had never wondered where the kid had gone.

He put some friendliness into his voice. "Long time no see. Listen, is your grandfather around?" Glancing at the nurse, still standing between them, he asked, "And Nancy, too?"

"You haven't been in lately, have you?"

"Not really. Just healthy, I guess."

"My grandfather's retiring." Grant gave a big smile. "And I'm taking over his practice. In fact, I've got a patient I'm attending right now, so if it's not an emergency, can we catch up another time? I'm really pretty busy here…"

Normally he would have apologized for bothering the man and walked away. But the gasp he heard behind him, then the curse in his aunt's frightened voice, made him insistent.

"As a matter of fact, it is an emergency. My uncle hit his head. I've got him in the waiting room and he needs—"

"Jake!" Aunt Pat's tone chilled his heart.

He had no idea how she did it, appeared and sounded solid in this realm when it was necessary, but her voice carried. Not a ghostly wail or faint whisper, but a full-on holler.

He turned and ran toward her cry. He dropped to his knees beside his aunt—technically, his aunt's ghost—and grabbed his uncle. She held her husband against her, but his limp form nearly sent her backward. Jake relieved her of the weight.

The doctor and nurse were right beside him. One checked the old man's pulse. The other pulled back an eyelid and flashed a penlight into his eye.

"Let's get him into a room." Dr. Jackson lost the old-friend routine, all business now. "And Darla, call for transport. We'll take him over to Placid General stat." He turned to Jake. "Put your hands beneath him, like this, and we'll make a sling with our arms. Ready?"

He nodded. They lifted his uncle off the chair. He wasn't heavy, and they carried him into the first empty room, put him on the paper-covered table, and gently pulled their arms from beneath him. Aunt Pat followed them into the examining room. As soon as Jake stepped away from the table, she moved forward. Her hands went to his uncle's collar, loosening the button holding his shirt closed.

The doctor obviously saw her, and if he was unsettled by her presence, he showed no sign.

"If you could wait outside." The doctor spoke to Aunt Pat in a gentle tone. His stethoscope already roamed across his patient's chest.

"Not a chance. I'm staying."

Dr. Jackson didn't act surprised that he got a wife attached to a patient. He glanced at Jake, who leaned down and placed a kiss on his aunt's cheek.

"I'll be in the waiting room." He left, passing Nurse Darla in the doorway. She smiled her approval, then quickly closed the door behind her as she went into the treatment room.

Chapter 36

"They say a bark is worse than a bite, but that isn't true. Not by a long shot—especially if the teeth doing the biting are as sharp as the bark!" ~Lola Delaney

The upper hand—the bandaged upper hand, unfortunately—was hers.

She recognized his voice as soon as she heard it. She was, after all, the patient whose room he'd barged into. The wide-shouldered doctor, standing in the doorway, shielded her from view, but she heard the whole conversation. When the medical crew rushed out, Kat waited in the examining room. Darla returned, running in and out again after giving her brief instructions and a small bottle of painkillers.

Kat wrestled with the bottle. Her hand, bandaged so heavily it looked like it belonged to Mickey Mouse, was no use. It throbbed steadily, an unrelenting *thump-thump-thump* that grew so insistent she grit her teeth.

Drastic times call for drastic measures. Fear of creating a dental issue where none existed lost the war to pain relief. She put the medicine bottle in her mouth, held it between her teeth, and twisted the cap with her good hand. The top shot off and the bottle tipped, dropping tablets onto her tongue. She gasped. Swallowed the pills.

They were bitter, and she wished she had

something to chase them down. Thankfully, they cleared her throat so they weren't stuck, but the nasty taste in her mouth didn't make her day any better.

She sat in the blue plastic visitor's chair. A poster of the body's muscles and bone structure filled the wall opposite. She examined it, shuddering over the sinewy strands of muscle covering some of the skeleton. How the hell could anyone ever want to be a doctor? In her opinion, a person's insides should remain firmly inside. At all times.

She shook her head, trying to clear the image of the bone man from her mind. He was the stuff nightmares were made of, and God knew, she didn't need any of those.

How long had she waited? The clock on the wall wasn't any help, since she hadn't looked at it when she sat down. Jake had to be gone by now. An eternity had passed since she'd swallowed the pills.

She couldn't cap the bottle, so she held both bottle and cap in her good hand and kicked the partially open examining room door with her toe. If it had been shut, she'd have been stuck in the stuffy room until someone rescued her. But it wasn't, so she hurried into the hallway, hoping to avoid the man who somehow had wrangled his way into her mind so completely she couldn't concentrate on much else.

If she didn't have shitty luck, she'd have no luck at all.

Jake emerged into the hallway just as she did.

She stopped short. His back, so strong and wide, brought a tremor of remembrance. Her hands—before one had been wounded—had embraced that smooth expanse of skin-covered musculature just hours earlier.

Then, she'd been free to kiss and nip any spot on his body. And, she had.

Now, if she had a free hand she'd have punched him. Hard.

She'd be damned if she let him see he'd hurt her feelings. Double-damned.

Wishing she'd had time to change into something more seductive than a plain white tank and white denim shorts, she straightened her spine.

"Hello."

Concern etched itself into his features. He smiled, but not deeply enough for his dimples to show. He looked ravaged.

"Kat." He didn't move, but his gaze traveled over her body. It rested on her hand, held high against her breasts. "What happened?"

Explanations? Now?

"It seems to me you're the one who should do the explaining." Her tongue felt thick in her mouth. A glass of something cold and wet would do nicely, but until she got back to the apartment she'd have to deal with the fat, dry tongue.

Lines creased his brow. She wasn't in the mood to feel sorry for him, however. Whatever was on his mind was no concern of hers, was it? He'd shown no care whatsoever for her when he bolted from the patio like an axe murderer was loose—and on his ass.

His tone was serious, and it pissed her off. "Really—what happened to your hand?"

"None of your b-business," she snapped. Only it didn't feel like a snappy reply when her tongue tied over the last word.

A stutter. Of all the luck—that monster duck had

infected her.

"Are you okay?" He closed the distance between them. Chlorine and cedar mingled with sweat. Her heart hammered, so she rubbed the spot with her wounded hand. "Really, Kat…are you okay?"

"What's it to you? Are you worried I gave you something last night? Hmm?" She lowered her voice. "Don't worry. I don't have any diseases to share with you. Or anyone else, e-e…either."

That fucking duck and its damn stutter!

"Hey, why don't we sit down somewhere?" He put a hand on her arm but she wiggled away. Her backside hit the wall behind her and she let it hold her up. Suddenly she was very, very sleepy.

Still, she was pissed.

"Why? So you can give me the hit-and-and-run treatment another t-time…ooh, it's hot in here. Are you hot in there?" She lifted the bottom edge of his untucked T-shirt with a fingertip to reveal the best set of abs she'd ever seen. Or touched. Letting his shirt drop, she fanned her face with her free hand. "Yes, you're hot in there."

A giggle came from somewhere deep, but she put her fingers over her mouth.

Jake put a hand on the wall near her head. He stared into her eyes. His other hand brushed her temple, sending shock waves through her body. Damn him, for being sexy enough to have that power over her.

"S-stop it." She pushed his hand away.

"Do you have a fever?" His gaze drilled into her eyes, so she closed them. Then, his question registered in her pain-fogged brain, so she opened them again.

"Asking if I'm hot? Hmm? Listen—if I'm hot—

and I'm n-not saying I am—that's not the sp-spot to ch-check!"

Oh, the floor was spinning. Fast.

How to get off a spinning floor?

Suddenly the Texas nurse—what was her name?—appeared. She and Jake talked, but Kat didn't bother listening. Who cared what they were saying, anyway? Someone, she wasn't sure who, took the pill bottle from her.

Then, Jake swept her off her feet. He did it carefully, not banging into her injury, and settled her against his chest. She wanted to protest, wanted to smack him and demand her release, but she didn't do any of those things.

No, he smelled too damn good. All cedar. And swimming pool. And man. Big, hot, sexy man.

She closed her eyes, rested her head against his chest, and took a deep breath.

His man scent was intoxicating.

It was also the last thing she remembered before she fell asleep.

Chapter 37

"A clear conscience is a soft pillow."
~Lola Delaney

Three things woke Kat, and they hit all at once.

Sunlight streamed through the sheers at the window. It was like a laser, so she squinted her eyes shut.

The aroma of fresh-brewed coffee filled her nostrils. She inhaled, savoring the scent.

Her bladder screamed more loudly than her eyes complained or her stomach demanded. She sat up. Reached for the bathrobe draped over the footboard.

That's when she saw them, tucked underneath her white-and-blue check summer robe.

Her shorts. The ones she wore to the medical center.

She looked down at herself. Luckily—or unluckily, depending on what had happened last night—her dark blue bikini panties were where they should be.

Damn. Losing her pants without remembering how they'd come off her body? Another first. One that didn't make her mood lighter.

She pulled the robe on, bunched it together in the front, and dashed to the bathroom. The hallway was short, the other rooms in the opposite direction, so she made it without having face time with whoever was responsible for the coffee smell.

Taking care of business required some planning. Everything, even the smallest things, like taking the top off the toothpaste tube, was a challenge.

By the time she washed her face, brushed her hair and teeth, she could have gone straight back to the bedroom. Pulled the blinds closed. Snuggled into the psychedelic cocoon and gone straight to Dreamland.

Except she couldn't do that. Not when someone—and she was pretty damn sure she knew *who* that someone was—roamed the apartment. After rendering her pants-less.

The kitchen was empty. Attila wasn't underfoot, as was her habit.

She looked under the table at the empty chairs. "Attila?"

No cat.

She called more loudly. "Attila?"

Still, no kitten.

Just when her heart began to jackhammer, Jake walked in through the door from outside. He had a green Fiestaware coffee mug in one hand and Attila in the other.

They stared at each other for one mind-numbing heartbeat. The sight of the man, so rawly masculine, in the small kitchen with the tiny gray kitten nestled in one palm made her wish she could change places with Attila.

Then, she remembered how he'd played and run. Suddenly she didn't feel inclined to nestle up against his anything. Much.

"You're awake." The stubble on his cheeks was sexy. His cleft chin drew her gaze. Seeing him like this, unshaven and in rumpled clothes, gave her a major hot wave. It started in her chest and worked its way down to her nether regions. When the heat crawled between her legs, she remembered the missing shorts and steaminess dissipated.

"Observant, aren't you?" Someone else might have been able to pull of cool and detached, but she just couldn't do it. It was too early. And her damn hand was beginning to throb. And, he'd taken her pants without asking first.

And, he held her pussycat as if he owned her.

She reached for the kitten with her good hand. Her fingers brushed the inside of Jake's wrist as he turned the furry bundle over to her. She'd kissed that spot, tasted the skin there.

The hell with cool and detached. Pissed would work.

Jake ignored her sarcasm. "We were on the patio. It's nice and quiet out there." He passed her, leaving plenty of room between them, and went to the stove. The old percolator, with a new glass knob screwed into its top, sat on the back burner. He filled the empty cup on the counter beside it before refilling his own cup. He spoke over his shoulder. "Why don't you go sit down there? I'll bring breakfast out to you."

"You don't need to bother."

Her turncoat belly took that exact moment to rumble. The noise filled the small space.

He turned and stared at her.

She scowled. It was a standoff. Silently she dared him to say something smooth and sexy. Anything at all. One hand might be bound up, and the other filled with a sleeping kitten, but she'd figure out how to hurl something his way if he gave her an opening. The view from the edge wasn't pretty, and all she needed to step over was the teeniest, tiniest provocation.

He didn't give it.

"Can you manage with Attila, or do you need help going down the stairs?"

She'd fall ass over teakettle before she'd ask him for help!

Using her shoulder to push and her elbow to press the door latch down, she sent the screen door flying as she forced it open and walked out. What's more, she didn't look back—not even when she heard him chuckle.

Not even when she felt his gaze warming her backside. No, not even then.

Chapter 38

"Sometimes your biggest blessing comes after your worst mistake." ~Lola Delaney

He was in the doghouse. It wasn't as if she tried to hide it.

But he'd suspected she would be angry even before she'd lurched out of the examining room. In his heart, he'd known. How could she not be upset with him? He'd behaved like a jackass after their encounter. Hell, he was annoyed with himself.

What had he been thinking?

Really, not much. He just wanted to get away because…well, as much as he hated to admit it, even to himself, what happened with Kat went beyond a casual hook up. She made him feel things he didn't want to feel.

He assembled a tray he'd found behind the toaster. Two cups of coffee. One plate of toast. Butter and knife.

Had there been a way to send the breakfast tray down ahead of him, so she could fill her belly and maybe soften the sarcastic edges of her temper, he would've done it. But there wasn't, so he pocketed the bottle of pain pills and went to face the music. He peered over the side of the staircase.

She was on the glider with Attila curled on her lap.

She stretched her legs out, leaving no room for anyone to sit beside her. It was fine with him. Safer to put some space between them.

He didn't look at her when put the tray on the table. Handed her a mug of coffee. She took it, also pointedly refusing to meet his gaze. He pulled a chair beside the glider, sat and reached for his own cup. They drank, the only sound the purring from the little cat.

When she didn't say a word, he buttered a triangle of toast. Handing it to her was out of the question. She held the mug in her good hand. The other lay across her lap.

He held the toast near her mouth. "Eat. Before it gets cold."

She eyed it. Then, she shot him a surly glance. Her mouth remained mulishly closed, the sweet-as-nectar lips unmoving.

Two could play the stubborn game. He held the toast in front of her. And waited.

"You'll feel better if you eat something."

She met his eyes, and he saw the truth in hers. The angry bit was mostly an act. He'd hurt her. It showed so clearly it felt like a dagger to his heart. He'd treated her so badly, he'd trampled her feelings. And, just when she was probably at one of the lowest points in her life, right after another man had disappointed her.

God, he really was a jerk.

"Please, Kat. Take a bite. You'll feel better once you get something in your stomach. Then, you can have a pill for the pain." He snagged the pill bottle from his pocket and placed it on the tray.

She knit her brows. Scowled at the bottle.

"Right. Like I'm going to let you drug me again,

and do who-knows-what while I'm knocked out. Yeah, I'm sure *that's* not going to happen again."

"It didn't happen before. You took the two Darvocet, remember? No one gave them to you. The nurse counted the pills in the bottle. You swallowed twice what the doctor ordered. I didn't drug you—you drugged yourself."

A sideways look. The toast still hovered in the air. "What happened to my pants?"

"I took them off when I got you in bed." She hadn't been in any condition to do it.

"No surprise, that. You're pretty good at taking off women's pants, it seems." She tried crossing her arms across her breasts, but it didn't go well. The look of pain that contorted her face when the bandage bumped her shoulder told him all he needed to know.

"Take a bite, okay? I'll take any shitstorm you want to throw my way, but first you've got to get some food inside you so you can take a pill." He touched her lower lip with the toast but she pulled her head back.

"Did we?" The question lacked vehemence.

"Did we what?"

She opened her pretty green eyes wide. She nodded toward his crotch, then down toward her lap. "Did we? You know…did we?"

"No! Of course not—you were out cold! What kind of an asshole do you think I am? I'm not the type to jump a woman when she's passed out."

No one had ever accused him of anything so low. The slap to his pride smarted. Probably, he thought, the same way her self-esteem had been damaged. By him—damn it.

"Right. You're just the type who almost cuts his

own cock off zipping up so he can run from the party. That's right—that's your type, isn't it?"

The toast compressed between his fingertips, sending crumbs scattering onto the skin exposed in the vee of her robe.

"Let's concentrate on you now. First, food. Then, pill. Then—and I promise I won't rob you of this chance—shitstorm. But first, take a bite of the damn toast because I'm not adverse to coming over there and prying open those sweet lips of yours."

He held the triangle to her mouth.

She took a bite, sending him the most god-awful glare he'd ever received as she chewed. Then, a second bite. And a second glare, worse than the first.

Too bad he hadn't thought to bring an umbrella. When the storm hit, it was going to be one helluva mess.

Chapter 39

"Fuzzy is good for slippers. Heads? Not so much."
~Lola Delaney

Darvocet was a miracle drug. Ten minutes after it hit her system, most of the discomfort in her hand was gone. It still hurt but the pain was tolerable.

The betrayal piercing her heart? That, even narcotics couldn't eradicate.

That Jake didn't flee after he'd hand fed her before opening the pill bottle and giving her just one pill to take with a swallow of coffee surprised her. She figured he'd bolt the minute he could manage it.

But he didn't appear in a rush to leave. He'd gone inside for coffee refills for both of them, bringing a saucer of cool water for Attila and placing it in the shade beneath the glider. Now their coffee cups were empty, abandoned on the table.

And Jake, aside from phoning to check that his uncle was okay, hadn't said a word.

She watched him out of the corner of her eye. His clothes were rumpled, his cheeks rasped every time he drew a hand across his skin and his eyes were bloodshot. Not the most flattering morning for either of them.

"Why don't you go home?"

Maybe it was mercy, she didn't know, but all at

once she didn't care to hear why he'd done what he had. Knowing wouldn't fix anything. Her life was screwed up, and her taste in men awful.

The experience reinforced her no-penis rule. She'd just have to cultivate self-control where penises and men were concerned. Especially the gorgeous one attached to the man beside her. Yes, his male apparatus was definitely off-limits from now on.

Jake cocked a brow. Shook his head. The mop of black curls, so enticing and as she now knew, silky and smooth, bounced.

"Nope. Not going until we get through the storm. I said I wouldn't move until you gave me your all—and, believe me, I realize I deserve it—so have at it. Tell me what an idiot I am."

"Let's forget it. I don't understand what happened...I just..." Fuzziness, not as bad as yesterday's episode, slowed her thoughts. "Let's just forget it, okay? It won't happen again, anyway, so why bother kicking a dead dog."

He met her gaze, a smile twitching his lips. She remembered how those lips felt pressed against hers, so capable and sublime all at once.

"I think the expression is 'kick a dead horse' but the dog thing works, too." He leaned forward, put his elbows on his knees, and loosely threaded his fingers together. They were so close she smelled chlorine and something inside her melted. Just a small softening, but a definite thaw. "The thing of it is, I owe you an apology. I'm sorry, I really am. I behaved like a fool, running out of here like...hell, I don't even know—"

"Like your ass was on fire. You accused me of it once, remember? In the grocery parking lot. But I didn't move nearly as fast as you did. You looked like your ass—and some other parts of your anatomy, too—was truly burning."

"That's probably how it looked. I don't know what happened. I just…I…shit, I'm not making a good job of this, am I?" He plowed a hand through his hair before scrubbing a palm across his chin. The cleft drew her gaze. Then she met his, and saw a glut of emotions swirling beyond his gold-flecked irises.

She'd been willing to let it drop. To let him walk away without an explanation. Just chalk it all up to one more crappy move on her part. But that was before he'd begun this conversation.

Now she wanted answers.

"Nope." She gave him credit for not flinching. "Just tell the truth. That's all I want. What the hell happened to you? One minute we were—you know. Then, you jumped up, ran off, and left me here like a twenty-dollar hooker."

Thinking about it, remembering how used and dirty she felt watching him leave, brought a chill. She sat up straight, tilted forward and stared into his face.

How could she have let him treat her like that? How?

"I never meant to make you feel that way."

"Well, that's how it felt."

"I'm sorry. I wish I could take it back, but I can't. All I can do is tell you how I feel, and hope it's enough."

"No," she demanded, bringing her face still closer to his. The distance between their noses was mere inches. Weariness showed clearly in his features but she couldn't drop this. Not now. "That's not enough. I want to know why—why did you do that? I thought we were, at the very least, friends. Or beginning friends. Or—damn it, I don't know. I thought there was something building between us. Something nice—but apparently I was mistaken. About a lot of things. About you, especially."

He placed a hand on her shoulder. Shaking him off would have meant moving her injured hand, possibly making it hurt more, so she didn't. But that wasn't the only reason she let his hand stay. She liked it. Pure and simple. Angry? Yes. Still under his spell? Evidently so.

"You're not mistaken. Please, don't say that." He squeezed, a small tightening of his strong fingers against her shoulder. "I'm an ass, Kat. I have this rule about women. About everything, but especially women, and I broke it. I just reacted like crap when it hit me. I broke the rule, with you."

"What's the rule?"

She held her breath.

"I don't date. Not with any real intentions, that is. I…well, I do casual dates, nothing more. Nothing that makes me feel for a woman in any real way." He took a deep breath. Let it out slowly. He shook his head, stared into her eyes so hard she couldn't look away. "I don't get involved. I can't fall for anyone. Can't feel responsible for anyone. I can't—I just can't do it."

"I didn't ask for that, did I? We were just…"

He shook his head. "No, we weren't. I thought so, too, in the beginning. I'm attracted to you, more than I like to admit, but there's more than sex between us." He searched her face but between the pill and his totally unexpected admission, she couldn't react. She stared into his eyes, not sure where the ride would stop but certain she didn't intend to let him pull out now. "Don't you feel it, too?"

She nodded. It was all she could manage.

"I thought so. Listen, it's amazing, what's growing between us. And as much as I'd like to say I have a place in my life for a real relationship..." He shook his head. "I just don't. I'm sorry, but I just can't let myself fall for anyone. I felt something for you when we connected that I haven't felt in a long time. It scared me. I ran. Stupid, I know. I've been kicking myself from here to hell and back, but that's it. It was a natural self-preservation reaction. Shitty, and I'm sorry."

So many scenarios, with a myriad of explanations, had crossed her mind. This had never been one of them.

For several heartbeats, they sat and stared into each other's eyes. Kat felt liquid beneath his gaze. She didn't want to. She'd give anything for more self-control, for not melting in his sight, but she had less power than a passenger did on a runaway train.

Yeah, she could see how feeling something this strong would scare someone.

She could see it—up close and personal.

"Forgive me? Can we be friends again? Please?"

Refusal wasn't an option.

She closed the tiny space between them. She rested her forehead against his, closed her eyes and said, "Friends. But, Jake?"

His breath warmed her chin.

"What?"

"Don't do it again. Promise."

"Oh, Kat...I promise."

Chapter 40

"There's only one thing to do when the world knocks you down. Get up off your ass, dust yourself off and move on." ~Lola Delaney

"You have to let me help you."

Jake watched as she stood in front of her open closet door. Leave it to a woman to insist on choosing an outfit when the only place she was going was to bed. The tank top, panties (blue, he remembered from removing her shorts the night before) and robe looked comfortable. Why change?

He would have lounged in his rattiest sweats for days had the hand been his. No need to get fancy.

Obviously, he didn't get it. Just another in a long line of female secrets that went right over his big, fat head.

"I don't need help. I can manage."

She pulled a lavender-striped one-piece shorts outfit off a hanger. A row of buttons, also lavender, ran down the front to the waist. Top attached to shorts, not a bad idea when it came right down to it. Kat opened a dresser drawer and pulled out a pair of lacy white panties. She shut the drawer with a clumsy thud.

Gathering up the clothes in her good arm, she turned and faced him. Tendrils of hair curled around her shoulders. Her eyes, usually so bright and inquisitive, were wider, a result of the narcotic, probably. She wasn't out of it, by any means. She was just…softer.

He hated himself. For hurting her. Letting her feel cheap and used.

Hated the fact he was so damn damaged that he couldn't have a normal relationship.

"You can leave, you know. I can manage just fine."

She swayed slightly. Yeah, she could manage. And his left testicle could drive a car. Right.

"You keep saying that, but I'm not sure it's altogether true. I think you need some help."

Her good arm tightened across her chest. The signal was clear—he wasn't going to get too close. Fine by him if she felt that way. But he wasn't leaving.

"I can manage." The scrap of fabric she'd squashed into the death grip she had on the romper slid out of her arms. It made a white puddle near her feet.

He reached down, snatched the panty and, before he straightened, ran a thumb over one toe.

"This belongs to you." He tucked the garment into her clothing bundle. "And I like those toes. What do you call a color like that? Amazing Pink?"

"Not exactly." Pink, a shade much paler than the one on her feet, kissed her cheeks.

"What, then? Passionate Pink?"

The bloom intensified. Stunning and adorable. The urge to kiss her was great but it was more fun to tease than ravish.

"Uh…nope, not that, either."

Jake put his arm across the open doorway. Trapping her symbolically, since she could easily duck beneath his arm.

"What then? I'm not going to let you out of here

until you fess up."

She tilted her head sideways a notch. "Scarlet Screaming Sex."

He couldn't stop the laughter that shot from his gut. Kat grinned, too. They both looked down at her feet. Suddenly the delicate toenails took on a whole new meaning.

"You're not kidding, are you?" He ran a hand across his cheek, rubbing the stubble against his palm. He'd give a lot for a shave.

"Nope." She tilted her head just a bit farther, studying him. "And I like your dimples. Have I told you that yet? They go real dimple-y when you laugh. I like it."

"No one's ever told me that before."

One eyebrow arched. "Really? I figured you must hear it all the time. I noticed them right away."

"Did you like them right away?" A small tease. The reward? She blushed again.

"I did."

He debated. Wanting to lean down and kiss her warred with memories of the friendship conversation they'd just had. Friendship won, but by the barest margin.

"I like your toes." When her gaze touched his cheeks, he knew the dimples made an appearance. Almost a secret weapon, those dimples. He filed the news of their effectiveness away. He might need them again sometime.

"Thank you." She took a step toward the doorway. "I should go shower. And really, you can leave. You must have stuff to do."

"Not really. My uncle is fine. My aunt is watching

over him the way she watches Clarence." He stopped, remembering her hand. Clarence had never bitten anyone before. Knowing he'd done so was almost impossible to believe, even with the proof right in front of him. "Hey, I'm really sorry my aunt's duck bit you. He's always so even-tempered. I just can't think of a reason for him to do something like that."

She glanced over to where Attila curled in a circle on the bed. Sunlight warmed her and she purred her contentment. She looked like the front of a Hallmark card.

"The duck tried to eat Attila. I put my hand between the cat and the monster." She shrugged. "I'm just grateful it was my hand and not Attila's head."

"I'm sorry it was either. Look, I'm not leaving you here one-handed. Not yet, anyway. And I don't have anything to do, what with no guests at the motel until Friday and my aunt and uncle managing without my help. Besides, we've just made the friendship pact, remember? Friends don't let friends do the one-hand struggle."

Kat sighed. "Fair enough. But we're just friends, right? Nothing more?"

She tugged his heartstrings. He wanted to chase all problems from her life.

But he couldn't. His presence, and their very unfriendly feelings, was the problem—for both of them.

Well, they were both adults, weren't they? Somehow, they would just have to learn to deal with their feelings.

"Didn't we just agree to that? I thought I gave you my word." He couldn't bring himself to say the words, "just friends" when his heart screamed otherwise.

"You gave your word you wouldn't make me feel cheap. That's different," she pointed out.

"Friends don't nitpick." He grinned.

She grinned back.

"Fine. But I've got my eye on you. No funny business."

Solemnly he crossed his heart. "Not one bit of funny from me. Now, do you need help getting undressed?" The look she gave answered his question. "Okay, I get it. You don't need help getting into the shower. But I'm going to wrap your hand in a plastic bag before you go in so it doesn't get wet."

"How am I supposed to wash with a bag on my hand?"

"I could come in and do the honors." Images of wet, soapy skin flashed through his mind. *Lord have mercy.* He pushed them out of the way and brought the Yankees stats into his head instead. RBIs and games won versus games lost didn't do the trick. He could still imagine his hands gliding over her slick skin.

His internal war did not go unnoticed. The gleam in her eyes and small, satisfied smirk let on she knew exactly what he was thinking. Down to the last soap bubble.

"I don't think so. I'll let you bag me, but I'm not going to let you do anything else, if you know what I mean."

"You don't have to spell it out. Let's find a plastic bag so you can get in the shower. Too much more shower talk is going to send me straight to the icebox."

He turned her around and followed her into the kitchen. In a drawer he found a box of gallon-size plastic bags. He covered the large bandage and sealed it with some packing tape. When he was finished, he put the tape on the table and admired his handiwork. It should hold. Ugly, but it would keep the area dry.

"Now, you're sure you don't need me?" Who could blame a guy for trying?

"I'm sure. And, stay out of my icebox. I've got truffles in there—and I expect them to still be there when I get done."

"So, you were making candy again? When?"

"Yesterday morning. Before the monster duck attack."

She'd told him the other night that candy making was her relaxation. Apparently something had been on her mind—and it didn't take a genius to figure out what.

"Truffles? Are you going to share them with me?"

He put a finger beneath her chin and tipped her head back. She looked so vulnerable standing with the ridiculous bag on her hand and the dreamy painkiller look in her eyes. The desire to kiss her ripped through him but he fought it. This only-friends arrangement was brand new, yet it already tore at him.

"Please?"

"I'll think about it."

She took a step back and shook her head. Without another word, she turned and headed for the hallway leading to the bathroom. He stood there, listening to her light footsteps on the bare wood floors.

He didn't move until he heard the door close and the shower water start.

He exhaled the breath he'd been holding. For months, the rules he'd made for his life had worked. Now, it seemed they would never work again.

Shit on a stick, but he had it bad for her—and there wasn't a damn thing he could do to change it.

Chapter 41

"There's a reason we're born naked. Not quite sure what it is, but I know there's a reason—and a damn good one, at that." ~Lola Delaney

The shower was well worth the effort. Kat held her bagged hand out of the direct spray, poking out between the flowered shower curtain and the wall. The method was clumsy, and she skipped a few body parts with the soap, but it worked.

Single-handedly drying off was harder than showering had been. The vintage green terrycloth bath towel was huge and would have wrapped twice around her body. Great for collecting moisture, but burdensome to actually maneuver across her skin. In the end, she opted to just wrap in it for a minute, using her armpit to hold it in place.

When she was semi-dry, she dropped the towel and managed to slide into the panty. It kept rolling when she pulled it up but determination won against wet skin and tiny stretch lace because it finally covered what it was meant to cover.

Damn. Why is it all so hard?

Dressing wore her out.

Kat sat on the edge of the tub and gazed at her surroundings. Like the rest of the tiny apartment, the bathroom was outdated. Pink-and-white tiles covered the floor. The bathtub, toilet, and sink were pink. The vanity cabinet had been painted white at one time, but the paint had worn through in spots so bursts of yellow and blue gave it an odd, patchwork effect.

When she had first glimpsed the room, she hated it. She'd longed for her city bath, all gleaming ceramic tiles and polished brass fixtures. But something changed. She didn't compare one against the other anymore. The retro room had grown on her, providing comfort in an otherwise-unsettled world.

She grabbed her outfit off the edge of the vanity. She arranged the garment on her lap before she slid her feet into the leg openings.

She figured dressing with only one arm would be a breeze. All she had to do was stand, pull the fabric over her hips and onto her arms. Right, onto her arms. As in, over the big, plastic-coated bandage on her hand. Which, coincidentally, was once again doing its pulse-thumping dance inside its wrapping.

Nothing to it, right?

Kat pulled the romper to her waist with her good arm. She stretched her bad one behind her, thinking she'd gently slide it into the armhole. As she did, her hand collided with the wall beside the shower.

Pain ricocheted from her hand to her heart to her head—in a half-second.

She dropped the romper.

"Shit! Oh, shit!"

She collapsed onto the side of the tub again, cradling her screaming hand against her chest. Ripples of agony, beginning at the hand and spiraling outward, shook her. Tears pooled in her eyes, spilling over her lids and down her cheeks.

Jake burst into the room. He fell to his knees in front of her, landing on the puddle of fabric that she'd been so desperate to pull over her body.

"What happened? Are you all right?"

Answering was impossible. She couldn't form a cohesive sentence as she fought the tide of pain. He seemed to sense it, and pulled her against him. The top of her head, damp from the shower, touched his chest right above his heart. They stayed like that until her hand quieted.

He ran a soothing hand down her back. His touch, so warm and gentle, reminded her she was half-dressed. Not that she gave a damn. He'd seen her naked before. Why quibble now?

She lifted her face, let him thumb away the tears drying on her skin.

"You hit your hand?"

She nodded, still too pain-wracked to speak.

"Do you think you can stand? Or should I carry you?"

They were in dangerous territory, walking a fine line between friends and more-than-friends. Since his reaction to the more-than option sent him running, it seemed best to stand on her own two feet.

"I can stand. But I can't get my arm where it needs to be. I can't get my arm back far enough to get it in." She still hadn't straightened.

"Are you sure you want to wear that outfit? I'm not trying to tell you what to do, but if you can't get it on without help, you're not going to be able to get it off, either. Not that I mind helping you. It just seems like it's going to be a problem you don't need."

His meaning was clear. Why hadn't she thought of

it? Because her brain was foggy, that's why.

"Not a good move, is it?"

"Like I said, I'm here to help, but I don't think you'll be happy with this choice." Jake took her robe off the hook on the wall. "If it was me, I'd slip this on. You're not going anywhere. It looks comfortable. What do you think?"

She couldn't argue with rationale like that and managed a small nod.

"I'll hold the robe up. You stand, turn around, and I'll slide it onto your arms. Sound like a plan?"

Kat nodded again, relieved that someone had a plan.

"First, let's get this thing off your feet. You'll end up tripping, and we'll be back at the doctor's office to get something else bandaged. If you would, please move those pretty Screaming Scarlet Sex toes this way."

He removed the garment and tossed it to the side. Then, took a deep breath. He met her gaze.

She saw this near-naked exchange was taking as much from him as it was from her. Maybe more.

"Ready?" He held the robe between them.

She stood, turned and, with his help, slipped her arms in. She pulled it closed with her hand and turned to face him. "I can't tie it, Jake."

Grinning so widely his dimples rocked her world, he tied the sash in a neat bow. "I'd be stupid if I refused any offer that involves tying you up."

Being "just friends" was painful. She bit the inside of her lower lip, willing herself not to rise to the bait before her. But the bait was so strong and sexy…and she was so damn weak.

The words tumbled out, and there wasn't a damn thing she could do to stop them.

"So you've got a kinky streak in you—is that what you're trying to say?"

He sucked in a breath. Held it. His hands hadn't left the bow at her waist, and she felt a tug as they gripped the sash tighter.

She'd hit a nerve. Or, shocked him. Either way, she scored.

Jake's voice was husky, so low and deep it made heat pool in places that were off-limits to his touch.

"There's only one way to find out, isn't there?" He held her gaze and she fell into his deep brown seduction willingly. There was no fighting it, not even if she'd had the energy—which, after expending so much showering, dressing and now, flirting, she didn't.

"Let's get another pain pill in you. Then, it's time for you to rest on the couch. I'll scare up a movie—a G-rated movie—and we'll nap the day away. Sound good?"

Honestly, it sounded perfect—although she could think of other ways to spend an afternoon with him.

Kat swallowed hard. Her mouth was dry, but she said, "It sounds great."

Really, what could she say? "I want to have wild monkey sex with you" was out of the question. Wasn't it?

Chapter 42

"Love isn't for cowards." ~*Lola Delaney*

Spending the day in Kat's company made a number of things clear.

One—her intelligence wasn't limited to dinner conversation or seduction. She did both extremely well, but that wasn't where her brain talent ended. They laughed over the movies they found on an oldies television station. During commercials, they discussed the stock market, Middle Eastern politics, barn restoration, and Hemingway. She was genuinely well-rounded.

Two—this friends-only clause to his no-dating rule was going to be a challenge. It never had been before. No one made his no-relationship philosophy difficult to adhere to. Until now.

And number three? Kat knocked his dick stiff—whether she was awake or asleep. Knowing the woman gave him an erection without any real effort on her part didn't stop it from happening. His cock had a mind of its own.

Jake felt like he had in high school, when a stiff wind could bring him to attention. What was the use of maturity and wisdom—two things he hoped he'd acquired by this point—when a man's penis refused to adhere to its owner's insights?

She slept peacefully, curled up on one end of the hideous sofa. Attila nestled on the pillow by Kat's head, a paw stretched into the curls fanning out over the plush gold fabric. They were a stunning portrait of grace and beauty, serene and flawless—that is, ignoring the bulky white bandage on her hand.

Uncle Gordon was napping, too. He'd checked a short time ago and been informed by his aunt that there was nothing to worry about.

Easy for her to say, when she wasn't the one who was going to have to explain her existence. Or lack thereof.

It was generally accepted in Mill Pond that the resident ghost was no big deal. Not everyone could see her, but enough did that they just treated her as they had while she was alive. It enriched his uncle's life to have her treated thusly. After all, he was the reason Aunt Pat hadn't toddled off to the hereafter. She'd promised him she'd stay with him, and so far she had done exactly that.

On the phone she'd *pooh-poohed* Jake's concern, reminding him she knew perfectly well how to care for the man. His uncle had a goose egg on his head that might take a while to subside. In the meantime, he was still making plans for their retirement move.

The retirement move.

It all happened so fast. Backing out was an impossibility, so he'd have to make running the motel work. Uncle Gordon deserved a break, some peaceful days at the sunset of his life.

Clarence. That was the kicker. He'd agreed to take the cat-eating duck. There was no backing out of that, either. Could his life get any crazier?

"Son of a bitch," he muttered. A flash of annoyance. Not only did his cock not behave the way he expected it to, but he'd been hoodwinked by an old man and a duck. "I'll be damned."

"Hmm?"

Kat stretched and turned onto her back. Where her bathrobe met across her breasts fell open just a smidge. He had—nearly—a view of a nipple. If he leaned a little bit to the right, he could almost make out the deep pink—

"Enjoying yourself?" Her sleepy voice was a purr.

Nailed. The interesting part was that she didn't pull her robe closed. So, maybe being caught peeping wasn't such a bad thing?

"Can't say I'm not enjoying the view." He met her gaze. "Do you mind?"

"Can't say I do, no." She lifted a shoulder, then let it drop. When it rose, her robe parted, revealing the entire breast—nipple included. But when she dropped her shoulder, the robe hid her again.

Drawing a breath wasn't as easy as it had been while she was napping.

He stood and went to the window behind his chair. Pushing aside the filmy sheers, he undid the window lock and pulled the wooden window frame. It didn't budge. Years of painting had sealed it.

But, damn, the room needed some air. He smacked the four corners of the frame with the palm of his left hand while he grasped the old wood and yanked. Nothing. Again, he hit the corners, where the paint formed a bond where one shouldn't be. He used both hands and forced the pane of glass up. It rose with a reluctant screech.

"That sounds awful."

When he turned, she was sitting up with the cat cradled in her arms. The fur on the cat stood up, and its tail was twice as big as normal. Kat ran a loving hand down its back.

"We needed air."

He felt exposed. She saw right through him. He felt it, and the small smile she gave him cemented the idea.

Oh, yeah. She knew what was going on.

"Thirsty?" He headed for the kitchen. His throat was as parched as a riverbed in July.

Peering into the refrigerator, he saw that Kat wasn't big on eating. A container of yogurt, half a bottle of lemonade, and six sticks of unsalted butter. He let the door close, grabbed a glass from the cupboard, and filled it with water from the tap. He was midway through the first glass, mentally compiling a grocery list, when his hostess joined him.

"Slim pickings, I'm afraid." She gave him an apologetic grin. Standing there with bare feet, wearing just a robe, she was delectable. Never mind the fridge—he'd settle for licking every inch of her sweet body.

Pulling his mind out of the gutter, he shrugged. "I'll go get some groceries. Any requests?"

"No, thanks. I'm not hungry. You?"

He was hungry, all right, but it wasn't for anything on a grocery store shelf.

It was a good thing she couldn't read his mind.

"I'm a guy—I can always eat." He tipped the glass back, emptying it before placing it in the sink. "And you should, too, even if you're not hungry. All those pills will make you sick on an empty stomach. You don't want that, do you?"

"Definitely not. But, really, I don't feel like a big deal meal. Just something small and...I don't know...sweet."

Oh, she was testing his will power. Big time.

And she knew it.

The credit he'd given her for her brains? Double it. She could play him like a banjo at a country music festival. She was just warming up, he could tell.

Grinning, Kat crossed the room and opened the freezer.

"See? Sweet." She pointed to something in the compartment, but he didn't follow her fingertip. "And cold."

She boils a man's blood, then asks for cold? Good lord.

Chapter 43

"Chocolate is best eaten off a lover's fingertip."
~*Lola Delaney*

Tempering the chocolate to dip the truffles had been easy. Jake took direction well, and once she got him to stop trying to peek beneath her robe, he was all action in the kitchen. He stirred chocolate chunks in a metal bowl over simmering water, pausing only once to dip a fingertip in the molten mixture. When he licked his skin clean, her body zinged its response, but she ignored it. They were only friends, right?

It was going to take every ounce of self-control she had to remember that small fact, and respond accordingly. Organizing things in store windows was simpler—and less taxing—than straightening out her love life.

No—not her love life. That implied physical closeness that she and Jake weren't going to have. It involved loving, touching and—and she was off men, and especially penises.

Not to self: No penises. No Jake. No—

Oh, crap. He was doing it again. The whole finger-licking thing that turned her legs to Jell-O.

"Stop that." She used her good hand to swat his finger before it dipped onto the rim of the bowl a second time. "You'll, ah…"

His finger disappeared between his lips, pulling her gaze with it. Memories flooded her, hot, delicious sensations zinged in her core and her mouth went dry. His tongue had been so warm and insistent, his touch tender and knowing…

Jake took his finger from his mouth and grinned. The Lord-have-mercy dimples made her grab the Formica countertop with her one good hand.

"I'll what? Spoil my appetite?" She nodded, every word in her vocabulary stuck in the back of her throat. He shook his head, his grin widening. "No chance of that. I'm a man with, shall we say, a voracious appetite."

Eat me.

She rounded her eyes, shocking herself.

Oh, boy, did that just come from my mind?

"So, what's next?"

A mental shake before she turned to the double boiler, where the rubber spatula dwarfed in his hand turned the chocolate and butter into a smooth, shiny pool.

"We dip and roll. Take a skewer, spear a truffle, then dip it into the chocolate. Roll it, let the excess drip off, then put it onto the tray." Even with only one hand at her disposal, the process was a snap. She demonstrated as she spoke. Then she skewered a second candy and handed it to him. "You try."

He got the hang of candy dipping right away. He dipped, swirled, and placed truffles in an orderly row on the prepared tray. They worked in silence until the truffles were all coated.

"Now what? We eat them?" His fingers hovered over a chocolate but she pushed his hand aside.

"Not yet. We'll stick them in the freezer for a few minutes so the chocolate will firm up. They're way better when they're firm."

He snickered, picked up the tray and popped it back into the empty freezer compartment.

"Most things are, you know. Better when firm, I mean."

The explanation was unnecessary. Firm was a good way to describe candy. The image of Jake, hard and well past firm, fired her cheeks. Again. The man set her ablaze with hardly any effort. All the blazing and cooling were too much to bear.

Chapter 44

"People waste too damn much time denying the truth." ~Lola Delaney

"Keep the conversation friendly. Remember? Nothing else, Jake. We..." Damn the conversational topics. Stubbled cheeks, dimples, and a cleft chin made for more-than-friends-only sensations

Much more than no-sex feelings.

"We agreed." Jake exhaled a long, shuddering sigh. She bet that if she looked down at his jeans, she'd find evidence that this was as hard for him as it was for her. Maybe, ah...maybe harder. He looked her straight in the eye, forcing her to keep her gaze above his neck. "You make it tough for me, Kat. I'd like to—"

He put both hands on his face, pressed his palms against his eyes and groaned. An animalistic sound, torn from his gut. He made a similar noise when he climaxed. Kat held her breath, hoping he'd make the noise again, but fearful she'd completely melt if he did.

He didn't. Instead, he put his hands on the counter in front of him, on either side of the almost-empty chocolate bowl. After glaring at the bowl, he turned to her and said, "Tell me why you make candy."

The question caught her unawares. "It calms me."

"How?"

She leaned her back against the Formica edge. A

tiny shrug. "Hard to say. I guess it's the orderliness of the whole thing. The process, you know? If I'm upset or overwhelmed, or just don't want to think anymore, I pull out some sugar, butter and a few other things and get to work. One step after the other, just going from one stage to the next, is calming. It puts me in charge. And I know that as long as I follow the recipe, I'll be successful. And, there's always something scrumptious to eat when I'm done."

While she explained, he'd eaten some more chocolate off his fingertip. This time the gesture was contemplative. Dipping a finger again, he held it over the bowl while the excess chocolate dribbled off.

"You know what's scrumptious?" His tone changed, and she knew the answer but asked anyway.

"What?"

He met her gaze.

They hadn't made enough frozen truffles to de-ice their libidos.

Her voice. It had disappeared. She didn't trust herself to speak.

So, she did the next best thing.

She leaned over, took his chocolate-covered fingertip in her mouth and sucked. He hitched a breath, so she swirled her tongue across his skin, taking her time and enjoying every delicious second of the journey.

She kissed his fingertip.

"You didn't just do that, Kat Delaney." His voice was a low growl.

"I did," she whispered.

"Not when we're working on the just-friends rule…"

She touched the tip of her tongue to the middle of her upper lip, licking a dab of chocolate off her mouth. Jake's eyes were riveted to her face. A rush of power made her grin.

That big, strong, dimpled hunk was putty in her hands—even if it was only for the briefest time, she was in control. Not a bad position to be, finally.

"Just then, yes. Just when we're, ah, working on the rule." Kat gave in to the devil sitting on her shoulder and poked a finger into the chocolate bowl. She swirled it around, taking a huge dollop and bringing it to her lips. She sucked it from her finger. Then, she swallowed.

"You're not playing the whole platonic-only game fair and you know it. You're just—"

"What?" A steady diet of painkillers and chocolate sent her inhibitions—as well as her common sense—out the window.

He reached for her, placing his arm beneath her bad arm and pulling her to him without bumping her sore hand. "We're playing with fire. You know it. I know it. But we're doing it anyway. Is this stupidity or something else?"

"Something else," she breathed as his mouth found hers. Their connection brought the world to a crashing stop. Nothing else mattered, no one else existed. The man holding her close, making her feel as if she'd finally found her way home—that was all that Kat cared about.

Her hand slipped around his neck, twined in the curls above his collar. Skin rasped stubble, turning her nipples to stiff peaks.

Pushing aside her robe, Jake fondled her ass. Her

tiny underwear barely concealed anything, so his hand covered more than she wore.

"Playing with fire..." He nibbled a line across her chin and down her neck.

"Who cares?"

She placed her good hand on the bulge threatening to split the zipper on his jeans. She massaged him, feeling the length of his erection through the worn fabric. As she had done in the shop, in the darkness, she slipped a fingertip over the top of his pants, snaking her way past knit boxer briefs and onto his skin. When she caressed him, he drew a sharp breath.

The feel of his mouth on her neck, the lingering taste of his kisses on her tongue, and the flaming hot flesh pressing against her hand was almost more than she could stand. Jake's fingers inched closer to the moist spot between her thighs...closer, but not there, and she silently urged him to touch her. Caress her.

Love her.

She arched her back and moaned when he nipped her earlobe.

"Are you sure about this?" He growled into her ear.

Oh, God, yes. She was sure.

She opened her mouth, about to suggest they move their pleasure into the bedroom, when there was a knock on the kitchen door.

They froze. The knock came a second time.

"Shit," Jake muttered. He pulled away from her and tugged the sides of her robe into place. He tied a hasty bow in the sash.

How he walked across the room with a raging hard-on was beyond her, but he did.

He opened the back door. The postman, an

ordinary-looking middle-aged man wearing uniform shorts and knee socks, handed him a business envelope. He glanced into the kitchen, tipped the safari hat on his head, and smiled. He ignored her, except for the lightning-fast mini-acknowledgement.

"Hey, Jake."

"Freddy."

"It's for Miss Delaney. I know she wouldn't think to check the box on the front of the building, so I figured I'd better bring it up. Looks important, you know."

With a fast smile for the postal worker, Jake nodded. "It does. Thanks."

"No problem. Hey, how's her hand?"

"Better, I think. How'd you hear?"

"Oh, you know how things are. One person knows something, and we all know it." He started back down the staircase. "Give my best to Miss Delaney. And if you get a chance, show her the mailbox out front."

"Sure thing." Jake closed the door, walked over, and handed her the envelope.

She looked down at the return address. Passion turned to ice in her veins when she saw who sent the mail.

Damn it.

Henry's lawyer.

Could life get any more complicated?

Chapter 45

"Licking a wound only gives you a wet wound. Better to forget about it. Move on. Find something else to occupy your time—and your mouth." ~Lola Delaney

The worst junk was gone with the Dumpster. The rest was in a storage building beside the back terrace. The only boxes Kat hadn't investigated she'd placed on the window seat, where Attila slept in the morning sunshine.

With most of the Tip-A-Canoe gallery cleared out, it wasn't as hard to see what she was left to deal with.

"Not much of a new start, is it?"

The cat opened an eye but didn't even *meow*. Not the conversation she hoped for, so she went over to the desk she'd uncovered in a corner. Sat down at the old-fashioned wooden chair. Picked up the handset and dialed. The rotary dial took forever to get the call through, so she put her feet on the desk and sat back.

"Hello."

"Hey, it's me."

Joann gave a short laugh. "Listen, *chica*, I know. I can *feel* you, you know?"

The old joke brought giggles.

"Right. What're you doing?"

"Mixing batter for a carrot cake with cream cheese frosting. It's the first weekend of the month, remember?

And that means…"

"Brooklyn Bookies."

The Bookies were an eclectic group of women who met once a month in the back room of a coffee shop on Flatbush Avenue and talked books. Their differences were vast, but they all loved reading—and Joann's carrot cake. And not always in that order.

Kat harbored a desire to be part of a literary group but the life she had with Henry left the wish unfulfilled. Now, hundreds of miles from Flatbush Avenue, the dream was dead.

"And before you ask—"

"I know. They pay."

She glanced at the boxes beside Attila. Her choices for the morning were few: The boxes or the broom. The boxes looked tempting.

"Right. They pay. And I usually get a book or two, too. I don't mind that part, either." How she managed it with all she had on her plate was a mystery but she devoured books. "So, what's up?"

"Not much. Got the place cleaned out. Almost—there's just a couple of boxes left. When we hang up, I'm going to check them out. After that a cleaning and the place will be ready."

"For what?"

"I've been thinking of different things, but I just don't know. The economy is down here. Tourists aren't coming this way and that, apparently, drives the town. So…an empty storefront and no ideas…not the best way to begin a new life."

Pity party, table for one.

"Don't tell me you're feeling sorry for yourself. You've got the world by the balls—you just don't know it yet."

"The world doesn't know it, either."

"So show the damn world! You've got the money to pull a new life together. You've got what sounds like a beautiful place to live. You're already involved—"

"I'm not involved. At least, not really."

"Okay, you're semi-involved with a hunk. And you've managed to lose the loser. What the hell are you complaining about? Damn, Kat—I'd change with you in a New York minute."

When put that way, her life sounded pretty good.

"You'd never change with anyone, for anything. Remember Jena Rose?"

"How could I forget? Your goddaughter unleashed a whopping case of three-year-old-itis on me this morning. It's amazing that something so small can make such a fuss."

"What happened?"

"Her grandmother promised she could have a cherry turnover for breakfast. Me? I thought the egg I'd just scrambled was a better choice. But what the hell do I know? I'm just the kid's mother."

Three generations in one apartment wasn't always sunshine and butterflies. Fortunately, flares like this were generally over before they began.

"Who won?" Kat put her money on the kid. She'd seen her in temper-tantrum action.

"You know who won." Joann groaned. "Afterward, I sent the cherry-faced gobbler and her abuela to the park. So I could bake and drink. Really, I considered putting a shot of something in this coffee, but I was afraid I'd mess up the cake recipe so it's just straight Hawaiian blend. And, I didn't forget... I'd trade with you because you'd take good care of the monster. I can trust you to wipe the berry stains off her cheeks while I go off and find a new life for myself. No worries there."

"Thanks for the vote of confidence."

"Don't mention it. But, really, what will you do with the gallery?"

"It's not a gallery. It's a shop—an empty one. I don't know what I'll do with it, but I don't have to figure that out right away. Something that might entice tourists, that's what I've been thinking. But the exact 'thing' that'll grab the tourist crowd? I don't have that answer yet."

"You've got time." Kat heard the sound of an electric mixer starting up. "Hey, have you heard from Henry?"

"Just his lawyer."

"What does he want?"

"A meeting. Probably plans to scare me into recanting what I've told the police. But I'm not going to see him. My lawyer says they're only trying to intimidate me, hoping I'll pull back my statement. I won't, though. What's right is right, and I don't care if they like it or not."

She had called Stella Green, her attorney, earlier. Stella seemed convinced Henry had to know he didn't have a chance of avoiding prosecution unless he swayed Kat's accounting. Her advice? Go about her business. She'd left the schmuck far behind, and he didn't have a place in her new life.

The solution suited her.

"I'm proud of you." The mixer's motor sped up. "Listen, what are you doing now?"

"Not much. The place is clean, except for the

couple of boxes. I'll go through them. Then, who knows?"

"I've got to run or the batter will be so thick the book chicks will be able to use the cake for a doorstop. I'm thinking of coming to visit next weekend. Is that okay?"

"You know it is! I miss you." Her mind whirled, considering all the attractions she could share. Not that she'd seen any of them yet herself. "When?"

"Friday. That's the plan. And if the kiddo doesn't drive me nuts between now and then, I'll bring her, too."

"Sounds good." The mixer stopped, so she knew the conversation was over. "Love you!"

The prospect of seeing Joann and, hopefully, Jena Rose in a few days put light in her heart. When they hung up, she walked to the window seat and sat beside the sleeping cat. She opened the top box.

It didn't matter what the boxes held. She was having visitors, and nothing could diminish her excitement over the fact. Nothing.

Chapter 46

"I've hidden my share of skeletons in the closet. Sure, I have. But really, who hasn't?" ~Lola Delaney

Kat had her back to him. She was on the window seat with a sleeping pile of fur on her lap. The scene couldn't be any cozier.

He wasn't there for cozy. He wasn't there for anything, really.

That wasn't true. He'd spied the open door and couldn't resist stopping in. For business purposes only.

Sure, that was it. Business. Nothing else.

Bullshit.

"Looks like you've been working hard, Miss Delaney." He removed his hat and tucked it beneath his left arm. His right hand naturally hooked over his belt, above the holstered weapon he wore.

She turned her upper half, carefully not disturbing the sleeping animal.

"Officer…"

He was so forgettable that she floundered on his name. Great, just great.

"Preston. Tom Preston, but you're supposed to call me Tom, remember?"

No wonder Jake had fallen for her. When she smiled, the sun dimmed. Damn, but she was a looker.

"Tom, then, but you agreed to call me Kat—

remember? And yes, I have been working hard in here. The first few times you saw it—" She stopped, color creeping up her neck. The effect was pure pleasure, on his part. Swallowing, she continued, "When you were here last, the place was kind of messy. My aunt apparently didn't organize well."

"That's one way of putting it. But you seem to have it under control." He looked around. Aside from the stack of books on the floor beside her and some cobwebs in the corners, the place was almost spotless. "What do you plan to do with the shop? Any ideas?"

"That's the million-dollar question." She stuck a finger between the pages of the book she held, nudged the kitten off her lap and onto the wooden seat. She stood, clasped the book to her chest with one hand and swept the other through the air. An ugly purple bruise covered the back of her hand, and one finger looked like a breakfast sausage. "I don't know what I'll do, but at least I'll have a clean slate to begin with."

"What happened to your hand?"

"Clarence. The little brown duck that walks around Main Street."

As if anyone in Mill Pond didn't recognize the local celebrity. He nodded. "I heard something, but didn't realize it was that bad. How'd you get bitten?"

"Just trying to keep Attila from being the duck's dinner." She held the hand out. It looked painful. "Clarence tried to eat me, instead. I guess I don't taste that good. He didn't even break the skin."

"Lucky for you. Ducks have strong bills and can do some impressive damage." Evidently, even ghost ducks. Not that anyone had to tell her, by the looks of things.

She dropped her hand to her side and gave him a curious look. Sunlight touched her hair, making it look like a halo. The green eyes trained upon him reminded him of Christmas trees. They were the same pure shade, with enough warmth that he had to fight not to stare into them.

"Is this a social visit? Or have I done something wrong? Broken some town ordinance, maybe?" Kat grinned, and he grinned right back at her.

He was charmed. The woman was pretty, intelligent, and kind enough that she sacrificed herself to save a kitten. Fascinating, to boot. Jake had finally found a keeper. Tom hoped he was smart enough to realize it.

"Nope, nothing like that. Our ordinances are safe, I think." Habit made him run a fingertip across his gun handle. "Mostly, this is a social call. But I do have something I'd like to discuss with you."

"What's that?" A smile, but the furrow in her forehead told the real story.

She knew it was coming. He could see it in her eyes, the knowledge that her past was upon her. It was a common sight in his line of duty. A lot of instances in a person's life could bring the deer-in-the-headlights freeze.

"You don't need to look like you're wondering how you'd look in an orange jumpsuit." When she grinned, this time for real, he smiled. Pushed the boundary between cop and human. "Although, if you don't mind my saying so, orange would look great with those beautiful eyes."

"Thank you. And I'm sorry for being so…jumpy. I don't mean to be but…"

She spread her hands, palms up, giving him a shot at the other side of the wounded one. That duck was a menace. If it bit anyone else, he'd have to take matters into his hands. Find the duck a home a long way from town, where it wouldn't hurt anyone. He couldn't stand by while it bit people at random.

"You've got reason to be jumpy. I know what went down before you got here. And before you think I'm prying into your business—which I'm not—I should say that Lola's attorney is also my dad. He didn't break client privilege by telling me what happened with your ex before you came here. Technically, your aunt was his client. You're her heir, so he doesn't work for you. And the stuff we talk about is strictly between us—he doesn't share anything with anyone else, so don't worry your business is all over town."

He watched her shoulders fall. They'd risen when her forehead furrowed. At least she wasn't as tense.

"That's good to know."

"The point of my telling you this is I want you to know I'm here if you need anything. If you feel unsafe at any time, all you've got to do is dial the station. I'm always available. And you don't have to go into details if you don't want to when the dispatcher—her name's Gail and she's very nice—answers. Just say you want to speak with me, and Gail will know what to do."

How to make her feel safe without letting her think he was nosing into her business?

Catching teenagers lifting Doritos at the Quick Stop was a walk in the park compared to this.

She looked down at the floor, her shoulders falling still more. This wasn't relaxation, though. She'd been beaten by the circumstances of her leaving New York

City. He saw that, but was powerless to change it.

She lifted her chin and met his gaze. "Thank you for your offer. I hope I don't have to take you up on it, but if I do, I'll know how to reach you. I'm sorry if my presence gives you any additional work. I don't mean to do that."

He was about to say she wasn't any trouble at all but didn't have the chance.

Jake sauntered into the shop. He recognized the I-just-stepped-in-shit-and-smell-like-a-rose grin plastered on his best friend's face. Before he could ask what had happened to put the goofy look in its place, Jake spilled it.

As he passed, he slapped his shoulder. "Uncle Gordon just did me a good one."

He spared Kat the slap, choosing instead to place a gentle hand on her shoulder. "Hey, your bandage is off. How does it feel?" He took her hand in his, turned it over and swore. "Does it feel as bad as it looks?"

"It hurts," she admitted. She took her fingers from his grasp, wincing as the hand brushed Jake's wrist.

"Your uncle's going to have to control that stupid duck. It can't keep doing this. Listen, either you talk with him about it, or I'm going to have to do it. Okay?"

Jake didn't meet Tom's eyes, which was strange. The brush-off was even more peculiar. "Gotcha. I'll take care of the duck." He turned his attention back to the woman. "I know what'll take your mind off that wounded wing."

"Duck stew?" Tom couldn't help himself.

"No, smartass, not duck stew." Jake raised both eyebrows and shook his head. "Shows how much you know, Deputy Dawg."

The childhood nickname never reached further than their immediate family. His using it—and so easily, at that—now just showed how close he and the new lady in town were.

"What, then?" Kat leaned into the space between her and Jake.

He got a bird's-eye view down her tank top, the curve of one breast clearly visible, but he made himself look away. Just because something was in front of you didn't mean you had to ogle it.

"Just what do you think Uncle Gordon just bestowed upon me?" He didn't wait for an answer. "That's right—his vintage Cris Craft. Twenty-two feet of pure wooden delight."

"He's crazy about that boat! You mean he just handed it over?"

Jake jingled a set of keys dangling from a ring on his index finger.

"Keys and all. I tried to pay him, but he said it's part of our agreement."

"What agreement?" He had been a cop long enough to smell something fishy without having to be in the fishing boat.

"I'll explain that later." He got the no-more-questions-now look.

Fine. But there'd be questions later. Plenty of them. That old man loved that boat. He'd bought it new and he couldn't remember him ever letting anyone hold the keys to it.

"You didn't kill him, did you?" He flicked the guard off his holster, put a hand on the revolver, and narrowed his eyes. Jake met his stare without flinching, a wicked grin on his face. "Your uncle—he's still among the living, right?"

"As among as he's ever been. Shit, you don't really think I'd off him, do you?"

He snapped the holster shut. "No, but I had to ask. It's my job to investigate especially when I know old Gordon would sooner toss you his wife than the keys to his boat."

"Well, this time he kept the wife and gave me the boat." Jake turned to Kat. He jangled the keys in the air and smiled. "What do you say? A spin around Bear Spring Lake in a vintage boat?"

"You're not thinking of fishing off that thing, are you?" The old man would have a cardiac arrest if even one slimy scale touched the pristine mahogany decking.

"Are you crazy? Of course not! I'm just going to take the gorgeous lady here out for a ride. That is, if she'll go with me."

Kat scanned the near-empty shop. She looked down at the worn book in her hand. She seemed to be weighing her options. To his credit, Jake didn't try to hurry her, although he did give the keys an extra jingle.

She folded down the corner of the page she'd been holding with her fingertip before placing the book on top of the others piled nearby.

"As long as I don't have to put a yucky worm on a fish hook. Any gross worms and I stay here."

"No worms, I promise." Jake pulled her against his body, giving the woman a bear hug that might have crushed her had she not gone so willingly into his friend's embrace.

He loved it. Miss Big City had somehow managed to get closer to Mr. No Strings than anyone had in years. The biggest question was, how long before one or the other realized their hearts had pulled them in deeper than their heads wanted them to be?

Only time would tell. And he had all the time in the world to wait and watch.

And pray. Oh, yeah. He planned to do a lot of praying on this one.

Chapter 47

"If I had my choice between being stranded on a desert island with either a handsome hunk or an okay-looking smart guy, I'd choose the brainwave every time. Sex can be taught—and, oh, what fun it is to be the teacher! But brains? Either you've got 'em or you don't." ~Lola Delaney

Back in the day, Bear Spring Lake had teemed with activity. Even a few years ago, there had been floating-room-only weekends, when boat traffic was so high it was nearly impossible to pick up any speed without slamming into another craft.

That part, the shoulder-to-shoulder boat traffic, Jake didn't miss. The revenue brought by the tourists was another story. To find a mid-point, that was his quest. So far, the search yielded only dead ends.

But today, when they practically had the lake to themselves, he didn't mind the lack of visitor income. It didn't cross his mind once.

Maybe the successful morning meeting he'd had in Placid lifted his hopes for their town's future. It could be the generous gift from Uncle Gordon that let him steer into the warm breeze with a smile on his face. Or, and it was the most likely reason of all for his good mood, the woman standing beside him.

Pure and simple, Kat Delaney made him feel like

the future might not be such a bad place after all. He still didn't want to be tied down or responsible for anyone but the idea of having her in his life, the way he did now, worked for him.

He glanced at her. She looked happy. Smiling, with the wind whipping her curls into a gorgeous mess. And, when she looked his way, his heart nearly burst from his chest.

"This is fun," Kat shouted over the twin engines.

"I think so." He took a step back. "Why don't you take the wheel?"

She held her hands up in front of her, squealing as he took first one hand, then the other, off the huge wood and chrome wheel. The boat wobbled, as he knew it would, when he let go. Kat grabbed the wheel, as he hoped, and the boat steadied.

"What do I do?"

Leaning so near her flying hair tickled his nose, he said, "Just what you're doing. Keep her steady, and head that way." He pointed to the small island in the center of the lake. "We'll lap around Button's Folly, then head back to the marina."

She widened her stance, stabilizing her body. The boat was a peach to steer. He'd first taken control when he was ten, so he knew she'd have no problem, even with an injured hand.

Still, he stood behind her. Not to assist her in any way. He just liked the way she felt, her backside pressed against him. Each water chop bounced them together, something that only made the already good day still brighter.

"Button's Folly? Why do you call it that?"

Her grip loosened as she relaxed. A positive sign,

her taking control so naturally. He spent most of his spare time on the water, and it would suck if Kat didn't take to the lifestyle. But she did, apparently, because she steered a touch starboard, then straightened out, as if she'd been handling a boat all her life. The slight pitch didn't seem to affect her one bit.

"You ever steer a boat before?"

She shook her head. "Never. Why? Am I doing it wrong?"

He nuzzled her neck, planting a kiss just below her earlobe. It registered that she squirmed, just a little bit, so he kissed her a second time. Her breath caught.

"You're doing everything just right. Keep it up."

A sweet giggle ratcheted up his awareness. She was so close he inhaled chocolate and caramel wafting off her skin. He felt the warmth of her. Memories flooded back, reminding him of the smooth, sensual curves beneath her summer clothing.

Keeping it up was never an issue with this woman nearby. It was keeping it somewhat at ease that gave him fits.

"Button's Folly?" The reminder came after they'd hit a swell and he met her backside in an intimate, albeit fleeting, touch.

They were nearly even with the small, uninhabited island. Lush white spruces sprang from jutting rocks, dipped low over the water and cast gorgeous green reflections. Gulls swooped, circled and landed among grassy patches leading down to a white-sand beach. The outline of a building, nearly covered with kudzu, peeked out between the pines.

"See the house? It's almost obscured, but it's beneath the vines. See it?"

215

He pointed, bringing his arm level with her face. She squinted, then nodded.

He dropped his arm and placed his hand on her right hip.

"The man who built it was named Carlyle Button. He was in love with a woman he planned to marry. Trouble is, Priscilla was in love with someone else. Nobody bothered to tell poor Carlyle, so he went ahead and built a house as an engagement gift for her. He had it nearly finished, right down to massive stone fireplaces and local granite flooring, when he popped the question."

"Oh, no…"

"That's right." He guided her hands on the wheel, slowing the boat as they rounded the island. The house, overgrown but still enchanting, showed more from this side. He let her look, then throttled up. The wake was wide as they left Button's Folly. "You can guess what happened. Priscilla said no. Carlyle never went back to the island and everyone—probably meaning it as a joke but really being mean-spirited—called the place Button's Folly."

"So sad." A sigh. "Who owns it now?"

"Tom's father."

She whirled around. "The cop? His father, the lawyer, owns it?"

"You sound so shocked. Is there some reason he shouldn't? Got a thing against lawyers, have you?"

She rose to the bait, becoming nearly as indignant as she had when he'd insinuated she was a lesbian. He'd known better, but teasing her was like eating pepperoni. He could never stop at just one slice. One was good, two better and the whole package heavenly.

"Of course not!" She turned back to the bow. "It just seems strange, that's all. Why would he buy a place when he obviously didn't intend to live in it?"

"Tom's father and Carlyle were as close as Tom and me. He felt awful when his friend's heart got torn apart, so he did the thing he knew would help him. He bought the house, which gave Carlyle enough cash to move somewhere else. He began a new life, in a place where nobody knew he'd been publicly humiliated."

"What happened to Carlyle?"

He kissed her earlobe again. They were near the marina but he didn't want to dock yet so he turned the engine off and dropped the anchor. The boat stopped moving, bobbing on the current so gently he turned her around to face him without worrying she'd lose her balance.

Her eyes held concern. It was good that the story had a happy ending.

"He went on to live a long, happy life. Married, had kids and still keeps in touch with Tom's dad. They don't talk about the house or the island. It's in the past, and doesn't seem to matter much. Sometimes life throws a curveball and you've just got so many choices, you know?"

"What choices?"

He shrugged. "Duck, so you don't get beaned. Catch the ball, and maybe make the play. Or, and what Carlyle did, get out of the game. If you can't stand the curveballs, you're not playing the right game. Move on. Find something new. Walk through another doorway. There's always something."

"Baseball fan?"

"Of course. We've got the greatest team in the

world in New York. How could anyone not be a fan?" He nipped her earlobe playfully. "You *are* a Yankees fan, aren't you?"

"Does it matter?"

Not really. But he wasn't going to let the ball fall.

"Damn right it does. So, tell the truth, sweet Kat. Do you wear the stripes proudly?"

"I do. I even went to a couple of games last year. Had nosebleed seats, but it didn't matter. I just wanted to see the dugout with my own eyes." She paused. "So, it's more than a game with you? The baseball-as-life stuff is serious, isn't it?"

"Hey, it works. And whatever works…"

It was uncomplicated to be philosophical dealing with someone else's life. His own? Not so damn straightforward.

Chapter 48

"Rock me, baby." ~Lola Delaney

The cabin below deck had everything anyone could want. A tiny galley, tinier head, and a large, pillow-laden bed.

She loved every inch of gleaming chrome and polished wood.

They settled onto the bed, since it was just about the only place to sit. She reached into her tote bag, which leaned against the edge of the bed, and pulled out a plastic container. Popping the lid, she held it out.

The grin he shot her even before he looked into the container warmed her heart. No one, besides Joann, Juanita, and of course Jena Rose, had ever appreciated her candy making skills before. Henry had ridiculed her interest, calling it a "juvenile hobby" which she was bound to "outgrow eventually" so the way Jake rubbed his palms together was a supreme ego boost.

"Brittle?"

His curls had been blown wild by the wind. If she hadn't been holding the candy, her fingers would definitely have been twined into the thick, black swirls.

Just looking at the man made her heart flutter. Platonic relationship her ass; she wanted to eat him alive.

Forget the candy!

"Peanut brittle? Like they sell in boxes around Christmastime?"

He chose a good-sized chunk and took a bite. She removed a piece for herself and set the container on the bed. Between them. Just in case she got any ideas of messing with his hair. Or anything else. An insurance policy in a Tupperware container.

"Not exactly. I mean, yes, stores do sell peanut brittle around the holidays and this is similar. But I hope it's not like what you've had before."

Jake ate the first piece. She caught him eyeing the insurance candy, so she gestured and pushed it closer. He chose another piece and popped it into his mouth. Watching him eat mesmerized her and for a moment she forgot she'd been in the midst of an explanation. "These aren't peanuts."

"Ah, no, they're not. Pecans—they're pecans, which makes for a softer brittle. It isn't so teeth crunching and the pecans are much sweeter than peanuts. What do you think?"

His appreciation was obvious, especially when he chose a third piece.

"I like sweet. I like brittle, more than I thought." He finished chewing, wiped his fingers on the leg of his faded Levis, and leaned back. Crossing his arms behind his head, he stared at the ceiling. Then, at her.

It was damn near impossible to eat with her throat almost closed shut, the result of his careful perusal and the sudden dryness invading her mouth, but she managed. Sometimes his eyes showed everything behind them. Every thought and emotion, telegraphed clearly in the gleaming irises. Other times, like now, he was unreadable.

Kat preferred the transparent Jake to this closed-book version. Knowing what was coming was less disconcerting.

She swallowed. Then, she put the lid back on the container and placed it back in her bag.

She lowered herself onto one elbow and stretched out beside him. The bed rocked soothingly on the water. Sleep would come fast in a nest like this, but that wasn't on her mind and she doubted it was on his, either.

Every woman knew one of the basic rules of dealing with men was to never ask them what they were thinking. Unless you were crazy or had a relationship death wish, neither of which applied. Still, it was one way to find out what lurked in the gorgeous man's head.

Don't do it.

Kat took a deep breath. Then, she ignored herself.

"What are you thinking about?"

"You." He answered without hesitation.

She waited. Nothing else.

A second plunge.

"Good or bad?"

"Very good. You should know that."

She did. But it didn't hurt to hear it.

"Just asking." His body showed no sign of tension but the line across his forehead signaled otherwise. "What is it, Jake?"

Rolling over to face her, he put a hand beneath his head. Their faces, just inches apart. The nearness of the man did things to her she couldn't ignore. Heat pooled in places that, before she'd met him, had been cool for a long time.

"I've always followed my head, thought things through and decided on a course based on facts. Facts don't lie, Kat. They are what they are, and we get to deal with them the best way we can." He looked down and ran a slow fingertip across her wounded hand. It rested on the bed between them. His touch was so light it soothed. When he met her gaze, he was still unreadable but not as shuttered. "You're a puzzle to my brain."

"No one's ever called me a brain puzzle before. I'm not sure how I should take it."

He grinned, a slow, lop-sided expression that sent an electric ping up her spine.

"No woman's ever puzzled me the way you do. My head says one thing but other parts of me say another. Reconciling the two and making the head come out on top...hell, it's just not happening. I can't figure a way to be 'just friends' with you—which is what conforms to my—"

"I know, your no-dating policy. You're like Switzerland, for Pete's sake. Complete neutrality, no involvement except to dole out chocolate now and again. I get it. Really, I do."

It was a lie. She didn't get it—not all the way. She wasn't in any rush to jump into a new relationship, either, but damn it, these electric lust pings that shot through her every time they got within five feet of each other had to count for something.

"I don't mean to upset you. I just want to be clear here so when things between us end you won't get hurt."

It already hurt.

"End? I wasn't sure we'd begun." She withdrew

her hand.

"You know what I mean. And see? You're already hurt and all I'm trying to do is prevent that from happening. I'm doing a shitty job of it." He raked his fingers through his curls. "I'm sorry. I just don't see how we can do this, not when we both know it'll end badly."

"You've really been hurt, haven't you?"

He covered his eyes with his hand for a brief moment before he looked up at her.

"Not by a woman."

"What, then? You've got something in your past that makes you afraid."

"Afraid? Yes, that's it. I've hurt others, and I can't let that happen again." He held her gaze with his dark, unreadable eyes. "I won't do it. Not to you."

"We're friends, that's all. No big promises. No huge commitments. Friends. I told you, I'm not looking for more. Off men, remember?" She smiled, hoping to break the tension in the tight space.

It worked. When he gave her a small laugh she saw the familiar teasing glimmer in his eyes.

"That's right. How could I forget? You're so off men that we can't keep our hands *off* each other." He paused, then said in a low voice. "No matter what my head says, it's not easy to be platonic with you. You make it hard, Kat." He swallowed. "Real hard."

Desire urged her on. She listened to her heart, and placed her wounded hand lightly on his chest. The thought to place it lower entered her mind but why cut to the chase when the build-up was so much fun?

"Is that so?" She wiggled closer, so their bodies touched. "How hard do I make it?"

"Rock hard. Check it for yourself—but, first, be sure. Are you certain we can be friends with…this? Don't agree unless you know how you feel."

Her hand trailed along the hard contours of his muscular body. Over the broad chest. Down every ridge of his abs. Lower onto his lean hips. Then, her fingers curled around the prize.

Jake didn't lie. He was rock hard and it made her wet just to feel his desire.

"I'm sure." She met his gaze as she stroked the length of him. "I have to be, don't I?"

Chapter 49

"Be careful what you wish for. You just might get it." ~Lola Delaney

He'd given her the chance to back out. Hell, he'd given her so many chances to say no he'd practically talked her out of having sex with him. The "are you sure" questions lasted longer than some foreplay and they'd done nothing at all to dissuade Kat from being intimate with him. If anything, they'd provided the backdrop for her seduction. It was clear she was in charge and for once he didn't mind letting someone else set the pace.

Especially when the pace included mind-numbing kissing. And licking. And fondling.

She left a burning trail along his body, searing his skin everywhere she touched. They'd shed their clothes, tossing them over the foot of the bed.

Her tongue slid along his skin. She devoured him greedily, testing his limits of endurance with each nip and suck.

"Enough." He urged her upward, not satisfied until her face was even with his. Her pink lips were swollen, so he kissed them, whisking his tongue across her lower lip and tasting the saltiness of his own skin. When he pulled back, he gazed into her eyes and saw her need matched his. But the boat swayed beneath them, and cocooned in their own world he was in no rush to let their pleasure end swiftly.

Not when he still had uncharted territory to explore.

"My turn."

"Oh…"

Her hands settled on his shoulders as he kissed his way down her body. He found her breasts, suckling one nipple before giving the other its due. Her skin pebbled in his mouth and her body arched against him. Every time his teeth grazed her sensitive skin, she moaned. He palmed the breast not in his mouth, flicked a thumb across her peak, and smiled around her flesh as a desperate sound tore from her throat.

"Jake," she panted, squirming on the gently rocking bed. "Oh, please…"

He reluctantly pulled his mouth from her body. Glancing up into her flushed face, he teased, "Please? Is that all? How about pretty please?"

A wicked grin. "Pretty please with a cherry on top?"

The thought that they might find a suitable use for cherries and whipped cream in the future made his heart race. The strong, lean lines of her supple body would look amazing covered in cream, smothered in cherries and served straight up—without a spoon.

His mouth watered. His need screamed but he refused to listen. The agony of waiting was exquisite, worth every torturous second. He held onto his control, loving the way she wiggled when he brushed a fingertip between her parted thighs.

"Are you making a suggestion? Because the galley isn't equipped with anything fancy. No cherries…no whipped cream…" Her fingers gripped his shoulders when he slid a finger inside her. God, but she was wet. He swallowed hard, concentrating on the little game in order to keep himself from losing it. "Like I said, nothing fancy. You're the sweetest thing on the boat."

"You're a tease—oh…"

"Complaining?"

He slid lower on the bed. When she shook her head, denying the allegation as he knew she would, he reached for a condom. Rolling it over himself with one hand, he parted her flesh with the other and groaned when he saw how ready she was. Trouble is, greed made him hesitant to surrender. He wanted all of her— every bit of pleasure, every taste and touch, and it killed him not to taste each delicious inch of the ravishing woman in his arms.

The taste of Kat's hot need almost threw his willpower out the tiny portal above the pillows. She arched her back, pressing her flesh into his mouth. He found her center and sucked hard, making her buck beneath him.

"Jake…" She moaned, a primal sound that made him more determined to bring her release. "I can't— oh…I can't wait—"

"Don't wait."

It was all the encouragement she needed. He stayed with her until the crescendo passed before he moved up over her, supporting his weight on his elbows.

Satiation gleamed in the depths of the green eyes that met his. She swallowed, and the movement of her delicate neck nearly sent him into a frenzy.

"Your turn," she whispered, her voice sex kitten throaty.

Wrapping her legs around his waist, she tilted herself to him. The tip of his cock brushed her slick skin, but he didn't enter. Not yet. Just one minute more. One. Glorious. Agonizing. Minute.

When every breath seemed like it would be his last, Jake thrust and began the most intimate dance of all. The water beneath them rocked the boat, his hips moved in cadence with their labored breathing and, for a long, magnificent instant, he held heaven in his arms.

"Do it." Kat moaned as he pulled her to the edge again. "Oh, Jake…do it."

Speeding the motion of his hips, driving deep and hard into her, he dropped his head back and closed his eyes. No better sensation, no more satisfying endeavor, existed. He knew that as surely as he knew his own name. His body melted into hers, leaving no discernible line between their flesh. Where she began or where he ended, he couldn't tell. More importantly, he didn't care.

Not seeing her when he came wasn't an option. He needed to witness the glow in her eyes, to read the weight of his own release mirrored in her green gaze. He leaned forward and met her stare, holding tight to the invisible cord binding them together.

He moaned her name as liquid heat spilled from deep within him.

It occurred in that instant that they could never be just friends.

She'd already claimed his heart—even though he'd held so tightly to it, she'd stolen it…and that was bad news, indeed.

Chapter 50

"Sleep is an elusive bedfellow." ~Lola Delaney

Falling asleep after sex wasn't in Kat's history. It's not as if she'd never been wiped out afterward, it's just that it was more a hit-or-miss thing. More miss than hit had been her experience.

But this was different. Once they untangled themselves, he held her close, cuddling her in the strong circle of his arms. Post-coital conversation was minimal. Between the boat's gentle sway and their sated bodies, it didn't take long for either of them to drift off.

He still slept, an arm curled protectively around her shoulders. The stubbled cheeks upon which his long, black eyelashes lay inches from her face called to be kissed but she didn't do it. Watching his unguarded, relaxed expression transfixed her. She stared, her breathing falling naturally into the same smooth rhythm of his snoring.

Moving to Mill Pond had been a gamble, a long shot thrust upon her when everything else in her life had gone awry. Never dreaming she'd find anything remotely close to what she felt now, she'd leaped into the inheritance and all that came with it hoping for at the very least a modicum of security and contentment.

The security and new business venture was a bust.

But, the contentment factor more than made up for it. Finding Jake, feeling this peace in his embrace and experiencing the pleasure of his company—even if they were only "just friends"—surpassed any loss she'd experienced.

Temptation sent a pinging jolt to her already spent muscles. His cock lay thick and heavy against her right thigh, inches from the spot it had so recently filled.

Hunger for him overcame sensibility. She lightly traced a trail down his right hip. Across his smooth skin, moving forward on his body. He sighed in his sleep, rolling slightly backward so he was more accessible. She stole a peek at his masculine form. All muscles and tanned flesh, except for the outline of his shorts where he was paler. His penis, even at rest, was splendid. Kat put a fingertip on him, sweeping her skin against his so lightly he didn't stir.

What was she doing? The flesh she so lazily stroked thickened beneath her touch. Playing with fire, she knew she'd get burnt. His penis was off-limits, remember?

Still…

She'd already fallen hard off the no-penis wagon. Why not stay off? What could it hurt?

His eyes were still closed. Sleeping, although one edge of his upper lip curled, the tiny smirk making him even handsomer. She kissed the cleft in his chin. A butterfly kiss, so fast and tender his eyes didn't open.

Her hand curled around him, gentling his flesh with her palm and fingers as her own body heated in response. Jake had led the last lovemaking session. He'd played her like a fiddle, plucking notes from her body she'd never heard before. His touch was magic, the steady road to climax filled with heart-stopping twists and sublime turns.

Now, it was time to return the favor. Even slumbering, his body came to attention. She stroked the steely velvet smoothness, cupped her hand around him, and tugged ever so gently as he responded.

"Mmm…"

She gripped him harder, fondling him with more abandon when he turned fully onto his back.

Once with Jake wasn't nearly enough. Even though the flesh he'd pleasured so recently was the tiniest bit sore, she wanted him. Now.

Kat straddled his hips, rubbing against the erection lying taut on his abdomen. Sensually, he stretched, pushing himself against her body. When she leaned close, her nipples brushed his chest hair and liquid sparks shot up her spine. Nerve endings tingled. Molten heat spread when she put her lips on his.

"Mmm." The growl filled her mouth. Their hips rocked, her slick spots rubbing over his hardness. She slipped her tongue into his mouth. As he woke, he put his arms around her and held her close, commanding the lead and kissing her so thoroughly her knees turned to rubber on the bed.

She broke the kiss and smiled when she met his eyes.

"Nice way to wake up." He kissed her neck. He nipped her earlobe, murmuring, "Nice way to go to sleep, too."

"I hoped you'd like it." She kissed his eyelids. His temple, then his cheeks, lingering on the spot where his dimples lay. "You do like it, don't you?"

The way he moved his grip down her back and

chuckled, low and deep, was the perfect answer. His wide hands warmed her skin as he moved them to her hips.

"Like is an understatement."

Flesh turned silk and steel collided. Need grew, making her hips move without any conscious effort. Kat gasped when his tip touched her in exactly the right spot with the perfect degree of intensity. Lord have mercy, but his penis could make her sing—even when it wasn't inside her…

Drawing the experience out was a fine idea but if she didn't get some release soon—like in the next heartbeat or so—she was going to go mad. Lyrics from the song playing on the radio took on a whole new meaning. They'd been just lyrics before today. Now she knew what it meant when it hurt so good. The pain of want was exquisite. The satisfaction, even more so.

Enough.

She couldn't stand another second without Jake inside her.

Kat kissed him as if he was a cold drink on a hot day. As their tongues twined, she put her hands on his shoulders, held tight and lowered herself onto him. Arcs of lust lit a fire inside her belly, and she began to move. Slowly, for the first few strokes. Then, the pressure of impending orgasm spurred her on, and she gyrated with increasing speed.

"Kat." The word came from between gritted teeth. His hands held her hips in a firm grip, but she had found a tempo that couldn't be stopped.

It registered that he was holding back, but the thought that she was so close already flashed through her mind. He didn't need to pace himself for her, if that was what he was doing. There was no need to rein in, no reason not to give in to the madness, so she squeezed her muscles around his cock and kept moving.

"Wait—"

No waiting.

Even if she'd wanted to—which she definitely did not—she wasn't sure she could. Already the first waves of release gripped her, bringing her to the precipice and threatening to toss her over. Waiting—no way to do it. Not now.

But she didn't want to climax alone.

With the last of her self-control hanging in the balance, she reached between them. When she touched him, he groaned.

"Oh..."

The scream about to erupt inside her couldn't be ignored. Kat met his gaze, her eyes clouded by the sheer force building in her center.

"Yes...Oh, Jake, come with me. Come with me...oh, yes...oh—"

Her breath caught as she began to climax. Then, the long, low scream she'd held so far loosened, filling her mind and ears as insistently as he filled her body. Releasing her handgrip, she buried him as deeply as their bodies allowed, willing his restraint to evaporate alongside hers. Her spasms held him, and it occurred to her his penis was still hard as he held her in place and watched her orgasm.

Finally, she shuddered, completely drained by the power of her climax.

His erection throbbed. Shock that he hadn't climaxed with her was the first reaction. The second, that they still had some lovemaking to do, brought a grin to her face.

Before she could move, the boat struck something.

Oh, shit.

She tumbled forward. There was still a connection between them, but the boat thumped a second time just before he withdrew.

He pushed hair from her face. "Are you okay? Kat?"

"Fine," she managed.

He rose, snagged his jeans and pulled them on. Grabbing her hand, he lifted her to her feet and nudged her toward the steps that led to the deck. "Go."

Together, they wrapped a sheet around her as they moved.

The afternoon sun was still bright when they stepped onto the boat's wooden decking. At first, she couldn't believe what met her eyes. Then, reality crashed as hard as the boat apparently had.

They'd landed against the dock. Thankfully, the side that struck an oiled wooden piling hadn't burst at a seam. The end of a frayed rope lay on the deck. Jake picked it up, tossed it over the side and swore.

"What happened?" She watched the piece of rope bob on the current.

"Damn anchor broke loose." He looked at the side where they'd struck the piling, ran a hand across the gash in the wooden exterior and swore again. Then, he raised one shoulder in a resigned air. "At least we didn't crash into anything big."

Who could resist the opportunity?

"Who says? I definitely crashed into something big." She raised an eyebrow at the bulge in his half-buttoned jeans. "And from what I can tell, it's still big.

I'm not sure why, though…"

His brows came together. Placing a hand on her waist and pulling her against him, he said, "No condom, Kat. One of my rules, remember?"

Heat flooded her face. How could she have been so irresponsible?

"Jake, I don't have anything—"

He shushed her with a kiss. "I don't keep the rule for that reason." He looked into her face, then shrugged. "Although it's a good one. I just don't want to get you pregnant. I just don't want kids, so I wear a condom. And that's why I'm still hard—nothing to do with you. All to do with me."

No kids. Not ever?

Not the time to think about it. Not now, when there was something much more interesting to deal with.

She brushed a playful hand over his crotch, satisfied when he growled his pleasure at her touch. She held the sheet over her with one hand. The other played with his fly, opening the top button with a quick twist.

"You still have condoms down there?" She nodded to the cabin.

"Plenty."

"Good. Since we're already docked, why don't we finish what we started?"

He chuckled, pulling her against him when she reached for the next button. "We? I think you're the one who started it. Me? I was an innocent bystander, sleeping like a baby. But I don't mind finishing what you started. But watch out—if you're not careful, you'll have me doing the full Monty dockside. Only one button stands between me—*all of me*—and the world."

He kissed her, holding her hand captive between

their bodies so she couldn't undo the final button. It was fine with her, because the distance between the deck and the bed was only a few steps. Four, to be exact. And hell, even a woman with a screaming libido could hold out for four steps—couldn't she?

"Kat! Over here, Kat!"

No fucking way.

Jake broke their kiss just as the call came a second time.

"Over here, Kat. Hey, it's me."

She whirled, shock loosening her grip on the sheet. It fell, puddling around her ankles at the same moment Jake's fly button, strained by the force of his arousal, popped open.

Henry stood on the dock. Ten feet separated them but even if it had been ten thousand feet, it wouldn't have been enough. Her gut turned over, forcing her to swallow the bile that rose in her throat.

She'd have rather come face to face with Satan himself than stare into her ex's shrewd eyes.

But Satan? Obviously busy, so he'd sent one of his Manhattan minions instead.

Chapter 51

"A polished turd is still a turd." ~Lola Delaney

Kat picked up the fallen sheet, wrapped it around her, and said the first thing that popped into her head. "Go away."

Had he been a bird, nothing would have ruffled Henry's feathers. Not that she'd ever seen, anyway. His expression didn't change; same perfectly-arranged features giving her the blandest of appraisals. His gaze shot down to her bare toes before he reached her eyes.

"I thought I'd get a better welcome than that." He sneered. "You didn't even dress for the occasion. My, my...going country on me, are you?"

"Leave. Just leave."

All the time they'd spent together, she never realized his eyes were so small—or closely set. It hit her now, as she stared into the face that was a mask for the rottenness he hid so well.

Beady-eyed bastard.

Too late for recriminations. She'd been charmed by a snake—and was in good company. After all, her mistake had chased her from Manhattan which certainly was no Garden of Eden.

And Henry wasn't even close to being anyone's Adam.

Not even in his crisply-pleated khakis and blue

237

button-down collar shirt. She checked his feet. Loafers, sans socks.

Ugh. The wolf in sheep's clothing who lied and stole as naturally as he breathed. Just looking at him made the acid in her stomach churn.

Now he pulled his hands from his pockets, held them palms upward, and said, "I come in peace, kitty Kat."

It was all she could do not to fling herself out of the boat and onto the man. How dare he be so bold? Use the name he'd called her when they were in private?

Pushing the memory of their intimacy aside, she forced herself not to scream at him. "Go to hell."

Jake hadn't said a word, but he didn't need to. His presence, solid and just a few steps behind her, gave her added strength. Now, he took a step forward, brushing her hip with his.

It was embarrassing to have a witness to the evidence of her foolish past but it couldn't be helped.

Henry turned his attention to the man beside her.

Another phony half-smile. This one, tight—his lips drawn into a straight line. "I don't believe we've met. I'm Henry, Kat's fiancé."

"Liar! You're not my anything—and we were never engaged."

"Leave it to you to nitpick." When he shrugged the top button near his collar tugged, exposing a bit of neck. Her fingers curled, imagining them wrapped around the man's flesh. "It's only a matter of time before we make it official. You know that."

"I hate you."

Another shrug. Only a pathological liar could be

unaffected by the disdain his actions brought from others.

"I read somewhere that hate is the closest emotion to love. So really, it's all the same, isn't it?"

Discussing anything with Henry was like wrestling with a pig. Muddy, dirty business—but one participant enjoyed the activity.

"Go away—anywhere. Go to hell. Go screw yourself—I don't care what you do or where you go as long as it's far away from here!"

Her fingers tightened around the sheet, holding it in place. She turned, looked up at Jake and whispered, "I'm sorry" as she passed him.

Below deck, the unmade bed. She dropped the sheet and pulled everything into place. The throw pillows bounced off the back wall when she tossed them. Above her, the rumble of male voices. Then, silence.

She scrambled into her clothes, remorse bringing a sheen to her eyes. She knuckled away the one tear that threatened to fall.

Crying was a waste of time and energy. If Henry's appearance put the kibosh to any future with Jake...well, there was damn little she could do about that.

At least they'd had today—and it had been, hands down, the best afternoon of her life.

Chapter 52

"Hell hath no fury like a cornered woman. Or one denied access to the Macy's Shoe Sale. Either way, it's going to get ugly." ~Lola Delaney

Jake complied when Kat said she wanted to be dropped at the shop. He didn't try to stay when she asked him to leave.

He didn't try to kiss her, either.

It was as if they were done with each other. Her heart hurt, but she had to respect how he felt.

Unlike Henry, who followed them in his shiny black Mercedes. The poster boy for disrespect if ever there was one.

He parked it right outside the front door, staking a claim on what wasn't his. It pissed her off, but she slammed the door in his face when he tried to follow her inside.

His response? To stand scowling on the sidewalk, pen a note, and slip it under the front door. Block letters informed her he'd be at The Lake Placid Manor until she agreed to see him.

Well, he could take a steaming shit in his hat for all she cared. And he could rot in the ritzy bed and breakfast before she'd consent to meet him there. When push came to shove, she'd already been pushed out of her old life. Now it was her turn to shove the residual shit from her new one.

There were no window coverings in the shop so she carried the last box from the window seat upstairs into the apartment. Before she'd agreed to the boat ride with Jake, the old books had her attention. They called her back to the words on their pages, beacons from the past that might show the way to a peaceful future.

The dented percolator brewed a strong cup of coffee. She added a spoonful of sugar and a healthy dollop of rum before she stirred. She took the hot mug to the living room, set it on a macramé coaster on the coffee table, and curled her legs beneath her on the worn sofa. Reaching for the book she'd left on the top of the pile, she took a deep breath and opened to the turned-down page.

There was a voyeuristic aspect to reading someone else's private thoughts but now that she'd begun getting to know her deceased aunt through her old diaries there was no turning back. The handwritten entries came in almost daily. They chronicled the ordinary and lent insight into the spiritual side of Lola Delaney.

Lola's personality shone on every page, and for the first time in her life she thought she understood her aunt.

An hour passed. Then, two. Her coffee grew cold. It turned almost iced, but she drank it anyway. She kept to the scrawled tale, unable to look away from the long-forgotten doings of a young woman on her own in what had then been a thriving town.

When she finished the last page, she shut the volume and held it close to her chest. It was illuminating. Intriguing. And, on a whole different plane, frightening.

A pink phone on the side table was handy. She pressed the familiar buttons. Joann picked up on the first ring.

"Hey, it's me."

"Hi, you. What's up?"

"I…oh, now that I've got you, I don't know how to say it." Her mind worked hard, trying to get around the news she'd uncovered. "It's all so surreal that I can hardly believe it. But I read it myself, so it must be true. Right? And really, who lies to a diary?"

"No one. Most people tell diaries things they wouldn't dare say out loud."

"You've got a point. But it's still hard to say. I'm not sure what to make of it, besides."

"Make of what?"

"I've got a cousin." The admission, out loud and without any trace of a doubt, made the thought reality. She said it again, this time with more force. "A cousin, Joann. I've got a cousin. It says so here in Lola's diaries."

"So you've got family, then. What fabulous news!"

Joann had been the shoulder Kat cried on when she lost her mother. She'd heard all the what-ifs, why-nots, and wouldn't-it-be-greats. She was the one who told her that she didn't need blood relatives, not when she had the three of them. Families were made, she insisted, and they'd been one together. But that had been when they'd believed Kat was without blood relations. This gave the story a new twist, and they both knew it.

"Where is she? Do you know?"

"The book says she's in France. A small town near Nice—there's even an address. And a phone number, too. The diary says Meredith—that's my cousin's name—lives with her father, who was a skier. Evidently my aunt and this skier forged a love connection and had a daughter. She gave him the baby after it was born." She did a quick mental calculation. "She's younger than I am, by a few years. What should I do, Joann?"

"You know what you need to do. Hang up and call her, right this very minute! Then, call me back and let me know how it goes. And remember, you've got family—even if things with this cousin don't work out."

She took a deep breath, held it, then let it out slowly. It did little to steady her wildly beating heart. "I know that. I'll call...hopefully she'll want to know me as much as I want to know her."

Chapter 53

"Don't let the bastards wear you down."
~Lola Delaney

Leaving the door to unit seventeen ajar didn't bring any cool air on the humid night, but it did give mosquitoes and moths a free pass.

Jake slapped at the oversized mosquito drilling for blood on the inside of his left wrist. He wiped its sticky remains on his cut-off jeans and muttered, "Take that, you little bastard."

"I recognize that tone of voice. It matches the old don't-stand-too-close-I'm-pissed mood you're so good at."

Tom, dressed in denim cut-offs and a faded gray Keep on Truckin' T-shirt, sauntered into the room. He leaned against the doorframe leading into the tiny bathroom and surveyed the mess on the floor. "Fixing something?"

"What brings you here, Sherlock?"

The screw ring holding the sink trap to the drainpipe was so old and corroded, he hated to put the wrench on it. But there was no other way to replace the trap, and it dripped so much that he couldn't use the room for guests. Changing it out was his only option.

He eased the wrench teeth together with a gentle touch, said a silent prayer that the damn thing would turn without his having to put his whole body weight behind it, and gave a slow pull. Nothing. He pulled the handle again, using just a touch more pressure. Still nothing. The thing was rusted and practically cemented in place.

Damn it.

"I could have you arrested, you know."

"For what?" He wiped the sweat off his brow with the dirty rag he'd used to wipe the pipe clean. He looked over at the other man, who grinned so broadly he looked like a cat with a canary in its mouth. "And what the hell are you smiling about?"

"For assault with a deadly weapon. Or at least assault with malice aforethought. Or something— somewhere in the books there's got to be a reason to ticket an engineer wielding a wrench without any idea what he's doing."

"I know what I'm doing." He used the rag on the teeth of the wrench, hoping it'd slipped instead of catching because the steel had oil on it. Nothing looked suspicious, but anything was possible. "I'm fixing this damn sink—or I was, until you came in here with all your stupid jokes."

"She's really got your nuts in her pretty little hands, doesn't she?"

"Don't say that." He rubbed the wrench handle in disgust. "She doesn't have anything. Besides, her ex is here. Did you know that? He dropped in, probably to haul her ass back to New York City—where plumbers fix sinks, ducks don't bite, she's got a real job and doesn't have to figure out what to do in a Green Acres kind of town. Shit, Tom, she's probably packing already."

He leaned down, put his head beneath the porcelain, and put the wrench back in place. Just above the ring joint, where he'd get the most torque for his effort.

"When did you become such a loser?"

His head hit the sink. The wrench clattered against the trap when he yanked it free. He turned, rubbing the egg beneath his hair. Tom stood there as calm as a game show contestant. He wished he had kept the crap he'd pulled from the clogged, leaky trap, but it was already in the trash. Good thing, because he pictured it sailing through the air and splattering on the clean shorts.

"What did you say?"

"You heard me. You're acting like an asshole, but I know there's nothing wrong with your ears. So, when was it? Must've been when you were off in Texas, because you were never a quitter before you left."

Being a widower or the police chief didn't give Tom free rein to say whatever asinine thing came into his head, so he called him on it. Waving a very large wrench.

"You're joking, right? Me—a quitter?"

"Do I look like I'm joking?" Tom folded his arms across his chest. His biceps bulged, thick and hard, straining the edges of his sleeves. Without Kathy, he had lots of spare time to fill. Some of it he spent at the gym. Arms like his didn't grow without encouragement. Serious, heavy lifting encouragement.

"I'm tired. I don't want to play games, so if you've got something to say get it off your damn chest. Don't call me names and act all holier-than-thou just because you can. I'm eyeball deep in crap already. Don't shovel more shit on the pile."

They stared at each other. When they were kids, they'd done a thing where they'd stare until one of them did something disgusting to break the stare contest. Farting and burping usually made the grade to make one—or both—of them burst out laughing. Problem was, now that they were men bodily function noises fell from the hilariously funny list.

Tom uncrossed his arms and squatted in the doorway, so they were eye level. He threaded his fingers together and held them loosely between his knees.

"Since you're home from Texas you're so beat up. I've never seen you this way. You've always been the go-to guy, the one who left this little town on a burst of glory. It blows to see you acting like the past will dictate your future. It can't—don't you see that? It just can't wreck your life, what happened. It wasn't your fault, and you've got to find a way to get past thinking it is." He held up a hand when Jake tried to protest. "I know, I've said it a million damn times already. But it's the truth, and I'm not giving up on your sorry ass just because you think you can—even if I piss you off."

The truth stung. And it was, he knew, the unvarnished truth. He'd known it for a while, but letting the past order how he organized his life worked. It kept everyone at a safe distance, and he could deal with that. Loneliness and regret were tough bedfellows but he'd grown accustomed to sharing his life with them.

Until now. He didn't know how Kat had dented his steel hide or why she meant so much more than any woman he'd met. He hadn't yet figured out what he was going to do with the feelings that—no matter how hard he tried to ignore them—just wouldn't quit.

He didn't know a lot. And it was all new to him, this not being in control. It sucked, but there was no solution that he could see for the mess his life had become. Every time he thought he might have a handle on things, something happened. A duck-ravaged hand. A business agreement—which he still hadn't divulged to anyone, thank you very much. A tryst in a crashing boat—with a city slicker ex watching everything.

Shit.

"You're a pain in my ass. But thank you. I mean that, Tom. Thanks for saying what you know I don't want to hear. Especially when I've got a big ass tool in my hand."

"You're welcome. You'd do the same for me, and I'm usually carrying a loaded pistol."

He paused, then added, "I won't ever forget how you were there for me and Kathy during the—well, during our bad time. And after. You never let me down, brother."

So much went unspoken, but no words mattered. They locked gazes, remembering the pretty young woman with cornflower-blue eyes, infectious smile, and loving heart. They shared so much, both good times and awful moments, that there wasn't a language invented that could give meaning to the life or loss they'd suffered.

Jake said a quick Hail Mary for Kathy's soul. He prayed her torment was over, and that she was truly at peace.

"We're brothers. They stick together." He saw the glaze of unshed tears in his friend's eyes, so he waved the wrench toward the bad trap. "Know anything about fixing a sink?"

The cop went down on one knee. He scooted closer and surveyed the mess.

"You really agreed to take the motel from your uncle?"

"How did you hear? I haven't told anyone yet."

Tom ran a testing fingertip along the corroded pipe. "I'm the head honcho down at the station, remember? I hear it all, one way or another. It's like the old plumber's saying…"

"What plumber's saying?"

Tom poked through the open toolbox beside the bathtub. He pushed aside two hammers, several screwdrivers, two carpenters' pencils, and a hole punch before he found what he wanted. Pulling out a smaller version of the huge wrench in Jake's hand, he nodded.

"That's right, the plumber's motto. 'Hot to the left, cold to the right, water goes up and shit floats downstream'." He held the wrench high. "We're going to finesse it with this. It'll come loose, you'll see. And, by the way, I know about your dockside fun. Now that I could arrest you for—both of you, from what I hear. Indecent exposure, lascivious conduct, and a bunch of other stuff. Lucky for you, the boyfriend's not pressing charges."

"Ex boyfriend." Jake laid on his side, jammed between the pipe and the outside of the bathtub so Tom could get close enough to help. "And I'll bet he's not going to press charges. He enjoyed the show."

"What do you think he's doing up here?" Tom scooted forward. When he was close enough, he put his wrench on one side of the pipe joint.

"I know what he's doing." Just remembering the

look in the other guy's eyes made him angry. He grabbed the pipe with the wrench harder than he needed to and clamped the teeth closed around the old fitting. "He wants her back. Shit, Tom, he was on her like a bum on a bologna sandwich."

"When I say 'three' you turn clockwise, and I'll go counter-clockwise. Gently, okay?" He waited until Jake nodded. "I guess you've got to decide whether or not the bologna sandwich is all yours or if it's okay to share with this ex. That is, if you don't mind him taking a bite now and then—"

"I mind. The sandwich is mine—what the hell am I saying? I don't want to share Kat with anyone—especially not some creep who swindles old ladies out of their social security checks. Now, are you going to count or what?"

"Gently, remember? I'm not the one who wants a bite of your girlfriend, so one-two-three—"

They turned. The fitting came loose. So did the trap.

And the pipe connected to it, the one going into the floor? That broke. In three jagged pieces.

That was bad enough, but the cold water line broke as well.

Neither man avoided being doused by a spray of ice-cold, rusty water. It hit the walls behind them, too. Jake tried stuffing the rag in the broken pipe, but the pressure sent it flying in a wet heap onto the tile. They grabbed the pipe with their hands, but the water shot between their fingers.

"You didn't shut the water off?" Tom's blond hair streamed into his eyes, much darker now that it'd been dyed with old motel rust water. He spat a piece of something fuzzy out of his mouth, then wiped his chin on his soaked T-shirt.

"I tried."

"Well?"

"Damn shut-off valve is rusted open. Won't turn!"

He hit the blue valve behind the spurting pipe with his elbow. Hard.

There was a cracking noise. Then, a wet pop as the valve broke loose. It flew off the pipe, narrowly missing hitting Tom in the head before it pinged off the turquoise bath tile. Without the valve, water gushed still faster, flooding the room at twice the speed.

They both sat back against the tub, too wet to care if they got wetter. And until one of them got up and shut the main for the whole motel, the water was going to flow.

A grin, and an elbow to the side. "So, you're staying in Mill Pond? Becoming a motel owner, I hear."

"That's right." Jake plowed his fingers through his hair, pushing it off his face and out of his eyes. "The place is mine now. The whole damn place."

"And what about the sandwich—er, girlfriend? You going to make that permanent, too?"

The tile floor was completely covered with water. Old hair, an ancient bobby pin, and bits of broken pipe floated around them.

"Damn right. I'll get that bum away from her and keep him away. But first, I'd better try to stop this mess."

He got another poke in the ribs. "Or we could just let the water float you across the street to Kat's place. That way you'll be sure no one's trying to take a bite out of her when you're not around. Just float on in, keep her company…"

"Come on, smartass. Help me with this so I can fix all the other broken stuff in my life."

He stood, water sloshing into his work boots as it dripped down his legs. He put his hand out and hauled his best friend to his feet. The water seeped onto the shag carpeting in the room outside the bathroom, but he didn't care. The whole place needed a renovation, so why not begin here?

And while he was at it, he could work on renovating his personal life, too. It was as cracked as the damn water pipe.

Yeah, shit runs downstream.

Chapter 54

"Sometimes the voices inside my head just won't shut up—no matter how tight I tie their gags."
                                                ~Lola Delaney

"I'm glad you weren't shocked to hear from me last night. I mean, you could have been as clueless about me as I was about you."

Kat hadn't slept at all, too excited by the late-night trans-Atlantic conversation. Suddenly she wasn't the only one in the world swimming in her gene pool which made the familial ache in her heart almost completely disappear.

"I knew you would eventually contact me. My parents told me about you. Also, about the distance between your aunt and my father. That will not happen with us, will it?"

Meredith, who preferred Meri to the more formal version of her name, was sweet. Her long-distance persona exuded poise and allure. Kat couldn't wait to meet her in person.

"No, of course not. My aunt was silly. How could she have done it to us?"

She visualized Meri's shrug, so slight and delicate and sublimely Parisian. *"C'est la vie.* We cannot turn back the hands of time, but we should not repeat the mistakes of our ancestors. In all fairness, I have always known about you, Kat. Oh, I love that name! Such a saucy name for an American!"

Saucy? Hardly. But if Meri thought so, it was fine with her. Besides, it would probably sound very lazy if she admitted the truth. Katharine had been too laborious to write when she was in grade school, so she'd shortened her name to match the neighbor's pet. Her mother tolerated Kitty and then Kat, and it had stuck.

"Thank you. And I guess you're right. We can't go back. Only forward, right? And I hope that includes a visit sometime. I don't have a passport, but I could get one. Or you're welcome to come here—" The timer buzzed. "Hold on. I'll be right back, okay? I've just got to grab something from the freezer."

She dropped the phone, ran into the kitchen, threw open the freezer compartment, and seized a frozen tray. She set it on the table as she went past. It slid on the polished top but stopped short of the chrome edge.

"I'm back." She dropped to the sofa. She didn't wait for the question she knew was coming. "I made fudge. It was getting solid in the freezer. It's one of those things that if it stays too long in the freezer it turns into an uncuttable block. Too short a time, it's still too gooey to cut. That's why I use a timer, so I get it just right."

"How long? What is the just-right time for making fudge?"

"Thirty-five minutes."

"No more? No less? Exactly thirty-five?" Meri hummed. "That is good to know, if ever I want to make this fudge you speak of. I have never had it, by the way. Perhaps when I visit, you will demonstrate the technique?"

Kat's heart skipped a beat. People with families took visits for granted. She could barely contain her excitement as she nodded. Tears pooled in her eyes, threatening to spill down her cheeks.

"Definitely. I will demonstrate...oh, I'm so happy..."

She tried to hide the emotions welling up inside her but her cousin wasn't fooled.

"Ooh, Kat... No, please don't cry. You don't have to teach me to make fudge if it will make you cry. I don't care about this fudge—*phooey* on the fudge! Don't cry, my cousin. Please—I probably hate fudge! And making it would undoubtedly be an international mess. We would—how do you say it? We would, ah—make headphones with the mess. That's right, so no fudge making for me and no crying for you. Is that better?"

Kat laughed, wiping tears from her cheeks with the backs of her hands.

"Headlines. We'd make headlines," she said with a grin. "And it's not the fudge that makes me cry. It's you—"

Meri gasped.

"Oh, no! I didn't mean it that way." She waved a hand in the air but of course the other woman couldn't see it. "I just meant that I'm so happy to have you, to know you're coming to visit and to be able to teach you anything at all—it just brings tears of happiness, Meri. That's why I'm crying. I'm happy."

She waited while Meri contemplated her explanation. With the cultural and language differences, knowing the right thing to say and how to say it was a challenge. She hoped she hadn't already put her foot in her mouth.

Finally, a giggle. "I understand. We cry, too, on happy occasions. This is a joyous moment for both of us. Forgive me, if I do not cry. I am happy but with dry eyes. That is not an insult, is it?"

She laughed. After a small delay, her cousin joined her.

"It's not an insult. Believe me, there are much worse things to have than dry eyes. I'm just glad you think our finding each other is as amazing as I do. Finally, I'm not alone."

Laughter faded.

The words were spoken from the heart and crossed all barriers, including distance.

"You are not alone, Kat. Never again. You have me—always."

Chapter 55

"Clear your mind and your heart might fill. Or maybe not. Who the hell knows with stuff like that?"
~Lola Delaney

The shop was finally empty. It had an enormous back room that she'd cleared out as well. Everything she couldn't part with she stored in a huge barn behind the patio. It seemed smarter to store things outside, even if just to give her a blank slate to ponder.

She sat on the window seat with Attila on her lap. The gallery was all hers, regardless of what she decided to do with it. After the conversations with Meri, she'd called Aunt Lola's attorney who confirmed that Meri had received a separate bequest from her mother. The gallery belonged to Kat. Lock, stock, and dust bunny.

"What now?"

Her voice echoed off the bare shelves and empty walls. Attila purred, but it was her only answer.

"You aren't a lot of help." She rubbed a thumb between the cat's ears.

An actual art gallery was out of the question. When she'd thought she was getting one, already up and running and filled with art, that had been one thing. But she knew less than nothing about art galleries, so starting one from scratch was ridiculous.

What, then?

A knock on the door saved her from giving herself a headache trying to come up with a solution to fill the gaping hole unemployment left in her life. She put the sleeping cat on the warm window seat and crossed to the door. Her hand stopped midway to the door latch.

She looked at the deadbolt. Locked.

Henry. Slicked-back hair. Expensive leather loafers, polished like twin black mirrors. The crease in his chinos, razor-sharp and the collar of his black oxford, its top button undone, set his casual wardrobe far beyond the degree of informal Mill Pond embraced.

The postman passed the shop, giving her ex an odd stare as he pushed his mail trolley. But when he saw her standing inside the door, he changed his expression. A wave and a smile, which she returned.

The look on Henry's face was a familiar one. Straight-line brows over light gray eyes. The same firm set to his thin lips. And the gaze, as cold and calculating as they came, trained on her.

His Intimidation Face. It worked for him in the past. Gave him what he wanted, when he wanted it. Many times.

It disgusted her that she'd given in to Henry, let him have his way in social situations, their home affairs, and even in the bedroom. She'd meant to keep peace between them, but she'd sold herself short. Way too short. But The Face had no effect now. He didn't intimidate her. He never would again. She'd changed— even if he, obviously, hadn't.

She didn't open the door.

He rattled the latch, but the old tumblers held. Frustration crossed onto his expression but he smiled around it. It was so false.

"Open the door." A command.

She crossed her hands over her chest. "What do you want?"

"Open the door so we can talk." He rattled the latch again, this time hard enough to make the glass clatter.

Too many more shakes and she'd be wearing the old door pane.

Not being intimidated didn't include being foolish. Henry had never given in on anything before, so there was no reason to believe he'd do so now.

She gave it a try anyway. "Go away. We have nothing to talk about."

Leaning in so his face was only an inch from the glass, he said, "We have a lot to talk about. Are you going to open this door—or am I going to do it for you?"

Damn it.

Damn him.

And damn her own stupidity. How could she have ever settled for this jerk? What shortfall within her personality let her believe she deserved to spend even one minute attached to someone so despicable?

No time for introspection. He rattled the door again. The glass jiggled but it didn't faze him. He didn't flinch or step back. And, he kept his fist around the old latch.

"Fine." It was clear he wouldn't go away until she heard him out. But she sure as hell wasn't letting him into the shop. "Step back, so I can open the door. We'll talk on the sidewalk. On that bench over there."

She nodded to a bench near the curb. A waist-high cedar wood planter box, overflowing with white and purple alyssum, orange and yellow cosmos, potato vines, and a center of white geraniums divided the bench. He could sit on one side while she sat on the other. They'd be out in the open and with the flower barricade she should be safe. She hoped.

The only other alternative was to let him into the shop, and that wasn't going to happen.

Henry didn't go for it. "On the sidewalk? You've got to be shitting me. Let me in. *Now*."

She held her ground. "I'm not *shitting* you—as you so eloquently put it. And it's either on the sidewalk or not at all. *Now*—step back, so I can come outside. Or don't—it's up to you. Either way, I'm not letting you in."

He took a step back, his hands fisted. His expression lost any trace of congenial. Behind the eyes she saw rage, pure and simple. If they'd been alone, she would have been frightened. But being stuck in a public setting made him impotent—didn't it?

When he took another step toward the bench, Kat unlocked the door. She slipped through, reaching behind her to relock it. It seemed less likely Henry would cause a scene on the sidewalk than he'd pull her into the shop and lock them inside. Giving him that chance, to get her alone, wasn't a gamble she was willing to take.

Spreading his hands wide, he asked, "Happy? You've got me out here like a stranger?"

She ignored the sarcasm and sat on the side of the bench closest to the shop's door.

"No, I'm not happy. How could I be, with you here? And you *are* a stranger, Henry. I thought I knew you, but I obviously didn't. What do you want?"

"Aren't you being harsh?"

He sat on the end of the bench, leaned forward so he was able to reach around the flowers, and placed a hand on her bare knee. She resisted the shudder that was her first reaction to his touch, instead scooting sideways out of his reach.

He looked annoyed, but he took his hand back.

She was beyond caring about his annoyance threshold.

"What do you want?"

A scowl. "So that's the way it is. Nothing nice between us until you make me grovel? What is it you want from me? An apology? Well, I'm sorry, Kat. There—I've said it. I'm sorry I upset you. Now can we stop this crap and go back home?"

"You've got to be kidding! You and I have no home. Not after what you've done. And your apology is worthless."

"So you're not going back to the city with me?"

Had he lost his damn mind along with his morals?

"I'm not going anywhere with you. Nowhere, do you understand?"

His jaw clenched. A vein throbbed in his temple. Before, she would have lifted a finger to gentle his emotions. Now, she hoped his head would burst. Right here on Main Street, where everyone could see what the inside of a swindler's skull looked like.

"Fine. But call your lawyer. Tell him you've changed your mind."

"Ha! You've got a problem—a big one—if you think I'm going to lie to get you off the hook."

Out of the corner of her eye, she spotted a low, slow movement coming along the sidewalk. Brown, with feathers. And waddling.

Damn it, but she was being stalked by the attack duck while the city creep tried to scare her into doing things his way. Lord, but it really poured sometimes!

His eyes flashed fury as he spat, careful not to soil his expensive shoes. Then, he spoke with such venom she recoiled. "I'm not the one with the problem. Believe me when I tell you it's in your best interest to recant your story. Tell the lawyer you had PMS. That you imagined the whole thing. Say whatever the hell you want, but act like what you said was a mistake. I mean it, Kat. Tell them it's not true—or I promise you'll be sorry."

"Fuck you, Henry."

If looks could kill, she'd be dead on the spot.

Time stood still, but she refused to be the first to blink. Their gazes locked in combat.

She saw the ugly truth in Henry's eyes. Had they not been in public it would have been even worse—she had no illusions about what she saw inside him, or how much he wanted to unleash the rage he restrained.

Qu-quack. Q-q-quack!

It was the only warning. A brown flurry of feathers, led by a strong orange bill, cannonballed between them. It knocked Henry backward. He rolled over, off the bench, and down the curb into the street.

"Clarence!" Jake's aunt appeared. She clapped her hands, as if trying to call unruly students to attention.

Kat stood and took a step away from the scuffle.

The beak clamped vise-like on his right hand. The man shook his arm wildly, hurling expletives as he tried to disengage but for his part, Clarence didn't seem inclined to let go.

"Get this fucking duck off me!" Anger mixed with

terror. She was too shocked to do anything other than stare as the duck sat on the man's chest, wings spread and flapping. Henry covered his face with his free arm. "Damn it—you bastard!"

"How dare you swear at my Clarence?" Today the elderly woman wore yellow—from the daisies sewn on the hat on her head to the daffodil-print Keds on her feet. She rushed forward like a yellow tornado. Wisps of white hair escaped from under her Yankees cap. She balled a fist, stood over the man, and yelled, "I'll wash your mouth out with soap, you citified asshole. Give me my duck—*now*!"

It was precisely what Henry tried to do—give her the duck. He grabbed Clarence by the neck. He tugged him off his hand and tossed the animal to the pavement. The old woman screamed, falling back onto the bench when the furious man tried to stand.

Kat moved without thinking, scooping Clarence into her arms and holding him the way she'd seen his owner do. The animal shook in her embrace, hiding his head beneath one of her arms and making no fuss over being held by a stranger.

Swirling lights intruded on the scene. Tom stepped from his cruiser, looked from the women to Henry, then at Clarence.

His question included everyone. "What's going on here?"

Jake's aunt stood, wiping her hands down her daisy-patterned sweatshirt with a look of disgust on her lined face. She pointed to Henry, who stood in the street cradling his hand against his expensive shirt.

"That asshole assaulted my Clarence. I want to press charges, Tom. A *lot* of charges."

Chapter 56

"Sweet and sour are different for everybody. Some people like pickles. Others, gooey desserts. And some of us like our pickles slathered with whipped cream. Go figure!" ~Lola Delaney

What kind of woman was she, that she could find solace in the candy aisle at the grocery store? Many women fled to find chocolate when life turned upside down, but most grabbed the nearest favorite bag of candy, paid for it, and gobbled it down. Not her. She examined all the rows, looking for inspiration. Nothing jumped out, so she walked to the end of the aisle and began her perusal again.

Jake rounded the corner. She wasn't so upset that her heart didn't react to his sudden arrival. It did, flipping and flopping in her chest like a fish thrown from a lake to the shore. It was exciting—and annoying—to react so strongly.

"I thought you might be here." He made no move to embrace her. No greeting kiss. No hug. His hands were in the front pockets of his jeans and he kept them there. It didn't stop his head to toe, then back up again inspection of her person, though.

A bug under a microscope got less careful examination.

Men—who could figure them out?

Exasperation made her snippy. "Nice work, Einstein. So, you found me."

One of his eyebrows disappeared from view, buried beneath a thick curl dangling over his forehead.

The die was cast. Bad attitude and snottiness, they were her window dressing. She wore them without guilt. She'd earned that right, after having been tossed from man to man without being given a clue about what little new game was on her horizon.

Enough with the man crap.

She grabbed a bag off the nearest shelf and turned away. Two aisles over, the baking necessities beckoned.

He followed, silent as a shadow.

Kat didn't peek at the candy in her hand until she stood in front of the baker's chocolate. She turned the bag over, glad she'd chosen something she could easily replicate.

Chocolate-covered peanuts. Ordinary, but semi-healthy. And delicious, to boot. Also, a simple recipe to copy, with a couple of adjustments to make it her own.

The small plastic grocery basket hanging over one arm filled quickly. Jake reached to take it from her but she turned her back on him. No man was going to do for her anymore. The no-penis rule she'd arrived in town with had been a good one. Stupidly she'd broken it. Now, whether he knew it or not, the rule was back in place.

Mr. Always-with-a-Condom could like it—or not. He hadn't consulted her on the condom thing, had he?

"Kat..." His voice, so smooth and dreamy, threatened to melt the icy fence around her heart. He put a hand on her shoulder and stood in front of her but stopped short of actually forcing her to look at him. She didn't, staring stubbornly at the ugly industrial tiles at their feet. "Can't we talk?"

Talk, talk, talk!

What could any man say that could unravel the mess in her heart and mind? To say nothing of her life?

She sighed. Yes, Jake was a man. And yes, he did have a penis—a very spectacular one—but he hadn't done anything to deserve the deep freeze. He was paying for Henry's mess, and it wasn't fair.

But that didn't mean she wanted to make their relationship any more complicated than it already was.

Finally, she met his eyes. Nothing she saw made her feel uncomfortable. Frightened. Foolish. Nothing made her feel the way she'd felt when she looked into the man who'd put her in such a foul mood.

Tenderness. Kindness. Concern. They were the emotions Jake brought to the table.

And patience. Lots of patience. He waited for her to speak.

No pressure. No demands. Only the things every woman dreamed to see in a man's eyes when he looked at her—that's what she saw before her.

But damn it, she sucked at relationships. Even platonic ones like the one they were supposedly having.

"I don't know what to say."

"Are you all right?" He ran his hand down her arm to her wrist. He took her hand, turned it over and ran a gentle finger across the bruise still visible there. "I hear you had a run-in with Clarence."

"Not me. Clarence actually, ah…" She floundered, not wanting to bring the sour aftertaste Henry left into her mouth again.

He held her hand. "I heard. So, Clarence rescued

you?"

"Let's just say I have a different opinion of the little brown duck than I had before."

It was true. He'd been docile while she held him so Jake's aunt could give her version of the events to Tom. Then, when it was Kat's turn to give a statement, Clarence had seemed so comfortable where he was, she held on to him. Only after Henry got into Tom's car and headed to the medical center would the duck allow her to place him on the sidewalk.

"Glad to hear it. But really, are you okay? I don't want to press, but Tom said your ex was pretty out of control. Did he hurt you?"

Physically? No.

Mentally? Suffering a huge blow to her self-esteem due to his narcissistic personality wasn't great but he hadn't done any lasting damage. If anything, he'd taught her a number of valuable lessons.

"No, he didn't. I'm fine."

"You don't look fine."

Chapter 57

"When all else fails, run for your life."
                                    ~Lola Delaney

The events of the last weeks wore her out. The peaceful pie she'd envisioned partaking of hadn't appeared. Even the wild sex she and Jake shared wasn't enough to put her mind in a place where she didn't feel exhausted.

Bone weary. Her mother's voice came to her, along with the realization that she needed a break. A break from this new life. Definitely a break from the old life. Even, she hated to admit it, a break from Jake and all the emotions being with him brought up. Her vision of new experiences, wide-open horizons hadn't included the ache in her chest.

Cut the head off this relationship—or whatever the hell this is—now.

One swift slice, leaving the emotional risk behind and giving her a chance to deal with her circumstances. Alone.

"I don't know what to say. I just didn't expect to find…well, I thought I wouldn't get involved with anyone when I got here. I made that clear, didn't I?"

He nodded. "You did. I thought you were a lesbian, remember?" A small, tension-breaking grin.

"How could I forget? Then your aunt jumped to the

268

same conclusion. Honestly, I've never been asked that before."

He pulled her out of the center of the aisle. They waited as a woman with a screaming baby went by. She pushed her grocery cart with one hand, juggled the crying infant with the other, and coaxed a wandering toddler to follow her. Kat turned in time to see him shake his head at the noisy little parade.

So, he really didn't like children. A good thing to know, especially since it was her long-standing dream to have a big family. Lots of noisy children. Sticky fingers. Even snotty noses and loud tears. All of it—she wanted all of and it was apparent he couldn't stand the idea.

It strengthened her resolve to put a stop to whatever they had growing between them.

Kat didn't give Jake a chance to ask another question.

"Right now, I need to be uninvolved. I'm not as good at the friends-with-sex thing as I hoped I'd be. And as I said the day after we met, I'm off men. All men, remember?" She took a step back, breaking contact between them. His hand left hers slowly. He held on even after she straightened her fingers and let him go. "I think we should try to just be waving-across-the-street friends. You spend a lot of time at the motel, so I'm sure we'll see each other around."

He studied her face, looking from her chin to her eyes, then down at her mouth. Not moving, letting him absorb the fact she was stopping their relationship wasn't easy but she owed him that much. Bad enough to announce she'd had enough of him and whatever they were—or weren't, depending on how you looked at it—building together in the middle of the grocery store, but to run before he could respond was just plain tacky.

She was a lot of things. Tacky wasn't one of them, so she shifted the grocery basket from one arm to the other and waited.

He sighed, his shoulders rising and stretching his T-shirt taut against his biceps. He shook his head, regret as clear as his muscles.

"Is this some kind of retribution, this whole no-guy thing? Payment for the shit your ex handed you? Tom told me some of what went on down in Manhattan, and I don't blame you for not trusting so easily." He plowed a hand through his hair. Then, he swept the side of his cheek, his palm rasping on the stubble there. "But hell, you can't judge every man by the way one mistreated you. Can you?"

The fact was, she could.

Invariably, she got hurt—one way or another. It wasn't wrong to finally decide she wouldn't tolerate the heartache anymore. It couldn't be wrong to stand up for herself, declare she had had enough of men and all the garbage that went along with them. Could it?

She didn't know. And this minute, she didn't give a shit.

"Listen, I don't want to get into this now." Tired and disgusted with everything, she held the grocery basket against her chest. "I just want to go back to the apartment, melt some chocolate, and forget about everything. I'm sorry if that hurts you, but it's what I've got to do—for me. Selfish? Maybe. But, Jake, I can't think of another way to hang on to my sanity."

He put his hand on his hip, looking like he might

make one more argument, so she hurried on, pulling a small smile to her lips.

"And there you have it—I've got a date with chocolate and some peanuts. I can't be late, so if you'll excuse me, I'll see you another time." She didn't give him a moment to respond. She turned on her heel and walked away. As she rounded the corner, headed for the cashier, she felt him boring a hole in her back.

It was a strange feeling, but the hole in her back didn't come close to matching the size of the hole in her heart, so she kept walking. What else could she do?

Chapter 58

"Loose lips might sink ships, but tight lips do more damage. Believe me, I know." ~Lola Delaney

"I can't believe you didn't tell her how you feel. Damn it—haven't you learned a single thing in thirty-three years? Didn't watching Kathy and me show you that when you find someone who holds your heart, you shouldn't mess around? I'm so pissed off at you right now. I could slug you, but then I'd be fixing this sink by myself."

Tom held the pipe in place beneath the sink. The water had been mopped up and the broken pieces of old trap and pipe had been removed. They were close to setting the new stuff in place. Jake tightened the fitting with a wrench, enough that it wouldn't leak but not so forcefully he wouldn't be able to remove it if needed. Now that the motel was his, and the repairs and renovations were all up to him, he did not intend to do any half-assed jobs. Everything was going to be top notch—starting with this bathroom overhaul.

"You can let go." Tom did, so he gave the coupling a final twist. "I'll turn the valve on. You get the faucet. Let's see if we've got it. If we don't, I'll save you the trouble and slug myself."

The valve opened smoothly. Tom ran the cold water, then the hot. It drained without leaking beneath the sink. They looked at each other and shrugged. Fixing a sink was small potatoes. Organizing a life was an entirely different matter, and they both knew it.

Jake shoved his wrench into the toolbox. He wiped his hands, then tossed the rag into the box. He closed it, locked it and waited until his helper stood before pushing himself to his feet.

They walked through the motel room and out to the patio.

Tom turned, and was about to speak but he said, "I know. You're right. I'm pissed with myself, too. I tried to talk to her, but the grocery store isn't really the best spot to tell a woman you're having feelings for her. Really, not so romantic."

Tom had gotten most of the rust off his sandy-colored hair, but there were still a few tendrils near his temples that looked darker than they should have.

"Got to agree on that point. Still, what the hell are you doing with her? She deserves better than what she's getting."

They reached a brick wall planter that ran around the perimeter of the pool area. The red against fading turquoise did nothing to enhance the motel's appeal.

Tom put one butt cheek on the planter. He swung his leg and shook his head. His annoyed cop expression arranged his features into a grim pose. "Her ex is bad news. Between us, Clarence should've gone for the guy's nuts. Would've served him right. A broken hand was too good for the jerk."

His gentle manner disappeared. He was rarely so agitated. Jake waited, knowing there was more to the story.

Years of bonding paid off.

Tom snorted in disgust.

Then, he looked into Jake's eyes and said, "That woman is too nice for what you're doing with her. She isn't screw buddy material. She's not Chelsea, you know."

No one had to point that out. The women were so different it was almost ridiculous to insinuate they could have anything in common.

"No shit. And I get it. She's more than just an available lay—believe me, I know." Kat had been more from the beginning. Only, he hadn't known it then. "It's just that I don't know what I want. I've already taken on more than I said I ever would. Look at this—the motel. It's mine now. I'm responsible for it, and for the guests I hope will fill the rooms. I told you I made a deal with the Placid tourism center, didn't I?"

"Great deal. It'll be good for everyone. Having them add Mill Pond's businesses to their brochures will increase tourist traffic here by a lot." Tom tipped his head, a small salute. "Thanks for doing it. I know everyone will appreciate the cash coming in."

"I did it for myself, too. Yeah, I want the town to prosper, but it's also good for me. Now I've got the motel. And my house. And the new boat—in addition to my old boat, which I haven't decided what to do with yet."

Tom squinted against the glare of the afternoon sun. "What do you mean? What are you thinking of doing with the old one?"

Talking with his uncle about their impending move made Jake reevaluate his own priorities. Thinking about all Tom and Kathy endured made a lot of things clear to him as well. And Kat—just knowing her even a short time and feeling the way he did when they were together…it changed him. More importantly, it made him think.

"You know the old use it or lose it thing?"

Tom snickered. "When people say that they're not talking about vintage boats, buddy."

"I know that. But it still applies…if I'm not going to use the boat I should lose it. Let someone else enjoy it. It's not doing it any good, keeping it strung up in the barn the way it is. And I'm certainly not getting any enjoyment from it. So—I'm thinking I'll use it. Or lose it."

"Which will it be?"

"Use it, I think."

"You *have* been thinking, haven't you?" Tom put a flattened hand over his eyes, shading them. He sniffed. Then, he pointed. "Hey, isn't that smoke coming from the gallery?"

Oh, God, no—not Kat!

Chapter 59

"Too hot to handle? Happens to the best of us, honey..." ~Lola Delaney

They sprinted across the motel parking lot. His heart pounded so hard he thought it might burst from his chest—fear turned his blood cold but made his feet fly.

Black smoke curled into the cloudless sky, the stream originating somewhere inside Lola's gallery. Correction—Kat's place.

A small crowd gathered on the sidewalk, brought together first by the smell of something burning. Then, Ray pointed to the smoke.

"The gallery's burning!" He and Destiny carried boxes from the printer, which they promptly dropped to the bench on the sidewalk. Purple menus and pink placemats slid from one box, landing in a glossy stream on the concrete.

Destiny banged on the front window with her palm, making the glass jiggle while Ray shoved against the closed door with his shoulder.

"It's locked." The young waitress stared into the bystanders. "We'll have to break in."

Ray nodded, turning to find something to smash the glass. One of the people who gathered, the triple threat herself, snickered.

They pushed their way through. The smoke was thicker on this side of the street, sending Jake's heart pumping double time.

Get Kat out.

The words repeated in his head, the drummer beating loudly now that he was closer to the fire.

Teri stepped forward. She was dressed in her usual drab garb and pointed a finger so long and white it looked skeletal at the closed door. She put one hand on her wide hip and gave her loud opinion. "You can't break that door. You could lose your job for that. It could get you thrown in jail—it's breaking and invading, you know."

Destiny whirled on the ferret-faced woman. She was slight, but she came at Triple T with a vengeance. She raised her own finger, pointing it into the startled older woman's face.

"Lose my job? Are you that evil that you can't see helping another human being—possibly even saving a life—matters more than any damn job on the planet? How could you even *say* such a thing—insinuating *a job* is worth more than *a person*? You know what, Teri? You really are a waste of time—and space. Move— *now*—or so help me God I'll move your fat ass for you."

A ripple went through those who gathered behind the saucy waitress. Teri took two steps back, then turned and scurried away.

Jake pounded on the front door, but Kat didn't appear on the other side. His first thought was she'd burned her candy again, but the smoke was harsh and bitter.

Candy should be sweet, so it couldn't be that.

Besides, no smoke alarm. If she'd burnt candy, the alarm would be ringing.

"The back." He pushed through his neighbors. He heard Tom tell everyone to stay where they were, not to follow them. He called for Ray and Destiny to stand guard at the side entrance.

As soon as he turned the corner of the building, he saw the fire. The glider where they'd made love was ablaze. The cushions burned, sending coils of smoke and a chemical smell toward them. He covered his face with his arm, breathing into the crook of his elbow, and took the stairs to the kitchen door two at a time.

He banged. Hard.

Kat pulled the door open.

The phone cord was stretched tight, the receiver against her cheek. She had a wooden skewer, dripping chocolate, between her teeth.

She took the skewer from her mouth. "Jake? What is—oh, what is that terrible smell?"

She leaned out the doorway and looked down at the mess in the yard. Tom was spraying the glider with the hose. Light gray smoke billowed as the flames were extinguished. A cloud struck the landing and enveloped both of them.

Kat coughed, then spoke into the phone. "I'll call you back, okay? I've got a situation here. No, nothing big, just..." She coughed again. "Just a situation. I'll call you right back."

She stepped into the kitchen and dropped the phone on the table.

Jake pulled her into his arms. He'd tried to hold himself in check, tried not to cross the boundary she so clearly set, but seeing her alive and well pushed him over that line.

She didn't move for several heartbeats. She didn't embrace him in return, but she didn't pull away, either.

Finally, he had to let her go. She met his gaze, then looked back down to the patio. The glider was ruined but it had stopped burning. Tom, covered in black soot, watched it from a short distance, still holding the hose.

"What happened?" Her bafflement would have been cute had he not been struggling to steady his racing heart.

"You didn't hear the banging? Half the town is out on the front sidewalk, trying to get your attention to tell you the place is on fire."

A small shrug brought her tiny pink tank top up, then down. It had a wide neck and gave him a great view of her braless assets. Jake glanced down, but didn't stare.

"I was talking with Meri." She waved to the phone. "I heard something, but I ignored it."

He resisted the urge to swear. "You ignored all that banging? Why?"

She shrugged again. "I thought it was Henry."

No good reply came to his mind, so he took a deep breath and counted to ten. Then, he added five more. The city bastard had almost killed her. Fury boiled his blood, but he counted another ten measures. When he trusted himself to speak without letting his emotions seep into his words, he asked, "So you didn't know you had a fire on the patio?"

"Nope. I was rolling nuts in chocolate and planning a visit with my cousin. How could I know?"

"I guess you couldn't. When was the last time you were on that glider?"

Her cheeks bloomed. A sweet smile played on her lips. She shrugged again, and this time Jake did allow his gaze to linger on her nipples.

"Ah…" She looked up at him. Her grin told the story but he wanted to hear her say it, so he waited. "Well, I haven't been on the glider since you and me…you know. Since we were…"

He leaned close, so close he could have touched her lips with his. It was his plan, to steal a kiss, but first he had to make her blush one more time. "Since we made love?"

She met his gaze. Suddenly serious, she nodded. "Yes. That."

The phrase was intentional. He knew it. And now he saw, she knew it too. They had made love. Not hooked up. Not gotten laid.

Love.

They had made love. It was different from all the rest.

He was about to kiss her when the phone rang. Without taking her eyes from him, Kat lifted the receiver.

"Yes?"

He watched the color drain from her face as quickly as water drains from a tub.

"When?" It was a whisper.

She waited.

Then, her voice stronger, "Hold on, Joann. I'll be there as fast as I can be. Just hold on, honey."

Kat dropped the phone onto the tile floor. She turned and ran into the apartment, tossing the chocolate-covered skewer in the sink as she passed.

He followed, reaching her as she grabbed her

handbag off her dresser. Whirling her to face him, he asked, "What happened?"

Tears streamed from her eyes. "Jena Rose. My God—Jake, she's missing!"

Chapter 60

"There's no way to outrun a creep."
                                                    ~Lola Delaney

The New York State Thruway had its tricky spots, where troopers hid behind signs or among brush along the median, but Jake didn't care if he got caught speeding. He put his big white Blazer in the left lane, hit eighty and kept his foot down. Occasionally he glanced to his right.

The woman in his passenger seat looked small against the wide leather. He'd fastened her safety belt but almost wished he hadn't. He was sure they'd both feel calmer if her body was right beside his and his arm was around her shoulders.

But Kat counted on him getting her to Brooklyn in one piece, so he kept his hands on the wheel. He watched her every chance he got, just to make sure she was still holding up. She was. For now. Maybe when this was behind them, he'd have chances to hold her close. And if she refused him that privilege, he'd deal with it. For now, his only mission was moving fast.

Seven hours between places was a helluva lot when a child's life was at stake. Taking a plane had crossed his mind, but the airport schedule between the Adirondacks and LaGuardia didn't suit the get-there-now mindset she had. And he couldn't blame her.

Her car, without air conditioning, was an option, as was his Jeep, but both seemed impractical.

A shocked expression when he'd pulled up to the curb to pick her up in the luxury vehicle. He hadn't taken it out of the garage once since he'd come home to New York. Texas license plates still hung on its bumpers.

His old life. The new life. And the one he saw his present life turning into. All so different, but each one important in its own way. Every facet of these past years—even the God-awful times—had been a lesson. It'd taken him a while to learn anything, but things were finally starting to sink in.

Kat.

He shot a sideways look. She held a photo of her goddaughter like it was the rope that would pull her out of a raging river.

It probably felt that way for her.

She'd spent the first hour of their drive with tears sliding down her cheeks. After a while, they had stopped, replaced by contemplative silence. Miles rolled by beneath the wide tires, but she didn't speak and he didn't, either. Respecting her right to ponder what lay ahead of her, or to pray for her godchild's safety, was far more important than filling the minutes with mindless chatter.

She broke the silence just past the halfway point.

"You didn't have to come with me."

"I want to come with you." How could she think he'd let her go alone? No one should face something like this without support. He shot her a fast smile. "I've got your back, Kat."

An unladylike snort. He didn't expect it, so he

asked, "What's the meaning of that? Hmm?"

She smiled, but only slightly. "My front. You've usually got my front, remember?"

The teasing came naturally between them. It was one of the best parts of being with her.

"How could I forget something like that? I mean, you haven't forgotten my front, have you?"

A tiny giggle. Then, she shook her head. "That's a loaded question if I ever heard one. I'm not answering." Her tone changed. "But seriously, you didn't have to come with me."

"I told you. I want to be with you. I want to see your goddaughter come home to her mom and grandmother."

"She will come home, don't you think?"

"Definitely. This is going to be cleared up. You've got to have faith, remember? That's what you told me when we met—that you have faith in yourself so others will, too. Now, have faith in Jena Rose's coming home. Don't give up on her."

Before they'd left, there had been two more frantic calls from the child's mother. Kat had calmed the distraught woman. There was no sign of the little girl. The police had been called, but no one had any information. Yet. There had to be something positive soon.

"This must be torture for you."

"It's no picnic for anybody. Knowing that child is missing is hard—and I haven't even met her yet. I can only imagine what this is doing to you. And Joann? God only knows."

She faced him. "You don't even like kids."

The vehicle swerved when he turned to look at her.

He straightened them out, putting his eyes back on the road. Words were hard to come by.

"How can you say that?" He fought to keep his voice calm, to hide the shock her statement brought. "What gave you that idea? I never said I don't like kids."

"You don't have to hide it. I can see where you're coming from. A guy with no commitments, nothing to tie him down. No one depending on him. Except, maybe, the condom companies. They must depend on the revenue your rabid condom use brings them."

Shit.

So that was the deal.

Just when he thought he was on his way to straightening things out between them, something else came up. Usually, it was his cock. Now, condoms? What the hell?

"I don't use condoms because—"

"You don't owe me any explanations." She looked at the scenery passing outside. "Your business is your own."

"My business is…" *Son of a bitch.* She was one hardheaded woman. One gorgeous, brilliant, sexy hardheaded woman.

He concentrated on driving. His thoughts refused cooperate, leaving him no option other than silence. For now.

Chapter 61

"Screw the tortoise. Better to be the hare sometimes!" ~Lola Delaney

The miles couldn't pass quickly enough. Having a jet engine under the hood and rocket fuel in the gas tank so they could soar over congested lanes of traffic would have suited her better than this stop-and-go agony. Jake had kept them just under the radar all the way, miraculously avoiding a meet-and-greet with any state troopers, but now that they were nearing the city, there was no opportunity to speed.

For what felt like the billionth time, a car cut ahead of them. He braked and narrowly avoided clipping the Buick's rear bumper.

"You idiot," she muttered. It was the first thing either of them had said in hours. In the darkness, she felt his gaze on her so she turned and gave him an apologetic shrug. Pointing to the car in front, she said, "I meant him, not you."

"Glad to hear it."

He looked exhausted. They'd driven through the day and into the night. Around them, headlight glare reflected off signs and chrome. The approach to the bridge, with its bright lights, felt harsh on her weary eyes. She could only imagine how his felt.

Never once, during the entire breakneck trip, had

he complained. About anything. Part of her felt as if she'd dragged him into her mess but the other side of her brain, and even her heart, knew he hadn't protested so did it count? Really, could someone be pulled into a situation if they went without resisting? She didn't think so. Still, the vortex of her life blew her neat, compartmentalized, tidy way of organizing everything around her to bits.

How and why.

Driving up to Mill Pond, her mantra had been *horizons and experiences.* Now, it was *how and why.* Much less exhilarating than the first—which had been only a few days ago. Astounding that time passed in a heartbeat, that a life could change so radically, and a new reality could claim someone.

Pondering the how and why of it all only gave her a headache. A big one. She'd tried closing her eyes but the pain swelled, probably spurred on by a slight case of motion sickness. The handful of cashews she'd eaten wasn't enough to sustain her but every time he offered to stop she refused. All she wanted was to get to Joann and find Jena Rose. Nothing else mattered.

No one else, either.

Oh, God, what if someone hurt her sweet goddaughter? What if, even now—*no!* She couldn't think those thoughts, couldn't even let them into their world. No, the child had to be okay.

And, come hell or high water, whoever was responsible for taking her would pay. There was no doubt in her mind that someone had snatched the little girl. Jena Rose would never, ever willingly wander from her mother or grandmother. *Never.* So, it left only one logical explanation.

She was ready to kill anyone who hurt that child. Kill them.

"This is only the bottleneck leading up to the tolls. The bridge itself isn't as congested." He maneuvered them into a toll line. They were all long, but he chose the shortest one in their range. It crept along, agonizingly slow.

Kat clutched Jena Rose's photo so tightly her fingernails left half-moons in her palm. "Almost there." He turned and touched her, putting a hand on her left knee. Air conditioning kept them comfortable but his hand was warm. "How are you holding up? Are you doing okay?"

"As okay as I can be. Thanks for asking. You? I feel like a wimp, not trying to share the driving with you. It didn't occur to me until just a few miles back. I'm sorry."

"You've got a lot on your plate. Give yourself some slack. I don't mind driving. Actually, I like it. When I lived in Texas, I spent a lot of my weekends driving through the canyons, looking at miles and miles of steer and endless cactus. It's one of my mental getaway techniques. The way you make candy, I drive."

"Got it. And you fish, too. Right?"

"You've had your ear on the local grapevine."

"Hard to miss hearing about the guy who took the prize for winning the annual fish tournament two years running. You caught the biggest…ah, what is it called? You got the heaviest Shitty, right?"

He shook his head, moving the SUV forward a car length. Then, he faced her in the darkness, his eyes twinkling and a huge grin plastered across his face. "The fish is called a Crappie. And yes, I did snag the biggest fish award these past two years. I won once before I left for Texas, too. Just love to fish." He paused. "We still haven't gotten a pole—ah, a fishing pole in your hands yet. Do you think you'd still like to try it?"

Who could tell? Committing to anything at this point was a risk so she semi-committed.

"Maybe someday."

"Fair enough."

They reached the tollbooth. Jake handed the man in the small cubicle cash, waited for the bar to lift, then drove onto the George Washington Bridge. Lights from apartments, skyscrapers, and cars twinkled in the distance. Ahead of them, a necklace of tail lights in each lane. He pulled into traffic, hugging the right lane closest to the water. The view was best in the slow lane, so she didn't mind his choosing it. None of the lanes, not even the far left lane, moved quickly on the bridge. New Yorkers knew when to slow down.

"Why did you leave Texas? It sounds like you had a great life there. Big city. Culture. I'm sure you had women hanging all over you. A powerful job. You must have had it made. Why return to a tiny town in the middle of nowhere? Especially a place that's suffering an economic slump. Why?"

He kept his eyes straight ahead. "So, you've been talking to the locals?" The light tone was gone.

"I'm a local now, too."

It was a stretch but he didn't argue.

"Hasn't anyone told you what happened? Why I came back? Bought a house, settled in and became my uncle's handyman? No one's spilled that juicy bit of information?"

"If they had, I wouldn't be asking." Agitating him while they were just a few feet from the bridge's guardrail wasn't the brightest plan. But she hadn't known when she asked that the subject was such a sore spot. "Forget I asked. I shouldn't have pried. Your life is your business, not mine. I'm sorry."

She looked out the window at the lights. Every minute brought them closer to finding Jena Rose. That should be her focus. Not bothering a man who, after this trip, probably wouldn't be involved in her life.

"Listen, you're going to find out sooner or later. It's best if I tell you. Your opinion of me will change, but that's nothing I can help." He drew in a breath, then let it out slowly before he spoke again. "You've got it pretty much right about Texas. It was great. I loved my job, and everything about the place. Before I became Uncle Gordon's fix-it guy, I was a mechanical engineer. I worked with a small crew on a design for a twin-engine plane. I won't go into details, because they don't matter."

They were near the far side of the bridge. Everyone jockeyed for position, choosing lanes and generally snarling—then unsnarling—traffic.

"All that matters is this: I was to blame for three people dying. It was part my design, and I knew it had problems. I tried to implement changes, but the company wouldn't hear of it. So, three people aren't alive today because of me. I'm responsible for that. And after the accident I couldn't stay with the company. They wanted me to—the other guys from the team are still there—but I couldn't do it. Not after what happened. So, I came home."

Inside she flinched, wondering how one man could

feel so totally responsible for everything. And, evidently, everyone.

He sounded weary. Resigned. As if opening the vault on his secrets was painful.

"You tried to make changes."

"Trying isn't enough. I should have made them listen. And really, did I try hard enough? *Did I?* Can I say to those families whose lives are shattered I tried but failed?" He smacked a palm against the steering wheel. Even the darkness couldn't hide the man's emotions. "No, I'm accountable. And I can't ever be responsible for anyone's life again. Just my own, because God knows I can't screw it up any more than I already have."

His hands gripped the steering wheel so tight his knuckles were white. They'd gotten off the bridge. Every intersection traffic light gave him the chance to stomp on the brakes, so their seat belts held them as he made his way to the Belt Parkway. She waited until he made the connection. Traffic leading into Brooklyn wasn't a closed-eyes negotiation any hour of the day. She'd done it so often it didn't intimidate her. Before they left, she hadn't asked if he was familiar with city driving but he didn't seem put off by it.

Expert fisherman. Brilliant engineer. Family orientated. Bathing suit top rescuer. Proponent of safe sex. Racecar driver's instinct.

Yeah, and ready to leap tall buildings in a single bound.

A mental tally of his attributes put him in the superhero category.

Even with stress etched on his handsome features, he looked infallible. He handled the huge vehicle with ease, bringing them closer to their destination with single-minded determination.

He'd dropped everything to come with her. It wasn't a sacrifice a self-centered, careless man responsible for killing people would make.

"You can't carry the burden forever. I know you think it's all yours, but there's got to be more to the story." She reached across and put a hand on his thigh. No sexual connotation, just reassurance of the faith she had in him. He didn't look at her, so she rubbed her hand on his jeans, making what she hoped was a comforting connection. "Were there inquiries? An investigation after the accident?"

"Several, both internally and by the police."

"What conclusions were drawn?" She held her breath for a second. "Were there any charges made?"

"None." Jake closed his eyes, just for an instant, and shook his head. "They all said it was an accident. But still—three people are dead. Don't you understand? I contributed to that. Those people counted on me, and I let them down. Now, they're dead. There's no going back to fix it, damn it!"

They were getting close to Joann's apartment. The time for in-depth discussions was over.

She pointed at the next light. "Turn right there. Then, up four blocks and make a left."

He stopped at the red light. He put his hand over hers on his leg. Meeting her gaze in the glow of the streetlights, he said, "Now you know my dirty little secret. I'm not the man you thought I was, am I?"

Chapter 62

"A lady's lipstick should be smudged by a man, not by sadness." ~Lola Delaney

Jake looked shocked when she pointed at the Mobil station on the corner.

"Can we stop?"

"I thought we were just around the corner."

She nodded as she reached down and grabbed her purse off the floorboards. "We are, but I don't want to get there looking like this. It'll scare Joann."

There was no way to erase all traces of her tears, but blowing her nose and washing her face would make her look as if she wasn't scared senseless. Even if she was.

He pulled into the gas station but bypassed the line at the pumps and parked near the restroom doors.

She pushed the door open before he could shut the engine off. "I'll only be a minute."

"Take your time."

The view of her face in the cracked bathroom mirror above the tiny sink was a relief. She felt worse than she looked. Sure, her eyes were a little bloodshot and her face a bit puffy but it was no match for the agony swirling inside.

It took two minutes to blow her nose on a length of cheap, scratchy toilet paper. Throw cold water on her

293

eyes and dry with another few squares of rough paper.

She took a second to steel herself for what waited just around the corner. Joann must be out of her mind. And Juanita? She was an elderly woman; this had to be the worst night of her life.

She prayed she would be able to stay strong, whatever happened.

The door was heavy, but she pulled so hard it crashed against the grimy, tiled bathroom wall. She went out into the sticky night, breathing in the smell of the city. It was different from country air, less crisp and with a heaviness all its own.

The pay phone hung from the wall. Even though their destination was just blocks away, she lifted the greasy receiver and dropped a quarter from her pocket into the slot. She dialed, willing the clicks to hurry.

"Hello?"

"Joann, it's me."

"Oh, thank God!" It was a full-on Brooklyn-accent screech. Kat pulled the phone from her head an inch.

Jake opened his door and jumped from the driver's seat. He was around the bumper and at her side almost instantly.

"Joann—Joann—what's going on?" Her hand gripped the black plastic so hard her fingers hurt.

"She's home." A muffled sob, then, "She's here."

"Oh, thank God—is she okay?" Her hand went to her chest, but her beating heart couldn't be stilled.

Before Joann answered, Kat heard the sweet little voice asking for chocolate ice cream in the background. It was relief enough to almost send her to the moon.

Not for the first time, she dropped the phone. It dangled on the metal cord but she didn't give it another thought. She turned and fell into the arms of the man beside her.

Amazing how joy and fright, sorrow and laughter, all brought a woman to tears.

Chapter 63

"Everyone hides something. Not all things should be hidden—that is, unless the truth is dog-butt ugly. Then, keep it covered." ~Lola Delaney

The vehicle was roomy but space was at a premium on the return trip. Neither Jake nor Kat brought anything with them so the whole luggage compartment was available, which was a good thing because two women and a small child necessitated a multitude of bags. They had crammed every inch of the cargo area. Juanita, Joann, and Jena Rose—along with Jellybean— filled the back seat.

Police reports and updates filled the morning. By the time they'd convinced Joann and her mother that a vacation in the country, far from Brooklyn and any possible residual trouble from one of Henry's vindictive friends or, possibly accomplices was a smart move, it was noon. Between packing and stowing luggage, another two hours passed.

Finally on the road in late afternoon, Jake would have liked to speed them home to safety but couldn't justify taking a chance, especially with no emergency to dash to and a small child in his back seat. So, he kept to the speed limit.

He glanced at Kat. She half-turned, her hips swiveled to facilitate conversation. Her placid demeanor was restored as soon as she'd reunited with her friends last night.

Friends? The three women and Jena Rose were family. A very tight-knit family who loved each other dearly. There had been so many hugs, some tears but mostly laughter. Astonishing to see Kat in her element, at home on the city streets.

No one mentioned the kidnapping in front of the little girl. The police had sent a child psychologist who advised they let her bring up the topic. Or not, it was her choice.

They also didn't speak about the fire on Kat's patio or Henry's threatening to make her recant. And they definitely didn't mention that Henry and his new girlfriend, the one who'd lured Jena Rose from the swing set at the park, were behind bars. Probably for a long time. There would be court appearances and depositions, but no one talked about that, either. For now, it was enough that everyone was safe. And, he was taking them home.

"Jellybean will like your house, Aunt Kat." Jena Rose sounded sleepy but the excitement of seeing her beloved godmother, meeting Jake, and going on a long ride kept her eyes open.

"I hope so." Kat reached through the seats and patted one pink sneaker. "I hope you like it, too."

A big yawn. "I will."

He glanced in his rear view mirror, watching as one small fist drilled into Jena Rose's eye. She pushed her bangs off her forehead and settled comfortably into the crook of her mother's arm. God, but she was adorable!

"I'll like it better than the place the lady took me.

She said there'd be swings but she lied. No swings. Only a sandbox."

No one said a word for a long moment.

"You didn't like the sandbox?" Joann's voice didn't waver.

He had to hand it to her. By the time they'd arrived at the apartment, Jena Rose was bathed and tucked into bed. Even with her daughter out of earshot, she held her composure. And if she'd cried during the night, he didn't hear her. He'd slept on the living room sofa, where he heard Kat's voice mingling with Joann's for a long time, but there hadn't been sounds of weeping. A mother's strength was a miraculous thing to witness.

"Nope. Don't like sand. Gets in my sneakers and makes my toes itchy." Another yawn. "Do you have swings, Aunt Kat? At your house?"

"Sorry, chickpea, I don't. There is a park, though."

Jake bought his house from a doctor who had four kids. It left him with plenty of bedrooms, a huge yard, and a swing set. As a bonus, a playhouse nestled beneath a grove of poplars.

"I do." Dusk had fallen and the first touch of darkness surrounded them but he saw the delight in the child's eyes in the light in his mirror. It was cast by the sun setting behind them, and put the round cheeks, bow-shaped mouth, and brown curls in a pinkish glow.

"At your house? Swings?" She perked right up. "Mama, can I go to Jake's house? To swing?"

A noncommittal reply, a Mommy standard. "We'll see. Now, why don't you snuggle in and close your eyes? I promise, we'll wake you if we see a moose."

"Promise?"

"Mmm hmm…"

Chapter 64

"Life hands enough hard moments. Don't accept any that aren't yours." ~Lola Delaney

Joann stroked the hair on her sleeping daughter's head. "Are you sure you've got room for us?"

"Of course I do." Kat replied, keeping her voice low so she didn't wake the little one.

"I should have stayed home." Juanita held herself accountable for the kidnapping. When she rummaged in her bag for some money to buy ice cream for her granddaughter from a street vendor, Henry's girlfriend saw an opportunity—and took it.

If the abduction hadn't been at the park, it would have been elsewhere. Henry's sole purpose, to frighten Kat into backing down, wouldn't let him stop before achieving his goal.

"Don't you dare say that again." Kat turned in her seat. "You are not responsible for what happened. You take good care of her—don't you forget that. She loves you, and this would have happened regardless of who was with her. And if anyone's responsible for what happened, it's me."

"Don't say that." Joann placed a hand on Kat's shoulder. "It's not true."

"No, it's not your fault," Juanita added.

"Oh, it is. If I hadn't brought Henry into our lives,

hadn't gotten involved with him, we wouldn't be having this conversation. It's my fault. I'm responsible, and I'm so very sorry I've done this. We could have lost—" Her voice hitched.

"We didn't." Joann shook her head. "Don't even think about what could have happened. Remember what did happen. And be grateful, that's all."

"Amen." Juanita made the sign of the cross. Then, she put her head against the headrest and closed her eyes.

Jake waited until Joann leaned back as well. She, too, shut her eyes and relaxed.

After a few miles, he and Kat were the only two awake. There was so much he wanted to say to her. So many questions worked on his mind. Mostly, he wanted to hold her close, to touch her and feel her against him. He wanted to taste her lips, smell her hair and fall into the wonder of her embrace.

But wanting and having were worlds apart. Now that she knew what he'd done, how horrific his past sins were, he doubted she'd ever let him touch her again. And who could blame her? He was poison.

Her face showed the emotions she held tight. The dashboard's glow illuminated her drawn brow. Her lower lip, the one he loved to kiss, was caught between her teeth. She stared at the road ahead of them, but he knew she didn't see it. Her mind was far away.

"Hey, are you all right?"

"As all right as I can be, I guess. God, Jake, I'm still shaking. I don't know how Joann stood the terror of thinking—I can't even say it."

"Don't dwell on what could have happened. She's right. We've got to be grateful for what did happen."

Terrible thoughts of what might have happened to the happy child had occurred to him, too. Hell, every one of them, the police included, shared the same fears.

Before they left Mill Pond, Tom had all but spelled out—as if he needed to do so just to be sure Jake could handle whatever happened—what monsters did with young girls. He'd passed on the grim statistics on finding her at all.

Torturing themselves couldn't help Jena Rose. And that, he was sure, was the most pressing need. It would kill Kat to watch her goddaughter grow up with emotional scars from the past twenty-four hours. Whatever he had to do to help make sure that didn't happen was what he was willing to do. Even if it meant tightening the bolts on the swing set in his yard and cleaning out the playhouse.

"Oh, God, I'm grateful. But still, I can't help it." She wiped a tear from her cheek. Her sorrow was a knife to his heart. "I brought this into our lives. I'm responsible."

"There's no way you could have known what a bastard Henry is, or what he would do in his life that would affect yours so drastically. And if you could have changed it, you would have. Wouldn't you?"

"You know I would have. But I didn't know what was going to happen…"

"See? You can't beat yourself up over something that was basically out of your hands. It's not fair to anyone, especially you, to let this event control your life. Think about it. You know I'm right."

She remained silent for a long time. Darkness deepened around them and the distance to home shortened. Every now and then a small snore emanated from behind them. Otherwise, just the swoosh of tires on pavement and the hum of air-conditioning surrounded them.

Finally, she turned toward him. "You're right. I can't let my mistakes dictate my life. I get it, and I know I didn't mean for any of this to happen. So, no, I can't be consumed by a lapse of judgment." She paused. "You're right. But, really, isn't that the pot calling the kettle black?"

Chapter 65

"Home is where you make it." ~*Lola Delaney*

A short time ago Kat would never have believed she'd be relieved to finally reach Mill Pond. She'd changed so much that the woman she was now was a huge leap from the one she'd been then.

Those days, when her neat little world began to crumble, were an awful memory. But the bitterness of finding herself living with a liar, unhappy but willing to settle, was beginning to fade. Maybe just knowing Henry wouldn't get the chance to deceive anyone else for a long time—if ever again—was enough to begin to close the door on the past weeks. She hoped so. Being trapped in the past wasn't something she planned to do.

Jake pulled up to the curb in front of the dark shop. The back seat riders were still sleeping, so they sat in silence. The ticking of the cooling engine seemed loud.

She stared at the wide, empty façade windows. They would change, too. Window dressings, something bright and inviting, would make the exterior look less forlorn. The door, with its ornery latch and shaky glass, would get repaired. She'd keep the latch in place, a reminder of the morning she'd forced her way from her old life into her new.

She couldn't help herself. She grinned, remembering how hard she'd tried to open the door.

Jake made it look simple, the way he did with so many things.

Thank you. And goodbye.

Putting it off wasn't going to make it any less difficult.

The Brooklyn trip didn't dispel the facts. He wanted one thing and she another. They were wasting time, messing around with each other when their goals were so clearly divergent.

"We should go in. Thanks for everything, Jake. I appreciate the way you rescued me—yet again."

He opened his mouth. Hesitated. Then, closed it.

Two days' worth of stubble made him look sexier than usual. Dangerous—in a titillating way. Running her tongue along his jaw line crossed her mind but she squelched the thought. No more friends who had sex, remember?

Damn the unbridled lust just looking at him brought out in her. And double damn the deeper feelings, more powerful, even, that she forced from her mind.

He opened the door. The dome light went on but he put a hand over it, flicked the switch on the side and returned the vehicle to darkness. "No reason to wake them up yet. Let me grab the stuff."

He closed his door so gently she didn't even hear it latch.

Considerate. Sexy. Intelligent.

Off limits.

She helped bring in the endless stream of baggage. They took it all up to the apartment, where she separated Joann and Jena Rose's things into one pile in the bigger bedroom her aunt had used and Juanita's belongings into her bedroom. She grabbed her pajamas, one pillow, and a granny-square afghan from the hall closet and dumped it all on the sofa.

Jake raised an eyebrow when he saw her stuff on the hideous green sofa.

"Are you sure there's enough room here for all of you? The motel's right across the street. I'm sure we could work out something to give you all more space."

Attila wound around her ankles, meowing a welcome. She picked her up, held her close, and rubbed her cheek in the kitten's fur. "We'll be fine, once we get things figured out."

"Can I do anything to help?"

Lock the door, throw me down. and make wild crazy love with me?

"You've already done it, thanks." Attila leaped gracefully from her arms onto the sofa. She walked across the afghan, curled into a ball, and closed her eyes. No need to wonder about her sleeping arrangements. "We should go wake them."

Wordlessly, he followed her downstairs and through the shop. When they passed the shelf where they'd nearly ripped each other's clothes off she kept her gaze forward. While she ignored the space, her body remembered.

To go back to the night when the fire alarm rang and they were hot for each other—the stuff dreams were made of. Reality, with its annoying truths and inconveniences was nothing by comparison.

The women were already awake when they returned. Juanita, travel rumpled and yawning, looked around at the deserted street as if she'd stepped into an alternate universe.

Jake waved a hand. "Don't worry. It livens up during the day."

"I hope so." She didn't look convinced but she wasn't immune to his charm. She pushed a hand through her hair, patting the curls into place as she smiled. "I'll take your word for it, Jake."

Great. Now Joann's mother had hot pants for him, too. As if life wasn't interesting enough?

"Welcome home." Kat hugged Joann before she nudged her friend to the sidewalk. "I'll get our angel."

Jake appeared behind her when she leaned in to unbuckle Jena Rose's seatbelt. His hips brushed her ass. Despite her weariness, his touch sent a ping to her core. Inhaling sharply, she froze. The feel of him against her was almost too much to bear.

The devil pushed her to press herself against him, but for once she sent Satan packing. Smooshing herself onto a man after their relationship was over was wrong. Inviting, yes. Nipple-hardening, definitely. But, still— wrong.

He put his hands on her shoulders and she stepped sideways.

"Let me get her." The intimate tone reminded her of how he sounded when they were joined, when he touched her sweet spots and cajoled her orgasm to join his.

"But you don't like children."

He already had Jena Rose. Her arms dangled over his shoulders and her cheek rested against his neck. He held the girl close, cradling her against his chest. The picture would have been perfect if he wasn't scowling.

"I love children." He took two slow steps toward the shop doorway before he stopped. For a second, he didn't move. Then, he turned and said, "You really don't know me at all, do you?"

She stared at him, wishing for the chance to trade places with her goddaughter. If only for a heartbeat, to press herself against him and feel his strong arms around her.

If only...

It was too late for that.

Sadly, she shook her head. "No. I guess I don't."

Chapter 66

"Doors open. Door close. Sometimes closed doors refuse to reopen. And open ones? Well, sometimes they won't close." ~Lola Delaney

Seven days is forever when you spend every single minute kicking yourself in the ass. Jake couldn't stand himself, but there was no escape. Even when he hated his own company there was no way to change it out.

Living with himself sucked. Big time.

The good part of ass-kicking was that it made him move. Renovations on the motel were going at warp speed. Four bathrooms had been gutted and had new fixtures. He'd tiled two already and was working the other two in tandem, going from shower stalls to floors in rotation so he could simultaneously grout and polish.

Lake Placid's tourism push had begun in earnest. Fliers and posters mentioned Mill Pond as an overflow venue and attraction in its own right. Already winter reservations were coming in. At first they were a slow trickle, but the tourism bureau's ad space in a Manhattan winter travel guide had brought a substantial increase in interest. Not just for the Tip-A-Canoe Motel, but for the other businesses as well. All in all, a damn good deal—one he was proud of brokering.

But it put stress on his plans to renovate the motel. Eventual had turned instant. It would stink if he couldn't fill reservation requests because he hadn't shaped up the rooms. So he worked, almost around the clock most days, and the place showed it.

His bloodshot eyes showed it, too. And his pissy attitude. And the growl that replaced his normal speaking voice.

A shit mood all around. And yeah, he knew where it originated. Knowing and doing something weren't the same thing, however.

Kat knew the truth about him now, and he couldn't change it. Losing the only woman he could ever seriously consider spending forever with because he'd been irresponsible years ago was cruel punishment.

No way was he going to sit and cry in his beer, though. It wouldn't solve a thing, and if there was one commitment he planned to keep it was to move forward without being shackled by his past. So, he tiled his ass off and avoided speaking with anyone.

Anyone, that is, who would take no for an answer. Tom wasn't frightened by his nasty mood. He had been popping in during his off hours to annoy him.

Jake let him come for two reasons. One, telling a brother to go to hell wasn't worth the hard feelings. Two, there was no keeping him away.

When Kathy died, Tom had gone into a shell and refused to see anyone. He got drunk. Threw things. Railed at the universe for taking his heart from his chest. He pushed the world away—but Jake went to him anyway. He popped in, the way Tom was doing now. Even if Tom had thrown his ass out, told him to go to hell and stay away, it wouldn't have mattered. He'd have gone back. Again and again—because that's what brothers did. So he let Tom come, but it didn't mean he was happy to see him.

When he heard the familiar voice, he wasn't at all surprised. Their police force was a small one, but the rotation allowed every officer two days off each week. Today was Tuesday, and Tuesday meant Tom didn't report to the station. Usually he showed up with coffee on his mornings off. Today there was no coffee. And it was well past lunchtime.

"Are you still messing around with that tile? Jesus, you work slower than a turtle on tranquilizers." Tom squatted in the open doorway, his denim shorts hiked high on muscular thighs. He pointed to the corner, where there were no tiles. "What about that? You going to leave that spot or what?"

Notoriously good on the firing range, at the wheel of a car, and wielding the oars on a canoe, the cop stunk at home improvements. He had ideas about things but experience and how-to weren't strong points.

Each tile got a tiny twist when placed on the adhesive layer. Jake twisted, then squared, the tile in his hands. He placed rubber X markers in the corners where the tile met the ones in adjacent rows. Then, he sat back on his heels. Almost done, thank God. His knees felt like they'd been smashed with a pile driver and his back felt permanently hunched.

Straightening his spine, he shook his head. "How can you be so clueless about stuff like this? Seriously, there might come a time when you should know the corners and edges need to be measured and cut. I'm putting in the whole tiles first, then I'll go back and fit the pieces. Once it's grouted and sealed, no one will know how the tiles went down, and I'll save all the tedious work for one session." He turned to face his friend, who grinned despite his growl. "Shit. What the hell are you going to do if you need to replace your bathroom floor?"

"No problem. I'll call you. So, how close are you to finishing up here?"

A sparkle in Tom's eyes caught his attention. Since Kathy's death, the man's demeanor was all-business, all-serious, all the time. Now? Not so much.

"What's got you looking so chipper?" He wiped his hands on the legs of his jeans. He poked a bit of mastic from one thumb and waited. Sooner or later Tom would have to say something—he looked like he was ready to burst. "Really, what's up? You win last night's lottery?"

"Nothing like that." His grin grew. "It's nothing I can put my finger on, really. Just happy, I guess." He sobered, but the sparkle remained. "It's been a long time since I felt this good. I didn't think it was possible after—well, you know. After."

He didn't want to hear the words, the reminder of their pain, any more than Tom did, so he nodded his understanding. He hadn't thought it possible for Tom to look this peaceful again. Whatever the cause of it, it was good by him. So many times he'd worried his buddy would never smile again.

"I hear you. You're not using too much gun cleaning fluid when you shine your pistols, are you? Not breathing in too deep without the windows open, getting yourself high on fumes?"

"Don't be an idiot. Of course I'm not—I'm not high on anything. Just content. Not that I'd expect you to understand how that feels, you miserable pain in the ass."

"Yeah, I'm a screw. So what?"

"So you're making everyone around you feel like crap. I saw Aunt Pat outside. She's telling Clarence how much she'll miss him. And I heard her tell the duck to run if you come at him with a fork and knife. Any validity to her fears?" He poked him in the shoulder, just the way he'd done when they were kids. Despite himself, Jake grinned.

"Yeah, watch out. I'm thinking duck would make a good addition to the complimentary breakfast buffet. What do you think? Duck pancakes? Quack-quack muffins? Scrambled duck?"

Tom winced. "Disgusting. Don't let her hear you say that—or she won't leave at all. Uncle Gordon will have your head on the breakfast tray if he misses the chance to go to the land of peaches and honey. You know he's been planning this getaway forever."

He hadn't. He hated it that he'd been so self-absorbed that he didn't know Uncle Gordon wanted to retire and move. It never occurred to him, but now it made sense. The winters were harsh, and his uncle wasn't young, and running a motel—even a down-on-its-luck motel—required a lot of stamina.

"I wish he'd said something sooner. I would've tried to help him get down south before now." He held his hands out, palms up. "I just didn't know."

Tom sighed. "You've both been so careful not to squash each other's toes for so long. He wanted to let you do what you wanted most, to live in a big city and be—and these are his words, not mine—a 'brilliant engineer' with huge prospects. They didn't want to tie you down to our small town, not if it's not what you want. And you figured they loved this place, right? You had no idea they wanted out. How could you?"

Finally their lives were all on the same page. He had no desire to leave Mill Pond. Now that tourism statistics were on the rise, the world was coming to them, anyhow. And his aunt and uncle could leave their dream in his hands, knowing he was finally ready to settle down. All good, right?

Then how come he felt like such shit?

Chapter 67

"Don't fall for the newfangled crap women's magazines try to feed you. The best way to a man's heart is still through his stomach." ~Lola Delaney

Over the chemical smell of floor compound, a sweet scent made its way to his nostrils. He sniffed, leaning forward. He sniffed again. Definitely not tile cement.

"What've you been doing? You smell funny."

"Funny? That's no way to speak to a guy, especially one who came to see if you need any help. Damn, Jake, I just might go off in a huff now."

They both knew there would be no huffing.

"What's the smell?" His stomach rumbled. He'd been working all day. No lunch break. No breaks of any kind. Damn, he was hungry—and sniffing Tom was making him hungrier. Scary, but true.

"Okay, you got me. Cookies. I smell like cookies." He sniffed his armpit and gave a snort. "Could be worse. I could smell like you, all sweat and tile crap."

He let the last part pass.

"Where'd you get the cookies?"

He didn't know how he knew, but suddenly, he did.

The sparkle. The grin. The good humor. And the damn cookies. They all had to have something to do with the women across the street.

"You know where." Tom grinned like the Cheshire Cat.

"Don't mess with me, man. Where'd you get the cookie perfume?"

Tom tilted his chin toward the street. It didn't matter there were walls and rooms between them and the object of his gesture. They both knew what he meant.

"Joann knows her way around a kitchen." A subtle change came over his features when he said the words.

Someone who didn't know the usually serious police chief would have missed the flash, but he knew him better. It struck him hard, the sudden knowledge that Tom might be—surely was, by the look in his eyes—moving on after losing Kathy. It was good, because he deserved happiness. But it stung, too. They had been the ideal couple, totally in love and committed to spending eternity together. Jake never thought he'd see the day when that bond might shake, but here it was.

Cut through the games. "You like her, don't you?"

His head moved slowly but it was a definite nod. "Yeah. I do."

"I'm glad. It's all right to feel something for someone else." He put a hand on his friend's shoulder and gave him a man-to-man encouraging squeeze. "Kathy would want this, you know. She would."

Tom's eyes had a sheen on them when he met his gaze. "I think she would. I hope she would. Jake, I really hope I'm not hurting her with this."

When it looked like sadness might overtake him, Jake turned the squeeze into a casual shoulder slap.

"Of course you're not! Don't over think it." He met and held his best friend's gaze, drilling his words into the other man and hoping to soothe his heart. "It's cookies, that's all. There's nothing to feel weird about. You're just tasting her cookies." He paused, raised an eyebrow and asked, "That is all you're tasting, isn't it?"

Tom shrugged.

Jake shook him. "Come on, don't hold out on me. You're just tasting cookies, right?"

Tom pushed the hand off his shoulder, chuckling. "For now, that's all. But later—who knows?"

Chapter 68

"The only difference between sweet and sour is the taste." *~Lola Delaney*

Kat's life changed more in one week than it had in years. Of course, that excluded the past six months.

Nothing was as life-changing as finding out you lived with a thief, had to move somewhere you'd only visited through scraps of shared memories, and falling in love with a man who completely didn't do love.

Yeah, she'd admitted—only to herself, with no plans to include anyone else on the discovery—her feelings for Jake were more than platonic. Way more. And they far exceeded the bedroom, although there were no complaints on that score. Other than she wasn't ever going to be naked—in the bedroom or anyone else—with him again which just plain—

Shit.

What had she done? Falling in love was supposed to be all about magic. Glitter. Romance. Moonlight, damn it.

The only moonlight she saw was through the kitchen window when insomnia struck and she stirred pecans and chocolate with as much gusto as she used to fondle Jake's goodies. Damn, but love bit the big one.

Big time.

Still, there was a silver lining. She wasn't alone

anymore, was she? Her nearest and dearest were with her, and they all planned to make it a permanent situation.

Last night's candy-making binge cluttered the Formica countertop. She knew she should pick it up and freeze most of it but she didn't have the energy. Bone weary—she was as tired today as she had been the day she'd met Jake in the swimming pool.

That damn swimming pool filter. It had started this mess, it had been the one to eat—

Who was she kidding? The pool filter deserved a medal, bringing them together the way it had. Their affair was short but it was the best thing that she'd experienced. Thank God for the filter.

"Damn it." Her elbows on the kitchen table held her hands up, and she dropped her head into her palms and closed her eyes. "Double damn."

"No swearing, remember? Not around my baby. We don't want her mouth to be as dirty as her aunt's, do we?" Joann sat on the chair across from her and put her own elbows on the table. She looked luminous, olive skin glowing and the smile on her face dazzling in its intensity. No one could have guessed that she'd just survived the worst day of her life, and only a week ago. "Really, Kat, you can be a shitty influence when you want to be, damn it."

Joann never swore near her daughter.

"Where's the kid?"

"At the park with Meri and my mother. She loves feeding the ducks but isn't impressed with the swings. She wants to know when she can go see Jake's toys." She meant to rile her, wiggling one suggestive eyebrow. "What about you? When are you going to play on his equipment?"

"Never."

Meri showed up six days ago. When Kat hadn't called her back after hanging up on her, the French ingénue got a trans-Atlantic flight and made her way to their doorstep. It was exciting having a cousin, especially one so cool, sophisticated, and adventurous. Her black curls, svelte figure, and fast smile made her a sensation around town, but the one she'd really been the belle of the ball with was with Jena Rose.

The child adored her, and insisted Meri accompany her everywhere. She'd learned Frere Jacques. Her Brooklyn accent gave the song a whole new level of cuteness.

The family had grown. The apartment was filled to bursting. And Kat was happy. With some things. Others? Not so much, but she was trying to accept the things she couldn't change.

She pushed to her feet and went to the cupboard. Grabbing an orange Tupperware container, circa mid-seventies, she started to pile the haystacks she'd made at three a.m. "My time with the man's equipment is, I'm sorry to say, over."

"Are you sure?"

Was she? On her end, no. But he made it plain he didn't want a relationship. He hadn't been over once since they'd gotten back from Brooklyn.

Clearly, his playground was closed.

"Yeah, I am. It was great while it lasted, but he's not a long-term kind of guy, and that's what I want." She sealed the container, turned, and put it in the freezer. Several similar containers lined the back wall. It had been a week of serious insomnia-driven candy-making. She leaned against the counter and met the other woman's gaze. "It's better to be alone than with the wrong person. And even though I thought he might be the right guy…well, he doesn't want the same things I do, and I'm not going to settle anymore."

"He sounds like the biggest bear in the Adirondacks. From what I hear, he's been growling all week."

Tom.

He'd been hanging around Joann like a bumblebee on a marigold. More than once she'd spied them laughing. And he'd charmed Jena Rose, who called him "my Tom".

Meri seemed suspicious of the police chief, but perhaps it was a cultural thing. She had been polite, and laughed at his jokes, but she hadn't warmed to him. Not that it mattered, since Tom only had eyes for Joann.

Chapter 69

"Love makes a woman glow. But then, so does indigestion." ~Lola Delaney

Joann's eyes shimmered in a way they hadn't since before her daughter's birth. Before that, she'd been carefree and, she thought, in love. When she got pregnant, her "true love" dumped her and since then she'd scrambled to provide a stable environment for her child. All the responsibilities didn't leave much room for fun, let alone shimmering eyes.

Kat was happy for her. Tom seemed like a good man, and Joann deserved some happiness. A win-win situation.

"Tom's been giving you the inside scoop?"

A blush turned her cheeks rosy. "He's filled me in."

The devil sat on her shoulder—yet again. "How does he do in the filling in department? Hmm?"

Joann's mouth became an "o" and she shook her head, feigning shock. Years of candid talks—about sex and every other damn thing—made the expression laughable. There was no subject too scandalous between them.

"Ooh, you are bad! How dare you insinuate that Tom and I are doing the nasty?"

She snorted. "Well? Are you?"

The giggle was, surprisingly, girlish. "No, we're not. Not that I'm not tempted to jump him every time I see him in his uniform. But I don't know if he's ready for it. You know he lost his wife to cancer, don't you?"

"I heard that." She swept chocolate crumbs off her hands and into the sink beside her. "But it was years ago, I believe. Maybe he's ready for a new relationship. He sure seems interested in you. And in Jena Rose, definitely."

A sigh, long and shuddering. "I don't know. Some people aren't ever ready for a new love after they lose someone like that. It's not like breaking up, where both parties agree things are over. It's worse, so much worse. Maybe he won't want anyone else."

She crossed the room, knelt in front of Joann and hugged her close. She smoothed the long, thick, straight hair she'd coveted as a child, until the woman in her arms sighed again. This time, the pain and uncertainty was gone from the sound, replaced by acceptance.

Kat pulled back and met the eyes she knew so well.

"Maybe Tom's ready. Are you sure you are, too?"

"I'm just scared, I think. It's so soon, and we've just met, and—"

She stood, waving the protests off with her hand. "And you can think of a million reasons not to get involved with him if you try. But don't be an ass. There's only one reason that matters, and it's in your heart. How you feel about him, that's the thing. The rest doesn't count for shit. Remember that."

She pulled Joann to her feet.

"Come on, let's get out of here. Maybe we can get Meri, your mom, and Jena Rose from the park and go to the diner for dinner. If I eat one more piece of candy,

I'm going to throw up."

"Me, too. But there are cookies. Lots and lots of cookies, if you want."

"Oh, I don't think I can eat another cookie or candy. Seriously, have you decided what the first cookies will be?"

The empty shop was going to become a bakery, with Joann and Juanita making cookies and cakes while the four of them lived in the apartment. It would be tight, but together they could make a new life for everyone. The situation seemed ideal. A few things— like constructing a kitchen in the big back room downstairs—remained to be figured out, but the heart of the matter was solved.

"I think so." Joann had spent the morning baking and smelled like vanilla and chocolate. Her efforts were stowed in big containers on top of the refrigerator. A homeless shelter in Lake Placid had been using them for dessert all week at their soup kitchen. Today's batch still waited to be delivered, but they had time for that, since they wouldn't be needed until tomorrow. "Tom says the snickerdoodles are his favorite. And Jena Rose wants the half moons, of course. Mama says I should stick some crowd favorites, like chocolate chip and oatmeal, on the menu. She's got six varieties of cakes lined up. So, I've just got to choose two more cookies, and we should be set."

Kat smacked her palm against her forehead. She'd almost forgotten the one thing she needed to know before calling a contractor about installing the kitchen. While the others were occupied, this was the time to check the last item off her list.

She'd found a length of yellow rope beneath the

sink. She grabbed it now and headed for the back door. A staircase leading to the attic wound up the back side of the building, with an access door beneath the eaves.

"Where are we going?" Joann followed her up the stairs.

"Tom said something about venting the bakery ovens out through the roof, remember? I think that must mean we've got to have more than one chimney, doesn't it?" She uncurled the rope, tying an end around her waist. The other end she wrapped around the wrought iron staircase railing, tying it with three fat knots. "I'm going to make sure we've got chimneys for the ovens. I don't want Jena Rose to see me on the roof, so let's do it now. Spot me, okay?"

"*Spot you?* Are you crazy?" Joann took the rope but the horror on her face showed she hated the idea.

Kat smiled, despite the herd of African elephants dancing in her stomach. Her fear of heights brought bile to the back of her throat but she swallowed it down. There wasn't anyone else to go up on the roof, was there? And if she was going to live this independent, country lifestyle, she'd have to get used to doing shit like this. Punching cows. Moving moose from the patio. Scaling the roof.

Don't look down.

"Not crazy." She stepped onto the railing. Forced herself to not look down. Then, she crept on her knees onto the sloped roof. "Just saving a buck or two. Why pay a contractor to do this when we can do it? Hold the damn rope. I'm going that way to check the chimney. How many do you think we should have for ovens? Two? Three?"

She crawled away. Roofing pebbles dug into her

palms. Her toes, in running shoes not work boots, curled hard as she crept across the pitched surface. One chimney, at the peak, looked fine. Red bricks, with cement-looking stuff in the cracks between the bricks. They could use that but they needed more than one oven so there should be more than one chimney. Shouldn't there?

Vertigo passed, and she grew more confident with each inch she traversed. Confident, not comfortable. Thank God she hadn't eaten any more candy—or cookies—or she'd be tossing them right now on the hot black surface.

How come birds made it look effortless, walking on rooftops all day long? It was hard. And dirty. And scratchy, too. Her hands felt raw but there was no going back.

"Un-fucking-believable."

Swearing took her mind off the drop just four feet to her left. She'd left the peak behind and descended to a point where two rooflines converged, hoping against hope that just around the bend there would be at least one other chimney. That would make two, and maybe two would be enough.

She heard Joann calling her back, but she was too close to go back. Just a few more feet and she'd be able to see what they already had, so they would know how to budget for what they still needed. Everyone was depending on her to make their dream a reality and she had no intention of letting them down.

"I'm fine," she yelled over her shoulder. It was a lie, but if anyone should be on the roof it was her. Joann had her daughter to consider. She had no one. No one who'd care if she plummeted to the ground and smashed like a bug on a windshield against the sidewalk.

"Stop being an asshole," Kat whispered. She urged her hands forward. The edge of the roof, where it turned and joined the jutting piece that was the shop area, grew closer. Just a few more crawling feet, and she'd be able to see what they had. Just a bit more—

"Shit!"

Her hand slipped and her knees scraped the surface. She slid closer to the edge of the building, scrabbling for something to hold onto but there was nothing to grab.

Her life didn't flash before her eyes, but she nearly wet her pants as she fell off the roof.

"Oh shit—*oh shit*—oh—"

Chapter 70

"There's no feeling like falling in love…"
~Lola Delaney

The scream pierced the air. He and Tom looked at each other for a split second before they followed the sound at a run.

They hit the sidewalk just in time to see a body tumble off the gallery roof. Three stories up, the woman looked like a Barbie doll. But Jake knew it wasn't Barbie. He recognized the voice, the hair, the flash of ass as her shorts rode high when the rope jerked, then held her, swinging over a second-floor balcony.

"No!" His heart stopped beating, then hammered triple time.

"Hold on!" Tom yelled the order in full cop style. "Just hold on, Kat. We're coming for you."

Jake ran across the street, heedless of traffic, and raced inside the building. The stairs between her shop and apartment felt endless. He took them two at a time but it still wasn't quick enough. The balcony, off the spare bedroom, was small. To his knowledge, it hadn't been used in years. He hoped it wasn't rotted, and that she wasn't already lying on the sidewalk below.

He ripped the bedroom door open, ran to the balcony door, and nearly pulled it off its rusted hinges.

Tom put a hand on his shoulder and held him back.

"Hang on. Make sure it's safe."

Kat dangled close enough that if she fell he could grab her, so he put one foot out and tested the worn wooden flooring. It creaked, but held. He took a full step onto it. Tom's fingers wound into the back belt loops on his jeans.

He wrapped his arms around her body. He looked up into her wide eyes and smiled.

"You're okay." He'd feel better when she wasn't hanging over the sidewalk. "I'm going to hold you while you untie the rope."

"I don't think so." She shook her head.

Shit.

She didn't trust him. And who could blame her? She knew he'd been trusted with lives before and they'd been lost. Of course she didn't trust his sorry ass.

This time was different. He was different. And it was Kat's life—he wasn't going to lose her. Not this way.

"Trust me, please. I won't let you fall. But you have to untie the rope. I can't hold you and untie you at the same time, or I would." He smiled again, just to let her know he wasn't worried. Which was a total lie but it worked, because she smiled back. He nodded, tightening his grip on her body. "Okay, untie yourself and fall into my arms."

She shook her head again.

"I can't. I tried, before you got here. The knot is too tight—I can't get it undone." She pulled on the loose end. It had no effect on the knot cutting into her waist. "See? I'm stuck."

Tom released his hold. "You okay?"

"It feels stable. I think it'll hold us, but I can't get

her down without letting her go, and I'm not going to do it."

"Kat!" Joann's voice, behind them, carried all the emotions he was trying to conceal. Love and fear mixed with urgency. The rope could break at any time.

"We've got her." Tom moved to his side and pulled a knife from his back pocket. "I'll cut. You catch. Ready?"

As ready as I'll ever be.

He nodded. "Do it."

Tom stretched and sliced the rope. Kat fell into his arms. He stepped back, fast, before the little balcony had a chance to give under their combined weight.

She slid down, the rope rasping between them. He was dimly aware that Tom embraced Joann near the doorway, but they seemed far away.

Chapter 71

"Women might look like the softer sex but they're
stronger than any man can guess. And that's a fact."
~Lola Delaney

Jake searched for any sign of fear in her eyes.
There was none. If she were a man, she'd have brass
balls. But the curves pressing into him were definitely
not masculine. Still, she had guts. Most women would
be crying now, but she grinned up at him like she'd
been on a grand adventure.

Comforting her would have been a pleasure, but
she didn't need it. She made it clear the roof dive was
no big deal.

"Thanks. I don't know how I would've gotten
down if you hadn't come along."

He wanted to shake her for being in the situation,
but her charm stole his breath. And his mind. And gave
him a growing hard-on, which he couldn't help and was
in no mood to hide.

If she minded, she didn't show it. Instead, she gave
him the smallest, stingiest peck on the cheek and
murmured into his ear, "It seems like you've made a
habit of rescuing me, Jake. Sorry to be such a pain in
your ass."

She slipped from his arms.

Turning to Tom, Kat said, "We've got two

chimneys. Is that enough for bakery ovens?"

"Is that what you were doing?"

Joann had an arm looped in his. "You said we needed chimneys, didn't you?"

"I said you'd need vents for the ovens." Tom looked at Jake, put a hand in the air, and shook his head. "Don't look at me like that. I didn't tell her to climb on the roof. Tell him, Kat, before he tries to throw all of us out the window."

Jake wanted to jump out himself.

"What the hell have I missed? You look as thick as thieves." He couldn't conceal the irritation from his voice. "Did you tell them to go check the chimneys?"

"Of course I didn't."

Kat turned. Her neckline had pulled low when she'd fallen, exposing a shoulder and creamy expanse of skin.

He was only human. A man whose strength at resisting her charms was nonexistent.

She glanced down and her eyes rounded. She lifted her gaze with a head shake that sent her black curls tumbling.

"Tom didn't tell me to go out on the roof. I decide where to go. And what to do when I get there."

Chapter 72

"Love's path is never straight. Zigging and zagging? They're part of the fun—especially if his zig fits in your zag…" ~Lola Delaney

Jake couldn't be more disgusted with his life if he tried.

Sure, he had made progress in the moving on side of things. He wasn't lamenting over his mistakes, penalizing himself long after the rest of the world absolved him. That had to count in his favor, didn't it?

And that he recognized an opportunity to make a difference in a place he loved, surrounded by people he treasured was another positive move. Taking over the motel, insisting his uncle—and his ghost of an aunt— accept a sizable chunk of his nest egg to feather their own new, southern nest, was the best thing for everyone concerned. Repaying those who'd taken him in when he had no one settled his karmic debt. The olds were as excited as teenagers, and he was happy for them.

The duck waddled into the extra-large cage he'd installed near the pool house. If Clarence was to stay at the Tip-A-Canoe, he'd have to accept a few new rules. One, that his freedom to roam was curtailed, didn't seem to affect the bird. Clarence settled into his cage, fluffed his feathers, and snuggled into a sleeping posture.

The taming of the wild duck? It counted in his favor, too.

He tallied and re-tallied the good stuff and the pros far outweighed the cons in his life. He'd pulled himself out of the slide, found a purpose and went hard at it. Not just for himself, either, but for the rest of the town.

All that—and he still felt like shit. Any other man would be flying high, but not him. No, he felt like he'd been keelhauled, dragged beneath his own life and torn apart by the barnacles that refused to unstick themselves.

But he couldn't—by any stretch of his imagination—think of Kat as a barnacle. Never.

She was more like a blister on his soul. She touched him deeply. Insistent and unforgettable, she grew inside him. He couldn't get her out of his system but until she softened to him he was going to be in pain.

Damn.

"Good night, Clarence. Sleep tight." Nighttime endearments to a fowl felt foolish but he'd promised Aunt Pat so he spoke the words.

Then, he turned and headed for the pool house. A few more small chores before calling it a day would cut tomorrow's to-do list down considerably. Besides, sleep didn't come fast anymore, so why bother cleaning up and turning in when all he'd do was toss and turn?

"Hey. Still working?"

Tom appeared from around the front of the building. The shit-eating grin on his face told the story of where he'd been, and with who, but he asked anyway. "And you're coming from...?"

"I checked on the ladies across the way." Tucking his hands in the pockets of his jeans, he shrugged. "Just wanted to make sure they're okay. After today, you know."

Jake knew. His groin still ached from the memory.

"Are they?"

"Are they what?"

The laugh came out like a snort, bringing a sloppy grin to the other man's face. He looked like he'd been drinking but Jake knew better. Joann worked her spell on him.

"You're in trouble, man. Big trouble. And you don't even know it." He reached into the fridge in the corner of the small utility room and pulled out two beers. He handed one over before he opened his and took a long swig. The bubbles felt good on his throat, so he took another drink. Wiping his lip on his wrist, he asked, "Are the ladies okay? You checked on them, so you should know."

Tom downed a mouthful before he spoke. "They're fine. Meri was teaching Jena Rose to count in French. It was the cutest thing. And Joann's mom was watching an old black-and-white movie. Joann and I went for a little walk. Then, I brought her back. So yeah, they're fine."

He narrowed his eyes. Conspicuously absent from the account? The one who held his interest.

He wished he wasn't so damn hard up for information about her—anything and everything satisfied him—but he was. So he asked, feeling like a major loser.

"What about Kat? She okay?"

Wiping the foam from his upper lip with his tongue, Tom nodded. He jerked his head.

"Yeah, she's fine. Real fine, Jake. And I've got to

say this, even if it pisses you off." He took another swallow of his beer. "I think you're an asshole for letting that woman get away from you. She's the best thing that's ever happened to you, and I can't believe you're not making a move for her. That, in my I-know-shit humble estimation, makes you a world-class asshole."

He downed the rest of his beer and tossed the empty in the trash can. "You're right. I'm probably the world's biggest asshole. The world's *very* biggest."

Chapter 73

"Make a wave. Make two or two thousand, if you have to. Whatever it takes to swim to shore…"
~*Lola Delaney*

Trying not to make waves hadn't gotten Kat anywhere with men. And letting someone else determine her future never worked, either. If she knew nothing else after the crap she had just muddled through, it was that she was in charge of her life. No one else. Only her.

This experience was life-changing, certainly. But it was also empowering. She hadn't realized she'd been settling for run of the mill instead of reaching for anything extraordinary. She'd sacrificed happiness for status quo, organizing everyone else's life to its best advantage while compartmentalizing her own in an it'll-do nook.

All that was behind her. No more settling or being stuck in a so-so existence.

Just no more.

Barefoot and wearing only a short terrycloth robe, she walked across the street to the motel. She passed the closed office. Walked by Clarence's cage, where he slept peacefully. A sweet pet, but a lousy watch duck. She flinched as she crossed the gravel beside the pool deck, lifting her bare feet high and taking large steps.

Only two lights illuminated the pool, and they were both built into the tiled walls. Their bulbs looked yellow, as if they were throwbacks to an earlier decade. Maybe one where bell-bottoms and platform shoes ruled, she wasn't sure. It didn't matter. For her purposes, the dim lighting made the mood more intimate.

"Mind if I join you?"

Jake turned so fast his arms sent a plume of water through the air. Muscles glistened, droplets clinging to his tanned shoulders. The intense, water-churning laps he'd been doing left the surface choppy. He looked like Poseidon, rising from the waves. All that was missing was a trident.

And a crown. He'd look hot wearing a crown, and nothing else.

If her guess was right, the nothing else part was covered.

The hell with the crown.

"You're welcome anytime. You know that."

He trod water effortlessly in the deep end of the pool. The shadows surrounding his scissoring legs shifted with each ripple. With every movement. Watching his athletic physique in action made her mouth water. It moistened other body parts, too.

"I hoped you'd say that." She undid the sash at her waist and pushed the robe off her shoulders. His eyes were on her as the cloth slid down her body and pooled at her feet. She gave him a moment to witness her nakedness before she moved to the edge. "How's the water?"

"Not as good as the view." His voice was husky. *Good.* She affected him which was exactly what she hoped for.

Her toes curled around the flamingo-pink tiles. She shot a look toward the pool filter at the shallow end. It had brought her to this point, and she was grateful for that. Not willing to waste another precious moment, she held her breath, straightened her arms over her head and pushed off from the edge. Years of yoga, swimming at the health club, and aerobic classes let her fly through the air and slice the water.

Usually she fell on her ass into everything. Diving headfirst, and knowing she did it well, was liberating.

She surfaced near the far wall, as she planned, putting a few feet of watery distance between their bodies.

"That was some show. I've never seen a naked dive before."

"Like it?" The question was unnecessary. The admiration shone clearly in his eyes.

Jake grinned. "Very much."

"How much?" She grinned back, loving the way they always fell so easily into teasing. It happened early on, that they could banter. It was one of the things that first attracted her to him. That, and his ten-pack abs.

"You really want to know?" He raised an eyebrow and gave her a flash of the killer dimples.

And the dimples. Yeah, they made him easy on the eyes.

"I do. Tell me, how much did you like the naked diving display? Because, honestly, it's not a show I put on for just anyone…"

Cold water didn't keep her body from growing warm beneath his approving gaze.

His grin turned devilish. "It knocked my dick

stiff."

She laughed and swam closer to him. "Is that a good thing?"

A low growl, and he closed the distance between them. "A very good thing. And, honestly, it's not something that happens for just anyone…"

Words caught in her throat. Their gazes locked, and she plumbed the depths of his gold-flecked, brown-as-night eyes, searching for what she needed—what she *prayed*—was inside him. Her whole convoluted life, with her never-ending attempts to wrestle order from chaos, had led her here, to this one wet, life-changing moment.

Falling off a roof and diving naked were nothing by comparison as she took a deep breath and took the biggest plunge of all.

"Listen, Jake…I know you don't want a heavy-duty relationship. I-I, ah, I—"

Shit.

The curse of Clarence the Stuttering Duck had to hit her now?

One stroke of strong legs and massive shoulders put his body within kissing distance.

"I changed my mind, Kat."

"W-what? Changed your mind?"

A curveball. One she hadn't planned for when she'd imagined what she'd say when she actually swam skin to skin with him.

One of his legs brushed hers, sending electric sparks to every nerve ending in her body. Every single one. Her nipples pebbled, her mouth became desert dry, and her breath caught. One brush, that's all, and her body went into full meltdown mode.

"Actually, you changed my mind." He didn't look away when she blinked. A tight nod and tiny smile. "It's true. All along I thought I knew what I wanted but you've shown me I wasn't choosing. I was running away. I feel like a wimp saying it, but refusing responsibility for anyone for the rest of my life was a cop-out. You showed me that."

"Oh…"

He moved still closer. So close, her breasts nearly—but not quite—touched his chest. And, their more intimate body parts were still separated by water, but not by much. She sensed the arousal of the man. It matched her own.

"I'm not proud of what happened in Texas. I wish to hell I could change it. But I can't. And you've shown me that carrying a burden for that cuts my opportunity for happiness down to zero." He reached for her and wiped a strand of hair back off her forehead. Cupping her head, he shook his own. "Life is too short to waste."

Words flew from her head, probably pushed out by the swelling of her heart. She nodded, turning so her cheek fit into his palm. She'd missed his touch, missed it so much the thought of breaking her connection with him now wasn't even an option.

She wanted to wrap her body around his, pull him into her flesh and never let him go.

He, however, wasn't done. He turned her face to his and for a second she thought he was going to kiss her.

"You inspire me, Kat Delaney."

Chapter 74

"My motto? No regrets." ~Lola Delaney

Her arms stopped moving. Then, her legs.

She inspired him? With the screwed-up family and flight for country freedom over chaotic city life? She who—

Sank.

And swallowed water.

And, when Jake pulled her roughly against his chest, spat water into his face. Again.

"What the hell are you doing? Are you okay?"

She nodded, pushing her hair out of her eyes. "Fine," she gasped. Hitching a mouthful of air, she swallowed, the taste of bitter chlorine on the back of her throat. "I'm okay. Really, I am."

Okay enough to feel his muscular chest squashed against her breasts and to enjoy the thrill of his strong thigh between her legs. And she was no-doubt-about-it okay enough to feel the hard length of his erection pressed flat against her hip.

"You can't stop swimming in the deep end of the pool. What if I wasn't here to pull you out?"

She sighed. "But you are."

"Next time, I might not be."

"There won't be a next time. It was your fault, you know."

He swam them over to the side of the pool. The underwater lights were dimmer here, making everything more shadowy. It was as if they were the only two people in the world. Which, as far as she was concerned, they were.

He kept one hand around her waist. The other he used to grip the edge of the pool. Very little movement kept them afloat.

"How is it my fault?"

"You threw me with the inspirational thing." Her arm wound around his shoulders. She walked her fingers across his skin and wove them into the thick wet hair at the base of his neck. So silken, it was a complete contradiction to the other hard, solid planes of the man. "I didn't expect anyone to say that. Ever."

"You need to raise your expectations then."

She didn't reply. Couldn't reply.

That exact realization had hit her only recently. This was the first time she'd heard the words spoken out loud.

His eyes were gentle on her, pulling her into a spell only he could cast. "You inspire me to be a better person. You saw an injustice, and put yourself out on a limb to help others. You had nowhere to go, so you took a leap of faith and moved here. And, when your expectations were shattered, you built a new road forward. Maybe the most inspirational thing about you, the part that really blows my mind, is the way you hold up your family. You brought them back here and pulled them into your new life. Even Meri, who showed up from halfway across the world, fits right in. If that's not inspirational, I don't know what is."

"You do the same." News traveled fast, particularly

between Joann and Tom. She'd heard about the motel, his ghostly aunt, elderly uncle and even the duck. "You're making it possible for two people to move to a new life."

"Listen, you really do understand about my aunt, don't you? She's not really…"

"I get it. I listen to the word about town. The lady loved the man too much to leave him—an incredible love story that transcends time and space. It's amazing."

He nodded. "I think so, too."

"But just when your aunt finally decided to like me, you're giving them their dream—helping them move away. Bad timing, I think," she teased.

He grinned. "They'll be back. And I'm not all that altruistic. I'm getting my dream, too." A pause. She watched him swallow, and resisted the impulse to kiss his neck when it moved. "At least, I hope I'm getting it."

Crunch time.

There was no place she'd rather be than crunched up against Jake.

"Tell me."

He touched his forehead against hers. Their breathing synchronized. Their breaths mingled. His heart beat in time with hers, pressed against her so tightly she didn't know where his body began and hers ended. And, she didn't care.

"Don't you know?"

"Tell me," she whispered. "I want to hear it, Jake."

"You're my dream. You, me, a life here—or anywhere, as long as we're together." He pulled his head back and met her gaze. "I love you. I think I fell for you the first day. I fought it—fought wanting you and falling for you but…"

He shrugged. The transparency was back in his eyes. No more hiding. No secrets.

No remorse.

His voice was mesmerizing. His words, music. "No more fighting. And no more looking to the past. No more hobbling my future, either." He hitched a breath. "Our future, I hope."

Jake lowered his mouth. He paused to meet her gaze a fraction from her lips. It was torture, having him close enough to practically taste, so she closed the gap. Her lips met his, her mouth opened and they deepened the kiss in a heartbeat.

One kiss led to another. And another. They kissed until she couldn't stand just kissing him.

"Jake, I need you…"

He trailed a ribbon of kisses along her jaw. Then, he pulled away and looked into her eyes. His hand gripped the pool edge and the other arm wrapped around her waist. He throbbed, hard and hot, against her hip, but he hadn't made any move to push things further.

His kisses left her panting in the face of his serious, yet deadly sexy, gaze.

"No more casual sex. Not that it was ever casual on my part. I realize that now." He bent and kissed her neck. A husky moan against her skin made her spine arch. "Between us—it's more now. I won't go back. No matter how hard you make me or how sweet you taste, I can't go back. It's got to be real, or we can't do this."

She wrapped her legs around his waist. Her hands rested on his broad shoulders. A thrill shot through her when he brushed her center but the jolt wasn't caused only by his touch.

He loved her—enough to say no when he oh, so obviously wanted her.

"I love you, Jake. Don't make me wait, please. I've waited long enough for this. For you. For us. Please, no more waiting."

He claimed her mouth. Desire swept conversation away, and they writhed against each other, trying to become one instead of two.

A smooth thrust and he was where she wanted him. Her breath caught, and she savored the sensations turning her insides molten. He moaned against her earlobe, where his teeth swept against her tender skin.

"I've waited for you my whole life, Kat. Now that I've got you, I'm not letting go." He thrust his hips against hers, and their movement sent tiny ripples on the surface of the water around them.

"Come with me, Kat. Oh, baby, come with me..."

He ground his body into hers, his velvety thickness meeting her moist center with increasing intensity. If she'd wanted to resist, it was already too late.

But she didn't want to resist. She was ready for this. Ready for a new life. Ready for wild pool sex. Ready for Jake.

And, ready for love.

Kat took a deep breath. Then, she let herself fall into the waves crashing within her.

She knew Jake would catch her. Hold her up.

Most importantly, she knew he'd ride all the waves life sent their way because finally they were both ready to leave the past behind—one shuddering, glorious moment at a time.

Kat's Comfort Toffee

½ cup coarsely chopped, toasted nuts (Kat uses hazelnuts, walnuts and almonds)

1 cup butter

1 cup sugar

3 T water

1 T corn syrup

1 cup chopped chocolate (Kat uses milk chocolate but it's a personal preference)

Line one 13x9x2-inch baking sheet with aluminum foil. Drape the foil over the sides so none of the ingredients touch the actual pan. Sprinkle coarsely chopped nuts on foil, spreading so they reach into the corners. Set aside.

Melt the butter in a heavy saucepan. When butter's melted, add the sugar, water and corn syrup. Stir mixture frequently, until it boils. Then, place a candy thermometer in the pot. Reduce the heat until caramel boils at a steady rate. Continue cooking and stirring until the temperature reaches the soft-crack stage.

Pour caramel into pan, taking care to cover all the nuts with sugar. Let the mixture firm up for a few minutes. Then, sprinkle the chopped chocolate onto the sugar layer. Wait a minute, then use a spatula to spread the chocolate. Finally, sprinkle the remaining nuts over the chocolate.

Chill candy until firm. Remove by lifting foil off pan, turning candy onto clean surface and chopping into chunks. Store in tightly covered container.

No-Fuss Peanut Clusters

16 ounces chopped chocolate
5 cups nuts
Line baking sheet with wax paper.
In a metal bowl over a pot of simmering water, melt chocolate. Stir constantly until smooth. Remove from heat and stir in nuts.
Spoon clusters onto wax paper. Allow to cool.
Store in funky Tupperware container until eaten—which, in Kat's apartment, will be less than twenty-four hours.

Attila's Truffles

1/4 cup softened butter
1 tablespoon pure maple syrup
1 1/2 cups powdered sugar
1 teaspoon pure vanilla
1/4 teaspoon maple extract
1cup chopped toasted walnuts
8 ounces chocolate

Combine butter, maple syrup and powdered sugar. Add extracts and beat until creamy. Finally, stir in walnuts.

Chill for 30 minutes.

Scoop tablespoon-sized balls and place on a cookie sheet. Chill again.

Melt chocolate, then dip each truffle.

Chill before serving.

Peanut Butter Fudge

1 cup creamy peanut butter
1 cup (2 sticks) unsalted butter
1 teaspoon vanilla
4 cups sifted confectioner's sugar

Melt the peanut butter and butter together in a large bowl. Add vanilla and sugar, and mix until combined. Press into a foil-lined square baking dish. Cover. Refrigerate overnight, then cut into squares.

Pecan Brittle

1 cup sugar
1/2 cup light corn syrup
1/8 teaspoon salt
1 cup chopped pecans
2 tablespoons butter
1 teaspoon baking soda
2 teaspoons vanilla

Bring sugar, corn syrup and salt to a boil over medium heat, stirring constantly. Boil without stirring until a candy thermometer reaches 310°. Add pecans, and boil an additional three minutes until syrup is golden brown.

Remove from heat and stir in butter, baking soda and vanilla.

Pour mixture onto a buttered baking sheet. Allow to stand until hardened. Break into pieces.

Kat's Fudge Balls

4 tablespoons unsalted butter
2 tablespoons heavy cream
28 ounces sweetened condensed milk
4 ounces finely chopped semisweet chocolate
1 tablespoon unsweetened cocoa powder
1 cup chocolate sprinkles

Bring butter, cream and milk to a boil over medium heat. Add chocolate and cocoa powder.

Reduce heat. Stir constantly, cooking for approximately fifteen minutes.

The chocolate batter should be dense.

Chill 4-6 hours, or overnight. Use a tablespoon to scoop fudge, then roll into balls. Rolls each ball in sprinkles. Return to fridge, and serve chilled.

Kat's Caramels

11/2 cups heavy cream
4 tablespoons unsalted butter
1/4 cup corn syrup
1/4 cup water
1/4 teaspoon salt
1 1/2 cup white granulated sugar
1/4 cup corn syrup
1/2 teaspoon vanilla extract

Butter an 8x8 baking dish.

Heat the cream, butter and salt. When the butter melts, remove pan from heat.

In a separate pan, combine the sugar, corn syrup and water. Stir until the sugar is evenly moistened. Insert candy thermometer and cook the syrup. Do not stir as mixture comes to a boil.

A 250°F, the sugar syrup will turn transparent and boil rapidly.

Remove syrup from heat. Whisk in the contents of the first pot.

Return to heat and do not stir. When temperature reaches 250°F again, whisk in the vanilla.

Pour into prepared baking dish, allow candy to set and cut into squares when cooled.

Chocolate-Covered Peanuts

1 cup chopped milk chocolate
1 cup chopped semi-sweet chocolate
½ cup chopped white chocolate
2 ½ cups peanuts
Melt chocolates in a double boiler over medium heat. When completely combined, add nuts. Stir gently to coat before dropping by spoonfuls onto wax paper. Allow to cool before serving.

Haystacks

4 ounces chow mein noodles
8 ounces chocolate chips
8 ounces butterscotch chips
Melt chips over low heat. Add noodles. Drop by spoonfuls on waxed paper and chill until hardened.

A word about the author...

Sarita Leone loves adventure, whether it be in a distant continent or her own backyard. When she's not off exploring the world, she keeps busy writing, reading, and dancing beneath the stars.

Always a fan of happy endings, she's fortunate to have a job which allows for so many of those!

She loves to hear from readers. Easiest way to connect? Check out her Facebook page, where all the latest news hits the screen, or her blog, *Write. Travel. Repeat.* at: https://saritaleone.wordpress.com/home/

Thank you for purchasing
this publication of The Wild Rose Press, Inc.

If you enjoyed the story, we would appreciate your
letting others know by leaving a review.

For other wonderful stories,
please visit our on-line bookstore at
www.thewildrosepress.com.

For questions or more information
contact us at
info@thewildrosepress.com.

The Wild Rose Press, Inc.
www.thewildrosepress.com

Stay current with The Wild Rose Press, Inc.

Like us on Facebook

https://www.facebook.com/TheWildRosePress

And Follow us on Twitter
https://twitter.com/WildRosePress